A Divided Corner

Charles Dobson

Published in 2021 by YBZcoy
188 Hyndland Road, Glasgow

Book designed by Lumphanan Press
www.lumphananpress.co.uk

Cover design by Claire Adams

ISBN: 978-1-8380669-4-9

In memory of

Rob Jack Dutton

Acknowledgements

I wish to thank Philip Hatton for his forthright and incisive comments, Gerard McManus for his advice but especially his patience in proof-reading and Gerard 'Ged' Wilkinson for his insightful observations. There are others who must remain unnamed. And all for their encouragement, also their humour and irony. Where I have not followed their advice, was not due to its quality but to my obstinacy.

My thanks to Claire Adams for the design of the cover, and to Duncan Lockerbie of Lumphanan Press for his assistance in bringing A Divided Corner to publication.

Finally, my thanks to Sue Thornton-Grimes for her meticulous and thoughtful editing as well as her wise guidance throughout this process.

Background

This is a work of fiction. The real individuals and events mentioned are to set the story in the context of the period. In 1976, the British Government ended special category status for people convicted of terrorist offences, so that henceforth they would be treated as ordinary criminals. On 14 September 1976, the first prisoner sentenced under the new rules refused to wear prison clothes and wrapped himself in a blanket – the beginning of the 'Blanket Protest'.

In October 1980, seven republican prisoners began a hunger strike in the Maze prison as part of their campaign for 'political status' and the right to wear their own clothing. The strike ended in December. The British Government seemingly made concessions.

On 1 March 1981, Bobby Sands began a hunger strike, claiming no concessions had been made. Initially, the IRA leadership outside the Maze did not support the decision to go on hunger strike. Each week, another prisoner joined the hunger strike. Whilst on hunger strike, Sands was elected an MP, by winning a by-election in Fermanagh and South Tyrone on 9 April. He died on 5 May 1981. Nine other republican prisoners also died as a result of hunger strikes. The hunger strike received world-wide media attention. The families of some of the prisoners took them off hunger strike, which ended in October. Unofficially the demands of the prisoners were granted, including the right to wear their own clothes.

During the period of the second hunger strike, the IRA killed 13 police officers, 13 soldiers and 5 civilians.

There were a number of British Army units operating covertly in Northern Ireland. However, for simplification of the narrative, I include them all under the Special Forces Group, 'the Group'. For the same reason, I refer to the Irish Republican Army (IRA) rather than the Provisional Irish Republican Army (PIRA) created in 1969 following a split in the IRA, as well as omitting any mention of other armed Republican groups.

Northern Ireland was also called Ulster, the North, the Six Counties and the Province. The term used often indicated the user's political viewpoint.

List of abbreviations and terms

Armalite
automatic rifle made by the American Colt Company

Army Council
the decision-making body of the IRA

ASU
active service unit: it carries out IRA attacks

BND
West German Intelligence Service

Browning 9 millimetre automatic pistol
British Army's standard handgun

B–Specials
RUC reserve: reputation for mistreatment of Catholics. Disbanded in 1970

CIA
Central Intelligence Agency: American overseas intelligence service

COP
Close Observation Platoon

Craic
banter

Double-tap
two rounds fired in quick succession

GOC
General Officer Commanding

Lords
cricket ground in London

Mau Mau
armed group who rebelled against British rule in Kenya in 1950s

NATO
North Atlantic Treaty Organisation

OP
observation post

Op
operation

Peeler
Police

Peter, Paul and Mary
American folk trio

QRF
quick reaction force: usually consisted of 8 soldiers, sometimes more

RSM
Regimental Sergeant Major: senior non-commissioned officer in a Battalion

RUC
Royal Ulster Constabulary: Northern Ireland police

SAS
22nd Special Air Service, an elite unit based in Hereford

SB
Special Branch: responsible for political intelligence and countering subversion

SDLP
Social Democratic and Labour Party. A constitutional Irish nationalist party

SF
Security Forces: generic term for all British units engaged in counter-terrorism

SOE
Special Operations Executive: a secret British unit in World War 2

SOPs
Standard Operating Procedures: the rules for conducting operations

Squaddie
a soldier of lower rank

Taig
derogatory term for Catholics mainly used in N Ireland

UDR
Ulster Defence Regiment: locally recruited British Army unit

UFF
Ulster Freedom Fighters

UVF
Ulster Volunteer Force

VCP
vehicle check point: army term for stopping and searching vehicles

Yom Kippur War 1973
between Israel and a coalition of Arab states led by Egypt

Two cracks!

The two soldiers at the five-bar metal gate immediately dropped to their knees, though the gate gave no cover. Almost in unison, the soldiers cocked their weapons and brought them up into the aim.

'Thought they were fucking ours!' the heavier of the two soldiers said as he aimed at the man crouching about 150 metres away.

The second soldier, now standing and leaning against the gate for more stability, fired two shots in rapid succession at the standing target about 10 metres to the right of the crouching target. The man instantly fell back.

'Contact, Tirkane crossroads, wait out.' The QRF commander spoke into his radio, his voice nervous but controlled. It was his first contact. He and Corporal Mayne ran the few metres forward to the gate.

Two more cracks!

'There's another up to the right!' Corporal Mayne shouted to alert the others, at the same time raising his 9mm automatic pistol in the general direction of the third man who was now running towards the trees to Mayne's right.

'Seen. On.' The second soldier fired twice, a double tap.

'He's down!' shouted Mayne.

The heavier soldier was now standing to engage his target again. The man crouching had to clear a stoppage, but as he brought his Armalite back up into the aim, he was spun round and hurled back to the ground by two 7.62 rounds fired by the soldier.

The QRF commander spotted two armed, uniformed men emerging from the bushes at the corner of the field 200 metres to his left. Before he could act to meet the new threat, he heard the voice of his platoon commander.

'Don't open fire! It's alright!'

The officer who had been 100 metres further back had come running forward when he heard the shots accompanied by a long-haired, moustached man in combats, wearing desert boots, no headdress and holding a non-standard radio.

'They are Ken's boys.'

The renewal of 'The Troubles' in 1970 presented Simon Derwenter Ormsby with the opportunity to pursue his cherished policy of cross-fertilisation: the Secret Intelligence Service and the Security Service would learn from and cooperate with each other. Ormsby pressed his case for a much closer SIS input into Ulster.

In 1974, Ormsby circulated an official paper to the relevant departments – though not to the Prime Minister – proposing direct involvement by the SIS in the events in Ulster. In response to the paper, the Foreign and Commonwealth Office and Home Office agreed that it was an internal British problem. The head of SIS, known as C, reminded Ormsby that the Service already had a tolerated, limited involvement and that he did not want to test further the tolerance of his counterpart, the Director-General of the Security Service, usually known as MI5 or just Five. Moreover, C, in a Minute, signed with the customary green ink, stated that Ulster was a minor police action and the Service had greater threats to consider – in particular, the threat to Britain's and the West's oil supplies being a consequence of the Yom Kippur War, and our presence in the European Common Market, which would allow the Soviets more opportunity to penetrate and undermine the UK. Privately, Ormsby scoffed at that because the greatest Soviet penetration had been achieved by their own kind, the chaps from Oxbridge: Burgess, Maclean, Philby and the rest including some unknown to the British public. Betrayal by men like these was one of the reasons why, despite the objections of colleagues, he had recruited into the Service individuals like Arthur Godden – a working-class boy educated at the London School of Economics.

In an act of appeasement, it was agreed that MI5 would accept SIS liaison officers. The emphasis was on liaison, and it was expected that most of the flow of information was likely to be towards MI5, such as information on arms smuggling from overseas. Nevertheless, Ormsby did not give up on his quest for closer involvement and awaited another opportunity to pursue his argument.

Arthur Godden had joined the Secret Intelligence Service after serving as a colonial Special Branch police officer, during which time he had worked for the Service but as an 'unofficial'. He had been recruited by his mentor, Ormsby. After a German language course, Godden was posted to West Germany to work with the *Bundesnachrichtendienst*, the BND, attempting to recruit Soviet agents. He quickly reached the conclusion that it was virtually impossible to recruit *bona fide* agents. He suspected that many of his colleagues in the BND were already Soviet agents or were hedging their bets in case either the United States upped sticks and left West Germany in the lurch, or a Social Democrat Chancellor adopted a policy of neutrality. A hidden seam of concern within the BND and the German Foreign policy establishment was that the Americans, after they had used their battlefield nuclear weapons, might make a bargain with the Soviets, or resort to a strategic nuclear exchange. Either way it would leave Germany devastated.

Godden had been plucked from Germany by Ormsby to be his assistant, his factotum. He was subsequently appointed to be one of the SIS Northern Ireland Liaison Officers (NILO) to MI5. These posts were part-time in that the appointed officers continued to perform their normal duties. Some of his less-than-enamoured colleagues claimed that NILO stood for 'Not Interested in Life Over there'. Godden, however, was much more comfortable working with MI5 than with the BND. On occasions, he was briefed by Army intelligence staff, though the RUC Special Branch was off-limits at Five's insistence.

Moreover, Godden had an ongoing commitment in the Province, known only to C and three other officers including Ormsby.

– 2 –

For Christine Latham, the IRA murder of an off-duty UDR soldier, the father of a friend from school, was morally repugnant. After a few glasses of wine, she told her father.

Geoff Latham was from Bath. He had been a civil engineer travelling the world on construction projects. In his mid thirties, he had met and married a girl from Coleraine, Christine being their only daughter. His wife wanted to return home to Northern Ireland. He agreed but only if they lived in Belfast. His main concern was the quality of education there but she assured him that it was probably better than anywhere on the mainland. His wife was right.

Once retired, he watched cricket and met up with some former colleagues for drinks. He had been surprised by the number of his engineer colleagues whom he had met on various different projects in different countries, who were Irish or Scottish. They organised quarterly lunches alternating between Belfast and Glasgow.

The deployment of armed soldiers onto the streets of Belfast and Londonderry in August 1969, though anticipated, still came as a shock.

The beginning of the violence, especially the burning out of people from their homes, the shootings and murders led to unintended and unwanted tensions in their lunching group. The sectarianism, despite their best efforts, could not be ignored although he felt he was set apart from it. The Roman Catholics found reasons not to attend the lunches, usually due to the dangers of travelling from their areas. Amongst the Protestants there were strains, with some vocal in their support for Ian Paisley whose hate-filled rants appalled Geoff Latham. What Geoff found amusing, slightly ironic, was he could not recall either Catholics or Protestants, with one or two exceptions, attending church when they were overseas. Sometimes, they were out in the sticks with no churches near-by but mostly they were in places with churches but the local hostelries were their places of worship. On Sunday mornings, most would wrap their sheets rather than the cloth of their religion around them against the air-conditioning.

Their daughter Christine excelled at school and took an English degree at Glasgow University, followed by a PhD at Queen's University in Belfast. They had not been too concerned with her involvement in the Civil Rights movement: both her parents were broadly sympathetic to the demands for equal rights for the Roman Catholic community. They had become gravely concerned when their daughter took a break from her PhD studies to assist republican groups, and especially when she went to England to advise the Troops Out movement on campaigning and producing propaganda leaflets.

In disclosing her quandary to her father, she seemed to be asking for his forgiveness, seeking redemption, atonement. He did not want his daughter becoming involved with the RUC or the Army. Even from his limited perspective he was aware that everyone seemed to know who spoke to the security forces. Geoff Latham promised his daughter that he would help her. Christine went to bed.

Geoff had worked in British colonies and other countries which at times experienced civil unrest. Before and after most contracts overseas, he and colleagues had been briefed and debriefed on the colony or country by a civil servant. The civil servant was always interested in their impressions of the place; whether they had encountered any foreigners, especially Russian and South African, or had been approached by any of the natives, at least the educated, powerful ones. He and his colleagues knew that the civil servant was from British intelligence – not so much the James Bond variety, more akin to a banker. Latham was never approached, or if he had been he hadn't realised, so he had never reported anything of interest. He was too busy constructing.

Nevertheless, he did remember being told that if something came to them, even a few years later, that might be prompted by something they read or saw on TV, they were to make contact on the telephone number they had been given. He went to his study. Thankfully, being an engineer, he was organised and soon located the card of a Mr Wells, the name of the last civil servant to brief him. His last debriefing had been four years ago and he therefore presumed Mr Wells had moved on. Although it was nearly ten pm, he decided to telephone, recalling the directive that they could telephone at any time.

Geoff's call was answered quickly. He asked for Mr Wells. In reply to a question, he provided a few details of his last two overseas contracts. He was beginning to feel foolish. After a pause on the line, he was told someone would return his call soon, probably later or the next morning. A call came back in less than twenty minutes. The caller said that he was Mr Wells but sounded younger than Geoff had recalled. There were a few additional confirmatory questions.

The junior SIS officer, the so-called Mr Wells, seemed unsure on how to proceed. He mumbled about information or advice.

Geoff confirmed it was not about a previous assignment. A pause.

'Your present location?'

'Yes.'

'Well there are the local agencies. I can give you telephone numbers.'

'I would rather not... for personal reasons.'

He could hear a mumbled conversation at the other end. Probably Mr Wells was telling a friend that he had a nut on the line.

'Is your address the same as when you went on your last overseas contract?'

'Yes.'

'Would it be convenient for someone to attend there?' The junior officer was unsure why he had made this suggestion. It was not really within his remit, but had come purely on impulse.

'Suppose so. When?'

'Possibly tomorrow or the following day.'

'Yes.'

'Prefer if no one else is around. If that is not convenient we can meet at some other place.'

'Well, between two and four would be fine because my wife will be out.'

'Good. We will telephone tomorrow to confirm. Goodnight, sir.'

After the initial telephone call, the young intelligence officer checked the name and his background. Mr Wells had been his last briefer. He consulted with the senior duty officer who was inclined to pass it to Five; it was probably some gossip on the Troubles, not their territory. He reminded the senior officer of the dictum of Mr Ormsby: *never rush to judgement*. The senior officer instructed his subordinate to write up the contact including his recommendation for the reviewing officer. What neither did was a trace on the rest of the family.

The next morning, the report landed on Arthur Godden's desk. The name rang a bell with his intense, bald-headed assistant known as *'the accountant'*, an epithet given him by a fledgling female agent. Godden decided to do a trace using the still-embryonic computerised database for Northern Ireland. The caller's daughter had been active in the Civil Rights Movement and was now supporting the Troops Out lot which had been established in London. This IRA sympathiser was the daughter of a solid, middle-class, Protestant family. The *accountant* remembered the name Christine Latham. Whilst a student at Glasgow University, Christine had been identified as a student activist with republican sympathies. She had been referred to Five who had carded and then forgotten about her.

Godden noted that Latham had agreed to someone attending at his house. He wondered why the receiving officer, Bamford, had asked because he did not have the required authority. Nevertheless, it presented an opportunity. He glanced at his watch. He knew he should clear it with Ormsby. It was unusual for him to work outside the boundaries, rules and protocols. But anyway, it was only an introductory inquiry.

Geoff Latham knew neither of the two visitors was Mr Wells. They were colleagues and Latham was not interested in their names and department.

'If you are not the people I'm expecting then you might as well go.'

Godden confirmed they were expected, and were not based in Ulster or part of any local agency. They were not the police.

'Good. That's why I called you.'

They were in the well-furnished and elegant sitting room.

Mrs Latham was out but Christine was in her room, which she had barely left since the murder of her friend's father – the reason for her father's telephone call. Christine would not interrupt them because he had told her that he was having visitors who might be able to help her.

'How can we help, Mister Latham... if we can.'

Geoff Latham told of his concerns, his fears for his daughter, starting from her first involvement in the Civil Rights Movement. He emphasised that both he and his wife were initially sympathetic because generally the Catholics had not had a fair deal.

'Sometimes, I feel like an alien here,' he said with a sheepish grin. 'Felt more at ease in some of the so-called backward countries.'

The two visitors smiled.

Christine's father narrated her involvement with Troops Out. He concluded by informing the two men of Christine's reaction, almost despair, at the murder of her friend's father. Geoff had surmised that his daughter wanted to extricate herself from her present predicament. However, he did not want to go to the RUC or the army because he knew Northern Ireland was like a village and someone would find out. He and his wife were prepared to pack up and move to England if it would help their daughter. Godden frowned inwardly.

'I would like to talk to your daughter.'

'Here?' A nod from the intelligence officer. 'I will get her down. She's in her room.'

'I would rather go up.' A look of disapproval from Latham met with a slight smile from Godden saying, 'It's alright. I'm not James Bond.'

Geoff smiled. 'Right. Will I take you up?'

Her father introduced Godden to his daughter as Mr Wells, agreed on the way up to Christine's room. He was a civil servant. Geoff would wait downstairs to intercept in the event of his wife returning.

Christine lay on her bed, her back against the pillows piled high against the headboard. She consented to Godden sitting at her dressing table. The curtains were already closed in the room.

'I understand that you have been upset by the recent murder of a friend's father?'

She nodded whilst peering suspiciously at Godden.

'May I call you Christine?' A consenting nod. 'I want you to know that if you do not want to talk to me, I will leave and you will never see me again.'

'You're not a policeman.' It was a statement.

'No.'

'Thought not. You don't look like a policeman.' An inward smile by Godden remembering an old school friend telling him that he was not a policeman, even when he saw him in his colonial policeman's uniform.

'Are you intelligence?'

'Sort of... but my job is in a research department. My department dealt with people like your father when they were going away to Africa and places. We briefed them on local conditions.' He paused. 'I never met your father. In fact, last night he contacted us because he was concerned about you. He did not want to go to the local police.'

'I know.' She leaned forward. 'I wouldn't and I won't talk to the police, the black bastards!' He noted the genuine hostility in her voice. 'Or the army.'

'I understand...'

She interrupted angrily, 'Do you?'

Godden thought it was wiser not to respond.

'Have you seen the way the police treat people? Roman Catholics stopped and abused... even assaulted... Just because they are taigs!' Her voice rose. 'The soldiers are almost as bad... especially the Scotch ones. Most of them are in Orange Lodges in Scotland.'

A silence whilst Christine pushed herself back into her pillows. Godden made a mental note to investigate Christine's claim about the Scottish soldiers.

'But I... don't agree with the killings... or the bombings... And I won't join the RA to inform on them.' She caught the quizzical look on Godden's face. 'You were telling the truth when you said you're not based here. The RA is what people mainly in West Belfast call the IRA.'

'Not my job to infiltrate the IRA.' A slight smile demonstrating he was a fast learner. 'My interest is political. At some stage there will be more talks.'

Both knew he was referring to the IRA leadership going to London in secret to talk with the British Government.

Godden looked at himself in the dressing-table mirror. Older. Knew this was not his forte. If he had not accepted Ormsby's offer over ten years ago, he would probably be like Christine, a supporter of civil rights in Ulster and possibly a supporter, if not a member of Troops Out. He knew that to recruit sources you had to be hard and indifferent, like his superior in the colonial Special Branch, a Northern Irishman. But it had warped the Northern Irishman. Ormsby had warned him of the effects of such work, especially on Special Branch officers: the paranoia, the descent into insecurity. Insecurity! When security was the paramount consideration in agent running. The mirror reflected an oblique grin.

'Christine, we would... I would like you to report to us just the politics of the republican groups.' He paused then said, 'I promise you that I will never use your information to arrest anyone.'

She did not respond but was looking intently at him.

'I would not intend to contact you again for some time.'

'Think my father was hoping that you would persuade me to leave them and that we go to England. I know that's what he wants to do... and I was his excuse... opportunity.'

'Possibly. But I do know your father was, is, really concerned for you... for your safety. It might be better if your parents moved to England. I think if you suddenly packed up and moved to England, then suspicion might fall on you.'

He was not sure why he said it or even if it was true.

'Anyway, you still believe in Troops Out and the ending of discrimination against Roman Catholics.'

'Yes. Yes, I do.'

'My research department looks at how the police and army behave, conduct themselves in what we call internal security operations. What you tell us about grievances might help us to pass down information to the army and police about treating people... though it might take some time.'

She sneered, 'The famous British Army hearts and minds!'

'There are people who do believe in it.' Met with a disdainful snort.

Godden thought it was wiser to ignore the response. Instead, he explained that he did not want her to join the IRA. If she was approached, she should make it clear that she opposed pretty much all violence. It was political information he wanted. The first step was to continue her involvement with Troops Out. If she was invited to any meetings in London or any other city in GB, she should go. She would not be contacted in Northern Ireland. She should return to her studies in order to create a respected academic career for herself. Her parents should never be involved. She might think, even hope, that she had been forgotten: she would not be.

Christine did not move or speak. Instead she stared hard at Godden which discomforted him somewhat.

'Alright, we'll see how it goes.' A pause before she spoke slowly and deliberately, 'But that is not a commitment.'

Having completed her PhD, Christine obtained a lecturing job at Queen's University. She continued to argue that it was for the benefit of the people of Britain if its soldiers were withdrawn. Young working-class men on both sides were dying for the upper-classes.

She spoke at a number of Troops Out meetings in England. During these visits, she was debriefed, usually in the St Ermin's Hotel in London. Precautions were taken to ensure that Godden's source was protected and to ensure that the Security Service did not learn that the SIS was running an agent in Ulster.

– 3 –

The choirmaster was born in Derry in Long Tower Street just outside the City Walls. Unlike other Roman Catholic families, his parents only had three children, Damien being the middle one between his brother and younger sister. The McGlones were a relatively well-off, respectable family, though considered by some as stand-offish.

The family had had a coach-building business in the Protestant Waterside area before selling it to a larger firm for a considerable profit which enabled them to buy a substantial terraced house on Marlborough Avenue in the Bogside. The two brothers, Damien's father and his unmarried brother, continued to utilise their skills doing contract work. The unmarried brother was known for his frugal nature, never having being a smoker or drinker, and it was said that he had never been heard to swear.

Damien's father had joined the Royal Navy in 1941 after the Nazi invasion of Russia. This act had caused some strife and dissension within the wider family, but although well-disposed to the Republican cause, the father's sympathies were with socialist, working-class politics. This had earlier brought criticism from the local parish priest for his support for the wrong cause in Spain. The McGlone brothers maintained that in 1921

Dublin had sold out the Catholics in the North because it suited Sinn Féin's purposes, in particular not to have a substantial, industrial Protestant working-class in the Free State. However, they did understand the decision knowing that the Protestants could not have been coerced into the Free State – certainly not by the British Army, many of whose generals were Irish Protestants. The sense of betrayal by the 1916 Easter Rising would have brought many more ex-soldiers, many unemployed, over to defend and protect Ulster. The McGlone brothers believed that the only way forward for northern Catholics was through socialism, collective action, even cooperation with like-minded Protestants.

The choirmaster's brother was educated in his home town but their parents were unhappy with the schooling, and young Damien found himself being sent to Dublin for his secondary education, residing with his mother's sister. There, Damien discovered his passion and gift for music, mainly classical. The three McGlones all became teachers, with his physics teacher brother Colm moving to Belfast to pursue his career while his sister Maeve, an English teacher, followed hers in London.

Damien embarked on his career, teaching music in Derry. Initially, he had intended to remain in Dublin or even go to London but, being single, he returned to care for his mother after his father had passed away. Shortly after, his mother also died. He remained in his home town. It was proclaimed in the omnipresent Derry gossip that Damien had inherited the sensitive nature of his uncle, sober and staid.

Damien reinvigorated the school choir which became popular and in demand. His advice was sought to help both school and church choirs. Eventually, he became a peripatetic teacher, also providing violin and piano lessons in Derry, then expanding into County Derry, Ballymena in County Antrim and even to Belfast. The majority of his students, mostly from middle-class families, came by word of mouth due to his growing reputation. Even some Protestant families sought his services. He gained work in the Republic, initially through his continuing links with his Dublin school. More and more of his time was being spent assisting schools and churches in setting up or improving choirs. Consequently, he found he had little time for individual tuition except for a number of local Derry students.

In the community, Damien McGlone, denoted 'the choir-master' – a Derry penchant for titling individuals usually by their job, foibles or afflictions – was a respected, sober but grey man. He continued to live in the large family home in Marlborough Avenue at the insistence of his siblings who returned with their families for holidays or en-route to the family holiday home in County Donegal.

The outbreak of 'The Troubles' impacted on his services, making him reluctant to travel beyond Derry, but he soon real-ised that the incidents were mostly confined to the same areas, and provided he exercised caution, his travels across the North and even into the Republic were not affected. He was also glad to be on the move again because of the noise of constant dis-order in the Bogside with the army driving around in armoured vehicles. The cacophony of the vehicle engines, the shouting, the shooting and the explosions disturbed his life. He found that he was spending more time on his trips including visits to his brother in Belfast and to his sister in London.

He saw little of the army or the police on his travels, though at the odd road-stop he found them generally to be polite towards him, and it helped that he was known to most of the RUC officers around Derry. Indeed, he had had a number of friends in the RUC who had been in choirs, but that was no longer prudent. His only trepidation was being stopped by the locally recruited Ulster Defence Regiment, having heard tales of their harassment of Catholics. He became aware of the areas in which the UDR patrolled so he tried to travel only by day, never going off the main roads even if it increased the journey time.

He found the soldiers, the Brits, strangely amusing and varied; some soldiers wanted to talk, even discuss music when they saw his instruments, others were brisk and abrupt. Gradually, due to the number of times he needed to go through the permanent army checkpoints in Derry, he came to recognise some of the soldiers by sight, and by accent which fascinated him. He found that the Welsh and Scottish regiments were more aggressive, though he came to believe that it was possibly due to their accents and backgrounds.

He had marched for Civil Rights in the late sixties and early seventies. He had opposed internment in August 1971, but privately he did not feel too strongly, it having been a tactic even used by the Republic in the past. He had never been approached by the IRA though he was aware of the IRA leaders in Derry.

Damien had missed the Bloody Sunday march due to a long-standing appointment in Ballymena. On his return he had been shocked, appalled, by the smog of despair, bitterness and anger which saturated the Bogside. The British Army's so-called disciplined, elite paratroopers had shot many people resulting in the death of 13 innocent civilians.

There had been some stone-throwing by the youths – no doubt egged on by IRA leaders – but that was no justification for murdering innocent civilians. The British state claimed that the North was part of it, and they were British citizens, but now they were being treated like colonials akin to the shooting of the Blacks in Sharpeville.

Damien and his brother agreed that the shooting of innocent civilians would hand the initiative and momentum to the IRA because the Brits did not listen to moderate politicians. His brother Colm was a member of the SDLP, as well as a supporter and confidant of Gerry Fitt, a Belfast MP, though Colm predicted that sympathy would soon dissipate when the IRA responded. It was not a long wait, with the attack on the Parachute Barracks in England. Damien was even more shocked and angered when he heard through a friendly police officer that the local police and army commanders had not wanted the paratroopers deployed from Belfast. Like others, he now realised that this was not the actions of a few ill-disciplined troops. It was a clear decision from the highest levels of the British state. He was unusually vocal in his condemnation and the need to fight back.

The coroner had stated that it was sheer unadulterated murder but Damien felt that by the middle of 1973, the events of Bloody Sunday had been forgotten, and that people had developed a sense of fatalism and just wanted to get on with their lives. The blowing up on a quiet August night of the Governor Walker Memorial on the Wall overlooking the Bogside, a reminder of Protestant ascendancy, produced in Damien a quiet smile. One day, he had been in the Walled City when there was a shooting at the check-point at the Butcher Street gate. Later, he heard the two soldiers had not been killed but wounded.

By 1975 Damien's life was almost normal. He was mostly able to eliminate the presence of the security forces by an almost tunnel-vision focus on his music.

For one of his rare private lessons, Damien went to a detached bungalow in Cosquin near the Border with the Republic of Ireland. He recognised the man sitting in the kitchen, the brother of his pupil's mother. The father and the other children were out. After the lesson, Damien was invited into the kitchen for tea. After pouring the tea, the mother mumbled something about needing some shopping from town and left with her daughter.

Liam *Gaggie* McKenna was a known IRA figure. Damien knew that the stocky, bearded McKenna had a reputation as a hard man and there were rumours that he organised the punishment beatings, including the kneecapping, of those who breached the Republican Army's rules.

There was no small talk, no enquiries as to how his niece's piano-playing was coming along. They, no amplification, had heard that Damien wanted to help because of the recent events – a reference to Bloody Sunday even though eighteen months had passed. Damien's response that he could not do guns or anything like that brought:

'Don't be so bloody stupid. We've got lots of young fellas. Too many. As we get older, we need to take a step back.'

McKenna paused staring intently at the respectable man.

'You can say no and you can just fu...' He bit back the swear word in deference to the choirmaster's known character. 'You can leave but...' He leaned forward and grabbed the man's left wrist tightly with his own right hand 'But you must never mention this wee chat to anyone.'

McKenna's eyes drilling into the choirmaster's. 'Ya know what I mean.' He released the wrist, a slight smile for the first time. 'It would be simply taking messages, passing on stuff... being a postman as well as a choirmaster. Also keeping your eyes and ears open. You know people. Just listen and report.'

McKenna leaned back in the kitchen chair, still staring at the other man who was nervous, fidgeting with his tie, then his spectacles.

'Well do you want to help your country?'

Damien spoke quietly, 'Yes.'

'Sure? There's no going back. Ya understand?'

'I understand, *Gaggie*.'

'That's your first mistake. During meetings with me or anyone else, never use names.' He paused. 'We're okay here. But you never know where or when the Brits are listening in.'

'Sorry.'

'Ya not going to be sworn in.' Another hard stare at him. 'Not my fucking choice. Only two of us know about you... for the moment. But more will need to know or else you won't be able to operate. Now, I'm going to give you some...' A smile.

'Like a lesson. To get you started. Then I'll see you when I need to. For yersake, you better hope the Brits don't ever turn up at our wee chats.'

− 4 −

On a liaison trip in 1977 to Londonderry, Godden had been briefed by two army majors – one a brigade intelligence officer, the other an infantry company commander – both wearing the wings of the SAS.

Godden had been alarmed by the concerns they had raised about a Special Branch officer whom they claimed was in cahoots with an IRA member for financial gain, but one could never be sure what else was passing between them. Rumours abounded of other Branch officers being seduced by the IRA, and no doubt some Branch men were cooperating with the Loyalists. The matter had been raised with the army's Headquarters Northern Ireland in Lisburn eliciting the response of it being the odd, rotten apple. No need for concern.

At the end of the trip he flew back on the same flight as Christine Latham, each ignoring the other, but his mind was predominately on what he had been told about rogue Special Branch officers, and not on his upcoming briefing with Christine in the St Ermine hotel later that day.

Over drinks that Friday night, he reported both his debrief of Christine and the concerns of rogue – even traitorous – Special Branch officers to Ormsby who suggested that they ponder the implications of it over the weekend and consider possible responses. The information on the Branch officers was not to be committed to paper at this stage.

Later, alone in his small flat – his wife lived in the family home in Hertfordshire – Ormsby reflected on the information about corrupt Special Branch officers. There had always been and always would be crooked policemen and politicians, and secret agents. He was neither surprised nor alarmed. It was not just money or sex or envy which caused individuals to betray. Betrayal was the currency of the world's intelligence services, but, it was also the most pervasive drug of human society.

He subscribed to Blaise Pascal's theory: there was an inherent contradiction in each person. That is why he laughed when he heard politicians or commentators call on one another to be consistent in their positions. Consistency created a boring world. In Chinese, the word *crisis* had two characters, one for danger and the second for opportunity. Whereas Godden would be reflecting on the possible damage to the community and the security forces from the actions of rogue policemen, Ormsby was rehearsing in his mind the potential opportunity. He knew there was a need to place an agent, ideally two, near to the top of the IRA command, preferably in the Army Council. He was aware of previous attempts which had been blown or foiled. He pondered that Five and Branch might have good sources, certainly the Garda would have excellent sources but they would be used to further the aims of the Republic, not Her Majesty's Government. On reflection, it had been a sensible decision by C to declare Christine Latham to the Security Service as a SIS source who had been in place for two years. After some heated discussions, it was agreed that SIS would continue to run her, but only for political intelligence and the Security Service would share in the resulting information.

A smile as he imagined the IRA and Security Forces in a black and white film of cops and robbers. SIS must not pick sides. Controlling both the cops and robbers would enable them to do their duty to advise HMG of the threats and hopefully bring the conflict to an end. But it required a long term approach. Most importantly, the Security Service and the generals would need to cooperate without knowing the real purpose of the operation.

He already had options for the name of the operation: *Mythical* or *Chronus*. This operation would need to be totally under SIS's control and direction.

From the recesses of his mind, he recalled one of his instructors, from Edinburgh, in his genteel, understated manner enlightening Ormsby's intake:

'Our role is to paint a picture for our masters in order to enlighten them.'

A pause.

'The corollary is that we are required to paint a picture to hide our actions from our enemies.'

A further pause.

'And sometimes from our friends.'

The instructor had returned to Edinburgh to join a merchant bank or an investment company. Ormsby was certain that the instructor would paint a picture to hide his assets from prying eyes. It was not the upper-class English but the Edinburgh financiers who had honed the perfect understated manner. 'Ostentatious' was not in their dictionary. Nor 'wealth' in their conversation. A warm smile before he returned to the task at hand.

The essential element, the keystone, was to secure the support of the Prime Minister. He was confident that the present incumbent of Downing Street would consent to the operation, but he could not be confident that the present government could survive. The incoming prime minister might abandon it, even if only out of pique. Prime Ministers, with the possible exception of Ted Heath, never thought long-term.

His final thought was that Godden was able but that his subordinate needed an assistant who could think outside the box and was resolute.

In Germany, Corporal Mayne's battalion began training for their new role of stopping the mass tank formations of the Soviet Three Shock Army. The recently concluded tour in Northern Ireland had been a success. Peter Mayne had played a small, but significant part in that success. He had been part of the battalion's intelligence section but in a small detachment located in a police station away from battalion HQ. It gave him responsibility above his rank at an early stage in his career. He had established good relations with RUC officers of all ranks, from chief inspectors down to constables and in particular the CID and Special Branch officers. He was considered more sympathetic to the police than other soldiers.

Moreover, Mayne had developed a relationship with a local girl during the tour.

Mayne had accompanied the Quick Reaction Force to a crossroads to support a covert operation by a unit of Special Forces. His role was to gather any intelligence as a result of the operation. During this operation, the QRF had positioned itself at a five-bar metal gate, the entrance to a large field. The covert soldiers' liaison man, simply called Ken with his rank never disclosed, was positioned around 100 metres further back with the QRF platoon commander and another section in a civilianised van ready to deploy quickly to another location. Ken, in his briefing, had been rather confident that the QRF would be needed only to secure the area so that the police could undertake their investigation once his boys had departed the scene.

The QRF spotted three armed and apparently uniformed individuals moving towards them and presumed they were covert soldiers – a notion soon disabused when the armed men opened fire. Two soldiers of the QRF returned fire, killing two IRA volunteers, while the third ran off. One of the soldiers shot at him and believed he had hit him because the man fell to the ground. However, unhurt, the third volunteer crawled into the tree-line bordering the field. Mayne took command of the hunt for him, eventually finding him, kneeling with his arms up in surrender around 150 metres to the right of the metal gate. He had thrown away his rifle, which was later recovered, though he had a revolver on a lanyard round his neck.

Harsh words were exchanged with the two covert soldiers when they arrived at Mayne's position. They wanted the terrorist to join his comrades. Mayne ordered one of the QRF soldiers to arrest the terrorist. There was a stand-off only resolved when the platoon commander and Ken arrived. Mayne informed the platoon commander that the captured terrorist had been arrested. Ken appraised the situation quickly, realising the potential for a publicity and legal disaster. He led his cursing comrades away.

Mayne's star rose higher after the shooting of the two IRA volunteers at Tirkane crossroads. This was not because of his decision to spare the life of the third terrorist – most of the soldiers would have preferred the third terrorist to be despatched like his comrades – but his willingness not to be bullied by the elite soldiers. Mayne had also remembered his detachment commander's advice on capturing a terrorist. If you are going to do it, then do it immediately, no debate with others, no radio message saying you have captured him, followed by another stating that you shot him when he was running away.

At a family wedding during his post-tour leave, he was told by his brother – now a NILO – that there might well be a call from a colleague. Mayne was disparaging of his brother and his oblique references. He felt that he understood Northern Ireland better, though he did not see the reports that his brother no doubt did.

In Germany, Mayne was settled and happy, though missing Jo, but was determined to focus on his army career. He was popular with most, both officers and soldiers. Affable and knowledgeable, he was on an upward trajectory, highly likely to become RSM, possibly even a commission before that. His Commanding Officer never understood why the bright and reliable Mayne had never sought a commission. While waiting for his promotion to sergeant, he was attached once more to the intelligence section. He read up on the Soviet order of battle as well as their tactics. He, rather than the dull, dim-witted Intelligence Officer, ended up briefing the CO and the battalion on the Soviets. He was clearly the CO's favourite son, causing some officers and SNCOs to be wary of him.

The CO called Mayne into his office. The latter together with some other members of the QRF were due to return to Belfast to give evidence at the trial of the captured terrorist from the Tirkane ambush. Mayne was told by his CO that after giving evidence at the trial he was to stay on in the UK to give a talk to a battalion preparing to deploy to the Province. He had been booked into the Union Jack Club in Waterloo, London.

The introduction had been short. He was a colleague of Mayne's brother and wanted to take him to lunch. The lunch was in an Italian restaurant near to the Union Jack Club. The stilted conversation was of Mayne's family, friends, his army career. His host exhibited all the characteristics of his brother. Godden suggested that they move to a nearby house for a more private conversation. Mayne was intrigued and interested. Unlike most of the other properties in the area, which were two up and two down red bricked houses, this was a three-storey mid-terraced property. He was led into a small sitting room. There was one other person present, a Mr Ormsby. They sat in low chairs round a coffee table. Only tea or coffee was on offer.

Godden was direct. 'We would like you to leave the army and join the RUC.'

Silence for a while to allow the soldier to ponder the offer.

Ormsby spoke, 'If your answer is no, then go now.' A smile. 'We are members of SIS. You know what that is. I don't go round in circles. It's insulting to you... considering your background.'

'We want to put an agent into the RUC Special Branch.' Godden in his brisk, business-like manner. He turned to the other man.

Ormsby continued: 'Her Majesty Government wants to re-solve the Ulster problem. We want to solve the Irish problem.' A pause before continuing in a soft, accommodating tone. 'We want out of Ireland... which is not a majority view in our Service but it is the view of our more enlightened members as well as HMG's, despite the public stance.'

Not a fully accurate reflection of HMG's policy.

Godden again. 'We believe, know, that members of the Special Branch have two conflicting objectives: some wish to keep the conflict going for narrow prejudicial aims, while others are actively involved in helping the IRA – their motives are not clear.'

Like his superior, he did not convey a wholly accurate assessment of the RUC Special Branch.

Ormsby took up the narrative.

'If we can prove that one or other of the factions is disreputable, it would make it easier for the government to say a plague on both your houses... We are gone.' A pause. 'You are an intelligent man from a Roman Catholic background. You know the divisions... deep hatred in the two communities. If we can reveal to the British public that the Special Branch are engaged in an internecine war not for the wellbeing of the community in the Province, then, we might be able to convince the British public to demand withdrawal.'

'It's a long term project,' said Godden. 'We want you to join the RUC. Make your way up, which should be easy for a man of your ability. We want you to provide evidence of collusion whether with the IRA or the Loyalists. Evidence of the Branch's collusion in the killings of Catholics, or supporting the Prots would be sufficient. It would be sufficient for HMG to rethink policy.'

'You want me to spy on the RUC?'

'Monitoring is a better description,' said Godden.

'No. You are right. Spying,' Ormsby said.

'On my own?'

'No, we have other sources,' stated Ormsby.

Mayne was thoughtful for a moment, knowing that the SIS officers were acting beyond their remit. Mayne's suggestion of remaining in the army whilst joining the RUC had been considered, but his name would remain in the Ministry of Defence, and no doubt some officer or civil servant might leak it, inadvertently of course. Ormsby murmured in a confessional tone that there was something not quite ethical in having a serving soldier spying on the police force the army was supporting.

Mayne knew this was neither the time nor place for a discussion on the ethics of spying, no matter the means.

On his discharge, the soldier would have to start as a constable, but it was believed that with his intelligence, skill and adaptability, he would soon move up. He had a degree, which would help. It was hoped that he would join the Special Branch, but first a stint with the CID to give him a good knowledge of the force from both sides – the cross–fertilisation preached by Ormsby. However, the initial stage after he left the army would be to attend a short course in this same location, which would allow them to organise contact and reporting procedures.

– 6 –

His CO was astounded that Mayne was leaving the army, and also disappointed, because the battalion would soon be embarking on another operational tour in Ulster. A number of inducements were offered but to no avail. With an accumulation of leave, the CO said he could leave once he had handed over to his successor and could spend his leave in England. Whilst he remained a serving soldier, he could not return to Ulster without permission, which the CO would not consent to because he had a duty to protect him.

At his farewell party after most of the others had departed, Mayne found himself sharing a few beers with the Glaswegian, his former detachment commander. Murray and Mayne had worked reasonably well together in Ireland though there was little personal chemistry or shared interests. Mayne knew that Murray came from the poorer East End of Glasgow, of which he seemed inordinately proud. For the sake of keeping the conversation alive, Mayne asked him if he had ever come across Ian Barclay, his friend at university. Mayne said he thought it was Reid Place, no, Reidvale Street.

The Glaswegian snorted, 'Upper Bellfield. Thought they were posh.'

An interlude of silence while both drank their German beer.

Murray suggested that he was making a mistake and Mayne thought that the former had an inkling that love of a girl was not the real reason for him leaving.

'It's your decision but I hope you don't regret it.'

'We could meet up for a drink when you're in Derry,' Mayne suggested.

'Think that's unlikely. The CO has just told me that I'm doing COP.'

'Some time then.' They shook hands.

The ex-infantry soldier arrived at the three-storey terraced house to be greeted by Eileen Kanna who was pleased, albeit disappointed that Mayne had not recognised her from Glasgow University. Their time at university had overlapped only for a short period and they had been doing different courses – but she had floated around the politics students.

Mayne was to live in the house, maintained by an ex-chief petty officer, an SIS gofer, who cooked the meals and performed other required chores, and also a taciturn, security man. The living room to the front was used for relaxation in the evening, though the security man slept in it. A door from the small kitchen led into the back yard which had space for a van or a car and a couple of motorcycles. Access to the street at the back was through a double metal door. Mayne and the SIS gofer occupied the two small bedrooms on the third floor, which also had a toilet and a small shower room. Eileen had the en-suite bedroom on the first floor with the second bedroom used as a classroom. She would do most of the teaching but there would be some 'guest' instructors as well as briefings from Godden and possibly Ormsby. Certain elements would not need to be covered because of his military training and experience. This would be a bespoke course because he would not be operating behind enemy lines. Mayne noted her mocking tone.

Eileen Kanna had been recruited by SIS at the end of her time in the overseas civil service. During her colonial stint, she had been seconded to the Army to provide intelligence support. One of her reports had identified the real target of a planned attack by a group of communist terrorists. Godden had been lukewarm in his recommendation, pointing out that Special Branch had already identified the target from human sources. But Ormsby had pointed out that it was an unusual gift to be able to identify threats solely from various reports. Yes, the Branch and intelligence services usually acted only on information from agents or intercepts of communications, but, this was a skill that should not be dismissed and regarded as archaic. She would study languages because she had shown an aptitude for Asian languages and she would go to Glasgow University to study Spanish and Italian. She remained unmarried. It had been her sole aim in life to marry a reasonably intelligent but fairly rich man, though children did not appeal to her.

At university she was not to join any political clubs; she was reminded that she remained a fledgling member of the Service. Nevertheless, she was to hover on the side-lines of the politicos, hoovering up gossip. Glasgow University had a reputation for producing aspiring Labour and Conservative politicians as well as incredibly gullible Liberals. The University also had a growing reputation for increasingly left wing politics, such as opposition to the Vietnam War and especially to the dictatorial regimes in Spain and Portugal. She was to do some talent spotting, both of the potentially hostile and potential recruits. Under no circumstances, was she to attempt to recruit anyone. She had noted several individuals, one a tall Englishman with an easy charm and sense of humour who mixed with those of all political persuasions without causing offence to any. He would engage in political discourse, sometimes mocking the Tories and at other times the lefties. He never seemed to give offence, even to the bitter, red-faced socialist workers.

Her debriefings were always during the holidays. Her contact was a small, prissy man. She related the names of people whom she thought might be of interest, their habits, politics and foibles. He would make notes in a black A4 notebook, ensuring she could not see what he was writing. When she gave a name, it was met with a nod and occasionally a comment of 'interesting' or 'oh right'. The name or piece of information would be entered into the ledger, without any display of emotion or recognition. She thought of him as *the accountant*. When she mentioned Mayne, he said that he was already in the ledger, accounted for. When Eileen asked whether it was still alright to socialise with Mayne, he made the disapproving comment, 'Is he not a bit young for you?'

In her final year, *the accountant* had been replaced by a younger man who seemed less interested in her reports, which he viewed as tedious and unimportant, than in her. There were questions on her social life after the debrief. What pubs and clubs did she frequent? Maybe they could meet up in the West End. She found him oily and revolting. *The accountant* had never said for whom he worked: it was not necessary. She asked the young man, who freely admitted he was a member of the Service intending to gain promotion, but that his main aim was to enter Parliament. He was deflated and astounded when Eileen asked which party he wanted to represent.

'Conservatives, of course!'

'Oh, them!'

'You are not – a socialist?' Disappointment in his voice.

'One has to vote for what is best for the country. Don't you agree?'

The subsequent meetings were formal and professional. The young intelligence officer assumed that he was debriefing a red agent. He was reminiscent of the type of arrogant young man she had met and disliked in the colonies.

Her first posting was to Rome in 1974. She enjoyed Rome and the work was not onerous. It was an almost idyllic existence which ended in 1975 with her posting to Lisbon. She quickly picked up a working knowledge of Portuguese. Its dictatorship was in its death throes due to the disastrous colonial wars in Africa. By 1975 the Portuguese had ditched their colonies, with the ensuring civil wars used as proxies by the two super-powers. There was criticism of her for spending too much time with the military officers: a naive female easily impressed by colourful uniforms and medals. Initially her warnings of a communist coup were discounted, but her credibility was enhanced when the coup happened. The army suppressed it and the first parliamentary elections took place in April 1976 although Eileen was not there to witness them.

When the Spanish dictator Franco died on 20 November 1975, Eileen was seconded to the Madrid embassy. Franco's nominated successor Juan Carlos became King on 22 November. It was considered that the generals would remain loyal to Franco's nominated successor. Once more, the same criticism was made of Eileen: too closely involved with fascist military officers, police and judicial figures. Yet once again she produced the old regime's intelligence on the rising political leaders.

In 1978, she reported that elements in the military had not discounted a coup but were biding their time, waiting for the most propitious moment. This was discounted by the more experienced embassy staff. The ambassador asked for her recall following a request from the Spanish government citing her alarmist reports of a coup. However, Eileen knew – or suspected – they had been put up to it by the First Secretary at the Embassy because Eileen had spurned his advances. It was not because of his family and children; she simply did not like him. The suave First Secretary had been particularly upset when she told him that he could not afford her – not even on his expenses.

She returned to Rome but for a brief period only, because Service economising led to her post being cut.

On her return to the UK she was stuck in Century House reading Spanish and Italian transcripts, but was plucked from there to join Godden as his special assistant for a highly sensitive operation in Ireland. She was told it was directed at rogue Special Branch officers. Godden was not happy with being saddled with her and suspected it was one of Ormsby's japes. Likewise, Eileen did not want the job, having no knowledge of Ireland, no Irish relatives and never even having visited there. Her distaste for Godden, acquired when they served in the same colony, still survived, but the fact remained that she was in a form of purdah. Her only other option would be to resign from the Service and become a teacher of modern languages.

At the final conclave with Godden and Ormsby, Eileen Kanna had consented to Mayne's deployment, but with a sense of foreboding. She had reservations about Mayne: he might 'go native'. Yes, he ticked all the right boxes, was amiable, and full of *bonhomie* towards his current friends and people of the moment. She had not told Ormsby and Godden of her previous encounter with him in Glasgow. It was unlikely that either would have read or been made aware of *the accountant's* ledger. If they did, she could profess ignorance. Had *the accountant* not told her to ignore him? Mayne's stability was a concern to Eileen. Despite his appearing tough, there was a core of softness, sensibility – loyalty to immediate friends.

In Mayne's final briefing in the classroom, Godden sat in the teacher's position and the student on the other side of the desk. Eileen Kanna sat to Mayne's right, but behind, almost at the door. Godden explained that he would not be expected to report on a regular basis. He would be contacted only when he was in England. This was a long-term project. He should concentrate on developing his career. Finally, Godden in a slow, stentorian voice set out his mission, which was to identify rogue Special Branch officers who might be consorting with terrorists, Republican or Loyalists, for ideological reasons or financial gain.

The two men shook hands, then the new recruit turned towards his mentor/instructor with a quip primed but she was almost out of the classroom door, her head inclined slightly back towards him.

'Good luck.'

There was no guarantee that Mayne would eventually make his way into Special Branch. Although he could be dismissive of Eileen Kanna, Godden was not foolish enough to ignore her perceptive opinions, especially in relation to Mayne's suitability. Mayne possibly could be a good-time Charlie but his military record did not support that view. Kanna could be right in that he might simply get bored and pick up another interest. His relationship with his girl might fizzle out and he could decide to leave the RUC to return to England. There was nothing the Service could do. They could not blackmail him. It was not a problem for the present: Mayne was not even in his new uniform.

In Godden's next private meeting with Ormsby, he expressed his view that Mayne was not sufficient, a mere gesture. He did not disclose all his concerns, trying to alleviate this tokenism by being positive. If he did identify a rogue officer, even two, how do they exploit it? Surveillance of the targets would be needed. For Ormsby that was for another day.

– 7 –

Peter Mayne found the police training difficult but not demanding. Superficially, he found all to be welcoming, though there was some good-natured banter about him being a Roman Catholic, never just a Catholic, sometimes a taig. There were three other Roman Catholics on his course including one female with whom he felt a mutual attraction – but there was Jo.

His natural leadership quality and gregarious nature came to the fore quickly – which would not have pleased Godden, who had told him that he had to be the man in the crowd, the 'grey man'. Eileen, however, contradicting her superior, had told Mayne to be himself. The police would have received a report about him from the army. Further, his vetting process would have included speaking to police officers who had worked with him on his last tour. If he slipped into the background, it would draw attention to him. Questions would be asked. Why is his natural character not coming out? Is he unhappy? Does he miss the army? Is he really committed? Maybe he's not suitable to be a policeman? His mission could be over – not through choice but by being deemed not to have the right qualities for a police officer. Mayne had followed Eileen's advice.

He was seen both by his fellow recruits and the instructors as the leader of the squad. Apart from another ex-soldier and a plumber from Larne, he was the oldest in his intake. His compendium of jokes and stories kept them amused especially during the more challenging parts of the training. He began to discern the inbred Protestant or Unionist bias – not of the instructors, but of the structure. He and the other Catholics represented tokenism. His fellow recruit from Ballymoney had identified it before Mayne; later both had ascribed his slowness in recognising the tokenism to his English background. Mayne found himself trying to steer the Ballymoney man through the course, and concurred with him that it would appear that nothing he did was ever quite good enough.

In Belfast for the final section of the training, a few of them, led by Mayne, went to a pub in the reasonably safe Queen's University area. The departure of the others found Mayne and Ballymoney still drinking Bushmills. The latter had become morose, lamenting his treatment by the instructors and being certain he would not make it to the end.

'The black bastards.' He used the term most republicans applied to the RUC. Mayne used his open palms in a downward motion to warn his colleague to lower his voice. It was a Protestant pub. He did comply, but his words became almost indecipherable. He named two men, both detectives, who were on the take. One, Ballymoney knew personally and was sure he was a Branch man, but had only heard of the other who was stationed in Derry. He thought the latter was a Catholic. Mayne knew not to ask questions and tried to steer the conversation back to other, more jovial matters. Ballymoney decided that he had had enough.

Once outside the pub he blurted out, 'Peter, you're a good man but... you're a Brit. You can always escape this shithole.'

Mayne kept repeating in his head the two names until he was back in his room when he could write them down.

The next day, Ballymoney suggested that he had been talking a load of nonsense in the pub. He had just been mouthing off and Mayne should forget it. Mayne told him that with so much Black Bush in him, he had been almost inaudible, and what he had said was in any case mostly incomprehensible, as he had reverted to his bog accent. Both laughed.

Mayne completed his recruit training but Ballymoney did not; he had resigned a few days after their night in the pub. He informed Mayne that he was going to Scotland to work with his brother who had a small building business in Coatbridge just outside Glasgow. Mayne did not disclose his knowledge of the republican sympathies prevalent in that small Scottish town.

Mayne teased him, 'Who's fucking escaping now!'

'Doesn't sound right when you swear. Ya're too posh,' came the riposte. Both laughed.

His leave before his posting to a Belfast station was spent in England. On his final debriefing with Godden, it was thought unlikely that they would be in contact again until Mayne was deep into his police career, but there was the proviso of contact if either party thought it was essential.

The meet was to be in the Waterloo house. His sister Marie-Theresa, a lecturer at University College London, though presently on maternity leave with her third child, would take his fiancée Jo shopping to Kensington, finishing with afternoon tea in Harvey Nicholls. Marie-Theresa knew never to ask questions. Secrets – some respectable, others squalid and tawdry – permeated the Mayne family. There was never any question of refusing cover for a sibling, even from the deeply religious Marie-Theresa.

Godden was the only person in the house, having sent the ex-chief petty officer gofer away on errands. There was no requirement for security. They sat at the table in the small kitchen. The introductory small talk was perfunctory, in keeping with Godden's temperament. Mayne narrated his drunken conversation with Ballymoney, trying to remember all the details of the conversation as well as all his previous conversations with Ballymoney and his background. Godden made a number of notes in a black police-type notebook. Mayne had assumed that the house was wired for sound. It wasn't. Ormsby did not want any potentially incriminating tapes being discovered, seeing that SIS was acting outside its remit. The Watergate Scandal in America had illustrated the dangers of taping conversations.

'Are you sure those were the two names?'

Mayne hesitated, 'I think so... a lot of drink had been taken.'

'You have a great capacity for that.'

Mayne did not react. He had been surprised that his drinking had not been raised in the past, though undoubtedly it had been noted and filed. He fell back on his normal practice.

'I could not swear to it, m'lud... but think the names are right.' A winning smile.

'Your boyish charms are lost on me.' A blank face.

'Sorry, sir.'

'Do you think he was a plant? An IRA attempt to infiltrate the police?'

'I don't know. I didn't think so. Thought it was just bitterness.' He paused looking at Godden before continuing, 'There's a lot of it about across the water.'

'No doubt.' The same unresponsive face.

'It's when he told me that he was moving to Coatbridge near Glasgow to work for his brother that made me wonder.'

'Why? What has Coatbridge to do with it?'

Mayne felt his confidence returning. 'Well, Coatbridge has a large Catholic population, most of the families having been immigrants from Ireland. They are very republican minded. Provide financial and other support.'

He paused to allow Godden to complete the entry in his note-book.

'In my last tour, a Coatbridge band came over for the Hibernian March...' He looked at Godden. 'You know what the Hibernians are?' He restrained himself from mentioning the Scottish football team – his boyish charms lost on the other man – though there had been a connection.

Godden nodded. 'Read something about them. Go on.' He made a mental note to refresh himself on the Hibernians.

'Also, we came across a young lad from Coatbridge. About seventeen, probably around twenty now. His mother was Irish and had moved back but he was born and went to school in Coatbridge. We screened him once at the Branch's request.'

He felt sure that Godden did not know what he meant by screening.

'It was obvious he was on the fringes of the IRA, probably now a volunteer.'

'I see.' Now a contemplative face. 'Anything else on Ballymoney?'

'No. Sure Branch up in Glasgow could have a look at him.'

'Thank you, Peter. We know how to proceed.'

After he had made a long entry into his notebook, Godden asked if Mayne had identified any other potentially rogue or hostile types in his recruit intake. Mayne hesitated, saying that it was difficult to say, as it was unlikely that they would openly express support for any faction. Pressed by Godden, he gave the names of two Protestant recruits who, one openly and the other surreptitiously, had expressed support for loyalist para-militaries. To be even-handed he gave the name of a Catholic recruit but made no mention of the Catholic female recruit. Godden thanked him and gave him £40 so he could treat his girlfriend, enquiring whether marriage was on the horizon. Mayne shrugged in response. He had no intention of revealing to Godden details of his private life.

8

Following his visits to Ulster and Glasgow, Godden had to wait several weeks for a meeting with Ormsby, who had recently been appointed as a senior assistant to C with responsibility for liaison with all allied and friendly intelligence services. The new appointee had decided that it was a requisite of his new role to make courtesy visits to the headquarters of the most important of the foreign services, including Washington DC, Paris, Berlin, Istanbul, Amman, Wellington and Canberra.

There was some disquiet at Ormsby's promotion amongst other senior officers of the Service, who feared his next step might be to C. The new senior assistant had never recruited a source during his career. He was an organisation man, able to identify and recruit the best talents. Nevertheless, if he became C, the Service would become a well-maintained, shining Rolls Royce – but would never go anywhere.

Godden's report to Ormsby was brief and specific. The Special Branch man named by the two army majors in Londonderry was one of the names mentioned by the Ballymoney man. Godden had to be circumspect in trying to confirm the second man as a detective. The current intelligence staff officer at 8 Brigade seemed reluctant to cooperate. The second man had been a CID officer in Derry but had recently transferred to Special Branch in Belfast.

In Glasgow, he had spoken to the Branch superintendent whom he knew from his time in the Far East when they had both been colonial Special Branch officers. The superintendent confirmed the republican sympathies of many of the Coatbridge population. The name had been mentioned but there was nothing to indicate any involvement. The building firm McElroy was doing well. The superintendent said that he would have a closer look at them, in particular the brother newly-arrived from Ulster. If his investigation produced evidence of support for the IRA – and he stressed not just republican sympathies, otherwise they would need to open a card on half the population of the West of Scotland – he would report it in the normal way including to Five, but would alert Godden as a favour.

'I think this is another day.' Ormsby smiled.

Godden knew it was a reference to their last private meeting.

'We need the necessary assets to exploit this.'

'We could use the Hereford chaps.'

'Yes, but...'

'But what, Arthur?'

'I think it's highly unlikely they would provide people for a year, even two years – and to do what – follow suspected rogue policemen.' He shook his head. 'After a couple of months they would want to hand it over. It's too passive for them. They would argue it's a waste of their capabilities.'

'Yes, yes, I understand' Ormsby was good at strategy but not tactics, not the nuts and bolts.

'Means bringing in Five and their people.'

'No!' Unusually for him, Ormsby raised his voice, then quickly followed with a smile. 'You have a suggestion?'

A pause, while Godden rehearsed inwardly what he had already prepared.

'When I was a colonial policeman, due to the unavailability of the SAS, we had to set up a specialist troop – 513 as I recall.'

'Yes, Arthur, I do recall your report on it. They had some successes?'

'Yes. Two. Probably would have been more if we hadn't scuttled.'

Godden caught Ormsby's right eyebrow arching in disapproval.

'I prefer re-alignment.' A smile and the eyebrow dropped back. 'Which is exactly what we are trying to do in Ireland.'

Godden did not respond.

Ormsby thought for a moment before stating, 'We are agreed that we require our own surveillance and action asset .'

Godden nodded.

'Should we use our own people?'

'Can we withdraw them from other ops? Think soldiers might be better.'

'You might be right. Of course, I would need to clear it with C and the Chief of the Defence Staff. The GOC over there would need to know. But if...' He stopped.

'Arthur. Send me a Minute on numbers, training etcetera.'

9

The action and tasking paper was drafted, revised and presented to C within a day. Ormsby had had most of it prepared for a number of years; updated after his visits to friendly services, finalised after his meeting with Godden and now waiting to be signed-off by C. Ormsby was given fifteen minutes with C to discuss his paper.

'Read it. Godden's drafting?' C did not wait for a reply. 'Has his dour, ponderous, Calvinistic tone... like a sermon. Where is he from in Scotland?'

'C, he is not Scottish. Godden has not had sight of it. I wrote the paper.'

'He's probably a golfer... Did you? Simon, with your experience, you should know it is too long.'

A pause to allow his subordinate to digest the rebuke. C had a fondness – some said a passion – for rebuking his senior assistants.

'Yes, sir.' C liked at least one 'sir' during a meeting.

'The Prime Minister is a scientist. Knows nothing of economics or history. Indeed, like most politicians, history begins when they come to power.'

Another pause to allow Ormsby to reflect on the witticism.

'I have amended it... rather butchered it. No need for a

history lesson. We read the reports or watch the BBC. Here. Read!'

He thrust the paper at Ormsby who immediately noted the thick green lines through most of the paragraphs.

'To the opera tonight. You like opera, Simon.' Not a question.

'Er, yes... I do.' Trying to concentrate on the bloodied paper.

'I go. Can't stand it. All sounds the same. I go to Lords but I am bored by cricket. Do you go?'

Another unwelcome interruption for Ormsby. 'No, no... C.'

'It is duty. Surprising how indiscreet people can be at cricket. Seem to think we are all fellows together again in the dorm.' A wry smile. 'Finished? Good. Get it retyped. You did it yourself?'

'Yes.'

'Another skill we need to acquire. Our typists no longer the dozy daughters of dukes. They could be trusted because they did not understand.'

Ormsby ignored the spiteful barb at his wife.

'Return for my signature.'

Ormsby's proposal, albeit reduced from twelve paragraphs to four, finally gained C's blessing. After his signature, C had annotated, 'Details of plan should be briefed orally to the PM.'

The paper circulated on the PM's instructions to the Foreign Secretary, the Home Secretary and the Defence Secretary read:

Highly Sensitive

Top Secret UK Eyes A

1. *HMG's position that the continuing situation in Northern Ireland is purely an internal matter cannot be sustained. The Irish Republican Army (IRA) by its actions does not consider it as a domestic matter. It wishes it to be seen as a colonial conflict*

with an oppressed people seeking to cut the chains of a repressive colonial power. A War of National Liberation! They have not restricted their violence to Ireland, having launched attacks on the mainland. It is frustrating when the enemy does not play by our rules. Now they have taken their campaign to Europe.

2. *The willingness to murder Lord Mountbatten, a respected international figure and a member of the Royal Family; the IRA knew this would result in the murders of children. It conveyed their callous disregard for the government of the Republic and international opinion. They have no intention of playing nice.*

3. *In the USA, there is significant support for the IRA, with some politicians actively if covertly supporting the IRA. There are also Irish communities in the Commonwealth countries. There are Irish communities in France, Germany, Netherlands and other European states that through social and sporting contacts might influence governments to express concern over aspects of our security policies. German and Dutch intelligence have both reported ongoing activities by the IRA.*

4. *The present Troubles are not helpful to our relations with the United States or our European allies. The SIS considers that its resources and skills should be brought into play. The aim is to bring the conflict to an end. It is not intended to surrender the UK's position or scuttle.*

Prior to the meeting with the Prime Minister, C instructed Ormsby, 'Keep it brief. You are not presenting a treatise. And keep your answers short.'

The PM bristled as she read the memorandum, at times glowering at the SIS Chief and making comments on the paper including putting a line through 'A War of National Liberation!'

Ormsby was invited in to make the oral presentation outlining the Service's substantive proposal to the PM, though the other recipients of the paper remained outside the Cabinet room. The PM made no interventions and thanked Ormsby for his succinct, coherent proposal. He would be informed of her decision once she had consulted with cabinet colleagues. A terse smile.

The PM gave her approval, but outside of SIS only the Foreign and Home Secretaries, the Cabinet Secretary and the Director-General of the Security Service would be aware of the aim. The Defence and Northern Ireland Secretaries together with a limited number of generals would be aware of the new unit, though not of the aim.

The operation was time-limited despite C's objections which brought an agreement to review after three years.

C did not relay to Ormsby the PM's misgiving that the latter was not up to the job, 'Seemed rather wet.'

– 10 –

Braco was becoming bored watching the same crossing point on the Border close to Derry in what was called the Enclave. They had been briefed that this was a crossing used by the IRA to transport weapons and explosives from the Republic. When he had been in his battalion's Close Observation Platoon, known simply as COP, they had spent time observing another border crossing point. When briefed on the current operation, he had asked the Special Branch officer about the other crossing point. The jovial Branch officer admitted the intelligence had been wrong then, but not this time. Braco wondered how his COP sergeant would have reacted on hearing this, and whether he had been posted back to Ireland. He recalled his last conversation with the taciturn sergeant.

They were alone in the soon-to-be-vacated COP office. Sergeant Murray had not tried to talk him out of volunteering for special duties, merely stating that it was his choice and if he did not try it then he would always have regrets. Also, there was nothing to be ashamed of if he did not make it. Murray was aware of good soldiers who had failed SAS selection.

'You know you can end up becoming a Northern Ireland warrior which could affect your career prospects.'

'I know but there's nothing else going on.'

Murray nodded in agreement. The two men were silent for a few minutes before the sergeant asked if he knew about corner boys. Braco nodded.

'I'm sure you were never a corner boy. You're a blue blood.'

Braco laughed because Murray had decided that he was a posh boy. He had known that the younger soldier had spent time in Africa.

'In Glasgow... probably the same as Manchester, London or Belfast, the neds, the louts... most, but not all, unemployed, hang around the street corners of their dark, grey tenements. They smoke, drink... usually cheap booze. They'll swear, argue... a bit of betting even on spitting competitions...' He eyed Braco. 'Know what they are?'

A shake of the head.

Murray chuckled. 'To see who could spit the furthest.'

He shook his head, his eyes staring at the wall to his right, not talking to Braco.

'Sometimes they would verbally abuse people, but rarely. They would say hello to the women passing on their way home from the shops. Even offer to help them with their messages.' He turned to Braco and asked, 'Do you know what I mean by "messages"?'

Another shake of the head.

'Shopping. In Glasgow, people said they were going for their messages.' He held up his right hand. 'Don't ask me why. I think I knew once but have forgotten. Anyway.'

His head once more inclined to his right.

'Sometimes they fought with others from different street corners. For protection, for fun, even comradeship but mostly to mark out their space, their territory. Sometimes they formed gangs... the Calton Tongs... the Baltic Fleet. But the street corner was their university... their mess like the sergeants' or corporals' mess. The most important thing was loyalty. Looking after their own.'

He broke into broad Glaswegian. 'Dae wan of oors! We'll dae two of yoors!' Another pause.

'The IRA and the Loyalists are corner boys. They are fighting for their land, their ideology.'

He turned back towards Braco.

'If you get in, you're becoming a corner boy. Special Branch, Army Intelligence, the Security Service, they are all corner boys carving out their areas based on their ideologies.'

A slight, sardonic laugh.

'Of course, the Security Service also wants to sow the seeds of mistrust and jealousy in the other corners. No one likes to be accused of disloyalty. In the army, we know suggestions of disloyalty can affect one's career. No corner boy likes being accused of being a sneak. A traitor is hated by everyone.' He turned away from Braco. 'The blue bloods of intelligence gamble not on spitting but on how many lives could be lost by their actions. Maybe it is spitting... how far they can go.'

Murray told Braco that he himself might be getting a posting to Ireland, though nothing as exciting as special duties, but assured the young corporal that if he saw him in Ireland, he knew the drill and would never approach him.

As they shook hands, Murray said, 'You might bump into Peter Mayne. He's gone to join the peelers over there. Do you know him?'

A nod from Braco.

'Well, good luck and take care.'

When promoted to lance-corporal, Braco had shared a few drinks with Mayne in the corporals' mess. Mayne had always ensured new members were welcomed. There were many bitter, old, passed-over corporals who took a delight in abusing young and eager NCOs though never if they were in Mayne's protective company. Indeed, Braco felt a kindred spirit with Mayne.

Braco was halfway through his tour with the Special Forces Group, simply the Group. His tour so far had been successful, leading to a number of arrests and finds though no bodies. His surveillance skills, both rural and urban, had been acknowledged to be particularly effective, with all his colleagues recognising that it was his calm demeanour which made him such a skilled covert operator. Usually he was given the more difficult tasks, though not on this occasion. Sitting in bushes on the Border was a run-of-the-mill operation, though Braco knew it was this type which could suddenly explode into action. He was aware of similar operations which had led to the shooting of operatives. Alertness at all times was essential. Even if it could not stop other matters – such as the past – reeling through his mind.

His father had been an estate manager in the North East of Scotland for a distinguished Scottish family. When war came in 1939, Braco's father volunteered for his county regiment. After the war, his father returned to Scotland but the estate owners had decided to sell up and move to France. He took up a number of temporary positions around Stirling, helping estates to return to normal. While doing so he met a local girl and they were married.

Finding it difficult to settle, he moved to Kenya to manage an estate. There, he and his wife bought their own farm near Nanyuki which thrived even during the Mau Mau terror. When independence came, they decided to remain in Kenya with their young family. Braco's father then died unexpectedly due to the lingering effects of his war wounds. His mother returned to live with her sister in Scotland, leaving her elder son, Martin, to manage the farm.

Braco enjoyed life in Kenya. He travelled to Scotland to attend a course at an agricultural college with the intention of returning to help his brother run the family farm. Inexplicably, he made the decision to join the army, his father's old regiment. His father had taught his two sons field craft and shooting, living in the bush for several nights at a time. This was not something their father had insisted they do; they enjoyed it. It was fun not work. Braco thought that the decision to join the army was an inner homage to his father.

He missed Kenya, mainly his brother Martin and their friend and neighbour Judy, though her farm was thirty miles away. The three had travelled together to secondary school in Nairobi, where they lived in a rented home presided over by an intimidating lady in her early twenties, who told them that she was not a common Kikuyu but from the Lao tribe. Her father had been a prosperous merchant but with independence, previous contracts were given to Kikuyu rivals. Her English was almost flawless though the three pupils could speak Swahili – particularly Judy who teased the two boys about their inferior language skills.

He found that army life suited him, the basic training fairly easy. He had joined the battalion near the end of its residential tour in Ireland. In Germany, he was promoted and was a natural fit for COP. He preferred the Kenya bush to the rough gorse of Ireland.

On return to base after the Border operation, Braco was told to report to his OC in Headquarters Northern Ireland in Lisburn. In a brief interview, the OC of Braco's unit told him that he was being seconded to another unit of the Group. His OC did not know any more, except that he could have a few days leave before joining his new unit. Finally, he thanked him for his contribution and expressed regret at losing him. The OC did not tell Braco that he had been directed to nominate covert operators for extraordinary special duties.

After a few days of leave in London, Braco found himself in a two-storey building behind a large country house in County Fermanagh. Having dumped his kit in a first floor bunk, he was told to report to the briefing room on the ground floor. It was set up as a classroom with four rows of two tables, each with two chairs and a passage-way between the tables. He was the last of the 'students' to arrive. He counted fifteen people including three females, all in civilian dress, sitting at the tables. He recognised some of the faces.

The final arrival sat at the single table at the front, facing them. Braco was sure that the 'teacher' had been a senior training instructor with the Group. He stood up and spoke to them in an amiable, friendly style.

'Welcome. I will be known simply as Control. Now.' He looked at Braco. 'It is Braco, not Bronco?'

'Yes, Control.' He had selected it as his operational name when he joined the Group. Most of his comrades had assumed it was a name from American westerns. Instead, a memory of his mother, her home village.

'Thank you.' He indicated that Braco should sit down. 'You can retain your current code names or change them. At supper, I, or rather our unit commander, will approve or reject. So have two options.' He paused. 'You will meet the boss after the work-up training. I will disappear after the training.'

Another pause while he shuffled through some papers on his table.

'Your duties will be surveillance only.'

Control acknowledged that all of them had had experience in surveillance of some type but their vehicles would contain much more sophisticated communications equipment than they were familiar with. The first few weeks would be spent in working together and getting used to their equipment. Better to do it here than in England, with the added bonus that they would be getting to know most of the ground in which they would be operating. It would be both rural and urban. There was a small technical support team.

They would live in the two-storey building, though the bosses would live in the big house. Entering the big house was forbidden. It was the home of an elderly lady with powerful connections. There was to be no 'hanky-panky', which was met with some laughter. At the end of the work-up phase if anyone felt that this was not for them or simply wished to resume their normal career, they could do so. However, the requirement for security of the operation would apply even back in their parent units, and any breach would have grave consequences for the individual concerned. At the end of the work-up phase, they would be given a full operational and intelligence briefing.

During the next three weeks, the unit practised surveillance techniques, mostly in vehicles but sometimes on foot. It transpired that there was to be no long term static observation – for which some were thankful as that meant no peeing into plastic bottles. They criss-crossed most of the Province in both urban and rural areas. Mostly, they operated with a combination of one or two in a vehicle, known as one-up and two-up respectively, but occasionally had three in the vehicle, one always being a female. When two-up, Braco mostly found himself with the same female called Tring.

The operators were surprised and delighted with their concealed vehicle communications. There were two covert buttons which would alert the operations room to any problems. The controller manned the operations room for most of the training together with two Royal Signals specialists. They practised and refined their radio communications. All of them had operated in units using skeleton radio procedure: less was best. On foot, a male and a female acted as the targets, the former deliberate in his movements whereas the latter meandered, with most of the watchers feeling that they had been compromised.

Their final work-up training was an actual operation against three targets, a male and a female in Belfast and another male in Cloghmills in County Antrim. They would operate in three teams on a three day rotation, with each team following and photographing the target from home to work. The Operation *Mythical* team's nomenclature for this type of operation was 'shepherding' with the obvious inference left unsaid. They were issued with photographs of the targets together with code-names: *Dee*, the Belfast male, *Forth* the Belfast female and *Trent* the third male. Braco recognised *Trent* as a Branch officer who had been at briefings, though Braco had usually been unshaven at these so was unlikely to be recognised.

The operation was successful, though one team thought that they had been spotted by *Forth*. She walked from her home in Lawrence Street to Queen's University; *Dee* travelled from his home in Bladon Drive to Castlereagh police station, and *Trent* from his home in Cloghmills to Ballymena police station. The three teams reported that *Trent* was surveillance aware. Braco had deliberately walked past him just before *Trent* entered the police station. The soldier reported there was no flicker of recognition.

At the end of the training debrief, Braco thought it was significant that no one in the unit had an Irish accent and suggested it as a possible flaw. The controller seemed irked but made a note. Two of the unit, one male and one female, asked to be returned to their parent units, both claiming that they had had enough of following people. There was no quibble or any attempt to change their minds. They were to pack their kit and leave that evening. As for the remainder, they should have a meal then sort out their kit and be ready for the full operational briefing the next day at 1000 hours.

The briefing took place in the same room. Seated at the front table facing them was a man and a woman. Braco thought that he recognised the man, that he was a Guards officer – which he was, Major Tim Somerville of the Scots Guards – but he did not recognise the black-haired woman on the man's left, estimating her to be in her late thirties, attractive despite her impassive face.

'Good morning, ladies and gentlemen. Welcome. I am the team commander. I know most of you have served in special forces or other small units in which the commander is called "boss".'

He paused, an almost imperceptible smile on his lips.

'We are not a gang of navvies on a building site... though you might have to be on some occasions. In base you will call me "sir".' Another pause. 'If you are fortunate to go out with me, I will tell you what name to use.'

He inclined slightly towards the female to his left. 'This lady is our intelligence officer. You will call her "ma'am".'

There had been a slight disagreement between them beforehand over this. Reluctantly, Eileen Kanna had agreed.

'Likewise, if out with ma'am, she will have another name.'

The audience assumed that she was from the Army's Intelligence Corps.

The commander confirmed that their role would be passive surveillance. They would operate province-wide and also, to a limited extent, south of the Border. Sometimes their appearance would need to be changed, but there were make-up artists on call. Leave would be as required. They were not here to attack, infiltrate or follow IRA ASUs. Their targets would be specific.

'Our targets.' He paused. 'Unfortunately within the RUC Special Branch there are a few bad apples...'

'A few!' An ironic Walsall accent. 'The whole f***ing barrel.'

It was Tamworth. The commander was not amused but Braco glimpsed the fleeting, wry smile of the intelligence officer.

They were part of Operation *Mythical*.

They would not carry British Army identity cards, but would instead be supplied with identities – sometimes just passports – depending on the task. The army or police would not know of their missions. They would not carry weapons; some muffled disquiet. On rare occasions, however, they would be armed though never in the South. If stopped by the army or police they would have cover stories. If taken to a SF base they were to try to bluff it out. Only as a last resort were they to request to speak to a senior officer and ask them to telephone a given number.

There were no questions. The commander handed over to the intelligence officer.

She thanked them for volunteering for the apple-dooking mission. Laughter.

'We have identified a number of Special Branch officers who have gone bad.'

She paused, then smiling at Tamworth said, 'I have worked with some good Branch officers.'

Her listeners assumed she meant RUC ones.

'Now don't be surprised that the opposition should seek to turn police officers, especially Branch ones. Usually because of money or marital problems. We do the same.'

Another pause as she surveyed her audience.

'We are not interested in the Branch officers – they will get their comeuppance. It's their contacts. What we would call their handlers. We would...'

She decided 'guess' was not the right word, although accurate.

'... assess that their handlers would be trusted volunteers... maybe not initially but as the IRA exploit their asset it is likely they would use someone who could ask the right questions. What we call tasking. And the produce, the information from the officer would go to those at the top. Of course, the rogue officer might be using their contact for their own financial gain. I am not interested in labelling the targeted officers as corrupt or rotten, traitors. I'll leave that to those who have too much time on their hands.'

Another pause accompanied by a clucking of her tongue and the same wry smile that Braco had noticed earlier.

'Instead, an opportunity, a route to the top of the IRA. I appreciate we all know who the leaders are but...'

She seemed to scrutinise each one of her audience.

'Do we know who their most trusted lieutenants, aides are? Of course their families, but there are others. We can estimate, guess, but we don't know for certain. There are the leaders and the active volunteers but it is the seam between them. The equivalent of our staff officers.'

An impish smile.

'And we all know what the real soldiers think of staff officers!'

This remark was greeted by a ripple of amusement but a scowl from the commander.

'Our mission is to locate the seam and mine it.'

The commander frowned at this comment because she was supposed to restrict their target to rogue SB officers. He had been selected to command the team not only because of his previous special duties experience, but because his brother was a SIS officer and the major hoped to join the Service.

Eileen had expanded her briefing because at some stage, even now, the soldiers, certainly most of them, would be questioning why their skills were being directed at corrupt police officers and not at preventing terrorism and capturing terrorists. She would square it with her superiors.

'That is why security has to be water-tight. One inadvertent slip and you will be gone.' The impish smile. 'To our Siberia.'

A pause.

'Finally, there cannot be any guarantee of success. No doubt you all have taken part in operations which never bore any fruit. We might be searching for the intelligence equivalent of Fool's Gold. But it's worth the search.'

Another pause with a wistful smile.

'The sad thing is that none of us might ever know whether our search found real gold. Those who use the gold will never tell us.'

A broad smile.

'I know you have all heard it before but source protection is an absolute.'

— 12 —

Braco's team was given call-sign 2, with each operative using an individual call-sign of 2 alpha and so on; Braco's was 2 charlie. Their target was the same Branch officer whom they had followed during the final work-up exercise, still with the code-word *Trent*. They had shepherded him for three months without producing any evidence of his involvement with the IRA until one Thursday evening, when *Trent* parked his car in a busy hospital car-park. He spent forty minutes in a ward visiting an elderly woman. On returning to his vehicle, he was met by another man and both got into *Trent's* vehicle. Their encounter lasted for five minutes. The unknown man left and went to another vehicle with a driver. The two vehicles left the car-park, with one going towards Derry and *Trent* towards his home in County Antrim. Call-sign 2 divided their assets to follow both vehicles.

In the operational report – Oprep 047 – *Trent* had returned to his own home. In respect of the other man it was reported:

'The green Opel Ascona AUI 9218 drove directly to the car-park of the Altnagevin Hospital in the Waterside area of Londonderry. The passenger, not identified, who had been in *Trent's* vehicle left the Opel, which drove away immediately. Due to the lack of assets, it was decided to concentrate on the passenger. He got into a black Austin Princess AIW 6219 which was parked under the lights of the hospital entrance. Estimated the target was aged around late twenties/early thirties, black fuzzy hair and medium build. Photographs taken. Followed to the Creggan area of Londonderry where he parked in Iniscarn Road and walked towards Central Drive. It was decided due to lack of assets to exercise caution and to withdraw.'

Eileen Kanna had attached her assessment to the end of the report:

'1. Green Opel Ascona AUI 9218 registered to Keith Porteous aged 42, hospital porter in Altnegevin Hospital. No trace of involvement with PIRA. Possibly part of pool of ancillaries used for low-level tasks such as driving. However, not confirmed that Porteous was the driver.

2. Black Austin Princess AIW6219 registered to Declan McGuigan 23 b Iniscarn Road, DOB 12/12/1956, unemployed though known to work part-time in different pubs. Interned. 1975 – Served one year for possession of a rifle and ammunition.

3. Unidentified driver of Austin believed to be James *Bap* Morrin, 211 a Creggan Heights, DOB 30/11/54, 5' 10', medium build, black hair, blue eyes. Unemployed. Interned. Sourced to have taken part in attacks on security forces. Arrested on five occasions but never charged. His identity to be confirmed once C/S Two operatives view the photographs.'

Braco and Tring were already seated in the not-quite-full Ballymena pub when their target *Trent* entered. In the two months since the hospital encounter, *Trent* had had two meetings with *Bap* Morrin, one in the same hospital car-park and the other in a hotel car-park close to Coleraine. On this evening, the Branch officer did not meet with the IRA man. Tring had bought the drinks at the bar, a bottle of Harp and a white wine. *Trent* stood inside the doorway surveying the lounge, his face showing concern, even alarm. Braco realised that he was looking at two men at the bar. Braco knew the taller, bald-headed man was a Branch officer who had briefed Braco when he was with the Group. He was confident that the Branch officer would not recognise him because there had never been a one-to-one, and in those days his heavy facial growth was almost a beard. *Trent* turned and left. There was no point in following him because the other teams which had shepherded him there would pick him up and put him back in his pen.

Braco knew that leaving the pub without finishing their drinks might be spotted by someone, even the barmen, and he knew that the Branch relied on bar staff – as did the opposition. They would finish their drinks. The two men at the bar had apparently not seen Braco's target, another Branch officer. The two suited men were joined by another, more casually dressed man. It was his COP sergeant. Briefly, Braco informed Tring that he knew him.

The sergeant knew the two men and Braco surmised that the smaller, heavier man was also a Branch officer. There was laughing and good-natured finger wagging by the soldier at the taller Branch man, whose eyes were directed at a table in the corner occupied by three women and a man, with an empty chair in the corner. They were not members of the security forces, possibly UDR, but Braco thought that unlikely. His erstwhile sergeant returned to the table, sat down in the empty chair and sipped his orange juice.

Yes, it was Murray. He always sat where he could observe the door or doors and the whole room. The two Branch men left, pausing at the table for a quick, smiling exchange of words. Braco was intrigued by seeing Murray there. He told Tring to go out to the vehicle to find out what was going on with the others, but remain in the car to observe people leaving. When Tring stood up to leave, Braco sensed that the girl's movement had attracted Murray's attention, and he was sure that his former comrade had recognised him.

Murray and his group left. Braco was curious but alarmed. Murray would not be allowed to travel on his own even if it was in a relatively safe area. He was sure that he was not part of any special forces unit. Murray seemed to know the others; it was not just a first meeting in a pub. The two Branch officers had not seemed surprised that he was there. Also, as far as Braco was aware, Murray never had a reputation for being a womaniser. Nevertheless, his being in a pub on his own was a serious breach of SOPs. He resolved to find out what he was doing. It was for Murray's own good, even his protection. His first task, which would be easy, was to find out his unit. He would find a way of warning him off.

Braco would have been even more shocked if he had known that Murray had been to Dublin for two weekends without permission.

– 13 –

Damien McGlone did not want to attend the Troops Out meeting in London.

He was on holiday. It was a time for concerts, visiting museums and reading, notwithstanding that *Gaggie* McKenna had told, no, ordered him to avoid any pro-Republican gatherings at all times. Damien was to remain the clean-skin, respectable choirmaster.

His role as a messenger had initially been sporadic, taking sealed letters or small packages to locations both residential and commercial in Belfast, Ballymena and Dublin. The items to be delivered were placed through his letter-box, usually at night. On rare occasions, he collected letters, but only from Belfast to be taken back to Derry. Sometimes he was instructed to attend at the house in Coshquin or at another in one of the more respectable parts of Derry. *Gaggie* McKenna was mostly interested in whether he had been stopped and questioned by the Brits or the RUC. He had been stopped several times but only searched on two occasions. Damien had never felt people were watching him when he delivered the items or that he was being followed by cars, even helicopters. When questioned by *Gaggie*, Damien was adamant that he had never told anyone, especially his family, about his courier duties.

On a number of occasions, he was debriefed by the tall, amiable Hugh Devlin who was of a similar age to *Gaggie*. Damien surmised that it was likely they had progressed through the ranks together to senior positions. Devlin was friendlier than *Gaggie*, though Damien had heard that he could be more ruthless than *Gaggie*. Damien was aware that Devlin was a feared man in Derry, but unlike *Gaggie*, Devlin was respected – though Damien winced inwardly when he thought of some of the punishment beatings allegedly ordered by Devlin. The tall man told him the work that he was doing was vital and appreciated, but he should relax and not look for possible surveillance. Anyway, he would never be able to spot them

Initially, Damien's tension and fear had been eased by Devlin. Later he pondered that in Derry he was probably safe, but in the other towns, different people had seen him, though they might not be aware of what he was doing. On the other hand, if Devlin was relaxed, he should be.

For a period he was sometimes given short verbal messages to take to certain individuals, again mostly in Belfast or Dublin. He never understood the meaning or import of these messages, and again he surmised that these were only part of the overall message. The recipients were always middle-aged even elderly men, occasionally women, and he recognised a couple of them from newspaper or TV reports. He delivered his messages in restaurants, parks and shops, as if by a chance meeting or simply passing the time of day with a stranger but never in pubs. He was given a number of places to visit. The delivery of verbal messages ceased after six months. He did not know why and did not ask but he was relieved.

Over time, he became impressed by how security-conscious the IRA were. On one occasion, Devlin reminded him never to deviate from his instructions and especially, to keep things tight. They had to be tight because British intelligence was good, Special Branch in particular, who were a cute bunch of fuckers never to be underestimated. Too many, especially the city dickheads – Damien took this to mean Belfast people – thought they could outsmart the Special Branch. If he was ever arrested, he was to say nothing. It would be difficult but it was in his interests. On another occasion, Devlin took him outside into the garden of the Coshquin bungalow and confirmed that Damien knew what a tout, an informer, was. Devlin's eyes were piercing, his voice low and menacing.

'Don't ever.' A slight smile but still with an edge. 'It's the quickest way to meet your maker.'

In their second or third meeting *Gaggie* had also warned him against becoming a police informer, but Devlin's warning was more chilling and credible. Later, Damien pondered that the reason for the repeat of the warning was that he was now encountering more senior members of the IRA and Sinn Féin and carrying more important messages. He was aware of treacherous IRA volunteers being dumped, hooded and shot in the border lanes of South Armagh.

Previously, Damien's concerns and fear over surveillance by the army had been calmed by Hugh Devlin telling him that he would probably not spot any surveillance. Now, Devlin had sparked new and more terrifying fears in Damien on the consequences of becoming a tout. If he was arrested by the RUC, it was likely that he would name Devlin because of what he had heard of the police's harsh interrogation methods, he would crumble.

His sister was insistent. She wanted a break from her children, they could have a drink afterwards, and anyway she knew the speaker from Queen's University. Maeve had started a PhD at the same time as Christine Latham but unlike Christine, had binned it after a couple of months to go into teaching. She remembered Christine as very intelligent but intense, and very committed to the struggle for civil rights even though she was a Protestant.

Damien won one argument, in that they would sit at the back near to the exit. His mind had wandered during the speech, more a tirade, but he still heard the usual republican phrases and slogans. Even his sister wanted to leave at the end of the speech and not wait for the questions, preferring instead to retire to a local pub. Damien finished his half pint quickly but his sister won this argument and had another large white wine. Seldom away from the clutches of her family, Maeve was determined to exploit and enjoy her temporary bout of freedom.

'It's Maeve, isn't it? I thought I saw you in the hall.'

The voice was pleasant, the congeniality of an academic's voice. Christine told her male friend, her minder, to get her a drink and she would join him and the others in a minute. Maeve was an old friend from Belfast. She sat down.

Christine said smilingly, 'I won't ask what you thought of the meeting.'

Maeve returned the smile saying, 'To be honest, really an excuse to get away from the kids.'

She introduced her brother who was on a visit from the North. 'I had to drag him out. Not his thing. Music is ...'

'I know. I have met Mister McGlone before.' A tone of respect.

'Oh! I'm sorry. I don't recall. I am sorry.'

'No reason why you should. I was just part of the choir... and it was a few years ago. You came to my Church in South Belfast, Church of Ireland. Our choir needed some assistance.'

'Did I help?'

'You most certainly did.'

'Who was your choirmaster?'

'Mister Bryce, James Bryce.'

'Oh yes. I remember. How is he?'

Christine shook her head, a hint of sadness in the movement. 'I haven't seen him for a while.' An awkward pause, now wistful. 'Not in the choir now.'

Nods of understanding from the brother and sister.

'Better return to my hosts.'

Brief handshakes as Christine's purposeful look from the meeting flooded back into her face.

Despite his denial to his sister, Damien had noted Christine's sadness and the readjustment of her expression before rejoining her comrades. He thought about, but decided against telling his masters back in Derry of his attendance at the meeting and the encounter with Christine Latham. He had disobeyed their instructions not to attend republican events. He hoped, prayed that his breach of discipline would not be discovered.

Christine had no doubts about informing her handler of the attendees, including the McGlones. She narrated her limited previous involvement with the brother and sister. She did express surprise at the attendance of Damien McGlone, though with the caveat that he was probably there just as company for his sister who had used the meeting – understandably – as an excuse to get away from the children. Without revealing the source or the reason, the Metropolitan Police's Special Branch was asked to run a check on Maeve McGlone – married name not known – but it was low priority. The RUC's SB was not asked to do a similar check on Damien McGlone.

With Christine's information and the scouring of back copies of the *Derry Journal* and other papers, it was easy to obtain a photograph of Damien and identify his address. He was a well-known local personality, though his profile was not as high as in the past. Eileen noted that he did get around, including Belfast and Dublin. Despite Godden's note agreeing with Christine's assessment that Damien McGlone was unlikely to be involved, Eileen Kanna decided that at the first opportunity one of her teams would take a look at him. She also hoped that Godden's IRA equivalent would conclude that it was unlikely Christine Latham was involved with the Brits.

— 14 —

The three were in the first floor sitting room of the Waterloo safe house, which was also the nerve centre for Op *Mythical*. The only item on the agenda was a review of the Operation. They agreed that Christine Latham was providing good intelligence on the political side. Furthermore, with the ongoing Hunger Strikes, it was essential to monitor the current debate within republican circles on moving more towards the political arm, though at present the men of violence continued to be the dominant voice.

'Anyway, I think Christine is getting bored giving the same spiel at the meetings and rallies. Think she would prefer to concentrate on her academic career. I am sure she could get a post in GB.'

'Did she tell you that?' The curt riposte so beloved by a particular breed of English public-school boys.

'No. Just by observing and...'

'A female's feeling. What do they call it? Feminine intuition?' Ormsby's tone was condescending.

'Possibly.'

'Well, Arthur, she has been in place for what... seven or eight years?' A nod of agreement from Godden. 'She could be bored. We three have changed in the same time.'

Nods of agreement from the other two.

'Do we have any other coverage of the politics?'

'Branch and Five have good – though hate to say it – better than us.'

'Think a review of her position might be needed. But leave her in place for now.'

Ormsby did not divulge that the Security Service were extremely satisfied with Christine's information and were keen that she remained in place. The other two had not been made aware of Christine's disclosure to the Security Service, nor of the long-standing information-sharing agreement.

Following a discussion, it was agreed that the Special Branch officer *Dee* should be ditched. The corrupt Special Branch officer would be disclosed to the RUC but via an appropriate cover story by army intelligence.

The discussion turned to *Trent*, who was meeting an experienced, mid-level terrorist. Increasingly, the IRA were using counter-surveillance measures and the *Mythical* team had had to abort some operations to avoid compromise.

'Again, I'm not sure what value he is to the opposition. He is viewed as a run-of-the-mill Branch officer. Maybe reach inspector rank.'

In his liaison role with Five and Army Intelligence, Godden had made discreet enquiries about *Trent*. Their surveillance team had observed *Trent* meeting his own three sources, two middle-level loyalists and a low grade republican.

'Arthur, we do the same. We pick up a source. Discover that there is not much to exploit but we are reluctant to off-load... just in case.'

'But the IRA do not have the structure or resources to run intelligence operations.'

'Not sure that I agree with that. If you read the histories and review our papers, intelligence has always played an important part in the IRA's planning.'

'And you have read all the histories and papers, Eileen.' A statement rather than a question.

'Most of them, sir.'

'Why do they retain this...' turning to Godden. '*Trent?*'

'Yes, sir.'

His questioning returned to Eileen. 'Why do they retain him?'

'Same reason you gave earlier.'

'Touché.'

'But they do seem keen to retain him, shown by their increased anti-surveillance to protect him.'

'Certainly seems the case.' Godden did not want to be overshadowed by his female subordinate's knowledge of Ireland but he would focus on the present not the past. 'Also, sir, I understand from Five that due to the Hunger Strikes there have been less meetings with their agents by Branch.'

'That is simply preposterous... and negligent. Dereliction of duty.'

Genuine but controlled anger in Ormsby's voice.

'With these bloody fenians starving themselves to death, the Branch should be out collecting as much intelligence as possible. How can we advise the PM on how to respond if we don't know what the bloody opposition are doing and thinking. She's just willing to let them starve themselves to death.'

'Things are quite tense at the moment and the IRA will no doubt be watching for any increased Branch activity. Would not help if a few of their agents ended up shot in the back of the head.'

A patronising smile from Ormsby. 'Arthur, you can never forget you were once in Special Branch.'

'No...' Godden was silenced by Ormsby's raised right hand.

'The question is, do we continue.' He did not wait for a response. 'I think we have to. We know that these operations can take time.'

The others nodded knowingly, but what Godden and Kanna did not know of was the PM's review of the operation after three years. Ormsby suspected that the review was at the behest of C, who was under pressure for the Service to concentrate on the Soviet Union, the Middle East and increasingly Southern Africa. Resources were always insufficient and should not be wasted on Ulster, was the argument put forward by the other assistant directors.

Another reason was that the failure of Op *Mythical* would end Ormsby's chance of the top job. Ormsby was aware of this and rather suspected that C shared this view. He was conscious of his colleagues' open contempt for Godden, the nonentity who was the former colonial Special Branch officer, and for Eileen Kanna, the colonial typist who had had the gall to be disdainful and dismissive of experienced officers in Madrid, Lisbon and Rome. Ormsby knew that failure would end the careers of his two subordinates, but that was minor collateral.

'So we are agreed.'

Consenting nods from the other two.

'But, I think it might soon be time to pull *Trent* in.'

Both subordinates thought it was too soon, though both knew that Ormsby was not in the mood for dissent. Each had concluded that Ormsby was under pressure but he would not reveal it, a hallmark of his particular breed.

'Do we have a secure place to take him to?'

'We are recceing some at the moment.'

'Decide on one. Ensure you have an alternative.'

'Yessir.' In unison.

'Will you need anyone from the Joint Interrogation Centre?'

'I think we can manage with our team. Some have the necessary experience.'

'I agree with Eileen. Also, bringing people over could have security implications.'

'That's true.' Ormsby paused. 'Our offer needs to be realistic and positive. I don't want him running back to his superiors offering *mea culpas*.'

'Think he's a Prot.' Kanna's quip was met with disapproval.

'Needs to be offered total immunity.'

'The opposition will eventually find out...'

Ormsby interrupted Godden, 'Of course they will, and cry foul about British dirty tricks.' He grinned. 'Thankfully, people will think it is Special Branch or Five. I don't want our fingerprints anywhere on it, nor even a soupçon of our breath suspected.'

'Well, *Trent* will probably think it's Branch or Five he is dealing with... And that he's been picked up by the SAS.'

Ormsby said, 'You are absolutely right, Eileen. But it must be made clear, crystal clear to *Trent* that he does not talk to anyone else or he will face dire consequences.'

'I think he will enjoy that... being a super-spy.'

'You mean he's a fantasist, a Billy Liar. Do you agree, Arthur?'

'I think Eileen is probably right.'

Ormsby sat back in his chair, his eyes half-closed as if praying, then said, 'We will probably have to remove him to some remote place.'

'He might not be keen to go.'

'Arthur, he won't have a choice. We'll send him to the Falklands or...'

A mischievous grin.

'We will set him up with a bar in Thailand. Hopefully the drugs, drink and women will squelch his mind. Thailand does that to men. Saw it with the Americans on R and R from Vietnam. No one will believe him. Protecting the integrity of the Service is more important.'

Eileen Kanna wondered where Ormsby found the pinhead on which to dance this particular moral fantasy.

'Good. Anything else?'

'There's Mayne.'

'Yes. What's happening with him?'

Godden explained that he had not been in contact with him since Mayne had completed his police recruit training – which was not in itself worrying, as it had been agreed that he should build his career with the aim of joining Special Branch. However, the concern was that he was not making any effort to advance his career, seemingly content to remain in uniform as a constable.

'Yes, Arthur. I bumped into his brother at a drinks reception a few weeks ago. The usual chit-chat about families and he mentioned that his brother, our Mayne, had mentioned joining the Met. Heard anything?'

The other two shook their heads.

'I fear this is another cul-de-sac. But I would like confirmation that young Peter has deserted us. You were never convinced by him, Eileen!'

A consenting nod from the female officer. A pondering pause by Ormsby.

'I don't want to approach his brother. He seems to remain of the view that his brother joined the RUC for love. An approach by you, Arthur?'

'I would rather not, sir. Certainly not over there.'

'Yes, yes.'

'There might be a way, sir. One of our team was in the same regiment as Mayne. Saw it from the records. Each one had to produce a list of people in the Province whom they knew and who might recognise them. Mayne was mentioned by one of our operatives.'

'You suggesting that your operative sidles up to Mayne and ask him if he's still batting for our team?' Ormsby's smiling response was tinged with derision.

Godden was scornful. 'Same regiment! They will concoct a story to cover for Mayne. Regimental loyalty, huh. Disloyalty.'

'He wouldn't do that. He's one of our best, if not our best operative. My experience is that soldiers are more trustworthy than most.' Anger in her voice. 'And certainly have more integrity than most.'

'Eileen knocked Arthur for six.'

She resisted the temptation to say that she did not play cricket and that it was a stupid game.

A smile by Ormsby. 'I forgot about your little sojourn with the soldiery in the colonies.'

Another pondering interlude.

'It might work. Let me give it some more thought.' He stood up. 'Right, some supper. My treat. While you get your hats and coats, I'll say hello to the others. They like encouraging words from head office.'

His two subordinates stood up and waited for him to leave the room.

'Don't ever do that again.' A sharp whisper.

'What?'

'Propose something to Ormsby without running it past me first.'

'I just thought of it. Thought he was asking for solutions.'

'Never again. You come to me first. I'm your immediate superior.'

Again, Eileen thought it wiser to soothe Godden by not responding, but she knew it would not stop her from doing the same thing again in the future.

15

The 'seize and conscript' operation was set. The plan was to seize *Trent* after his meeting with the IRA and take him to an isolated building with the aim of conscripting him into the service of SIS. It was estimated that at most they would have one hour to convince, more accurately terrify him into co-operating. Refusal by *Trent* would create a dilemma, in that his treachery would, of course, be reported to his superiors, and that would then pose a threat to the security of Op *Mythical*.

The SIS operational team had technical support from a dedicated GCHQ desk with its product restricted to the Op *Mythical* team. Communications interception had revealed that the IRA contacted the target *Trent* on his home telephone, using a simple cover such as selling something or offering tickets for holidays, followed by the agreement of a date. It was assessed that the cover story for the next meeting was arranged at the previous meet, and assumed that there was a method for aborting any meet due to the target's work. However, since the monitoring of his telephone had begun, not one meet had been cancelled. This was considered further evidence both of the target's lowly position in Special Branch and of his lack of access to worthwhile intelligence.

Braco's concern, raised at the debrief after the final test

exercise that there no Irish voices in the team, had been addressed. Two Irish voices had been added.

Pimlico, a specialist covert surveillance officer, who came originally from Coleraine, was seconded from the Metropolitan Police to SIS as a trainer – part of Ormsby's cherished policy of cross-fertilisation. The police, the Security Service, H M Customs and other agencies paid lip-service to it, but it was useful to these agencies in that attachments could be used as a carrot for potentially bored officers, and there was also the hope of shining some light on the SIS, the most secretive and quirkiest service. Pimlico had been interviewed by Ormsby and accepted the offer of joining the *Mythical* team.

Ormsby's admonition that the Met must not know of his new role received a rueful smile and the comment, 'I don't think my bosses know who I am.'

A year's undocumented secondment was agreed with the Met. It was unlikely a senior officer would ask about him; out of sight, out of mind. Other officers in the same role were likely to assume that he was on another police covert operation.

Hennessy was a SIS officer. He came from Belfast, having being recruited by SIS when he was at Durham University. His patch was South East Asia; he had arrived in Bangkok as the Americans were fleeing from Saigon. He knew his time and efforts were fruitless and forlorn, despite recruiting journalists, former diplomats and military officers who had fled from South Vietnam. The intelligence officer knew the exaggerated claims of his 'agents' were made to recreate and finance their extravagant lifestyles in exile. Hennessy did not hide his scorn for the alleged intelligence he was producing, which brought him into conflict with the head of station in Hong Kong to whom he reported.

The head of station considered that Hennessy's dress, in particular the bushy beard, displayed visible contempt for the Service, further aggravated by the Belfast man's conduct in Hong Kong. He did not socialise with his peers, preferring to spend his time in the girlie bar areas of Tsim Sha Tsui and Wanchai.

Hennessy knew the owner of the Carousel Bar was not a local. She was elegant and haughty. She had suddenly appeared in the bar shadowing the owner, then the latter was gone after a few weeks. She now owned the bar, and had expressed her displeasure at the local Chinese girls. In the new owner's view, they were unenthusiastic in their work, and indeed displayed arrogance towards their customers – mainly British soldiers and some expat lawyers and accountants. It was true that the only time the bar girls were roused from their inertia was when there was a requirement to please the American servicemen on R & R. It was also true that their enthusiasm was largely sparked by the US dollar; the American servicemen were generous in their spending unlike the mean British soldiers. Young, lonely men from the mid-western states had never experienced anything like Hong Kong or Bangkok. However, with the fall of South Vietnam, it was anticipated that the flow of American dollars would cease, though the new bar owner anticipated there would be more American warships arriving, if only to salve the USA's conscience over their betrayal of their ally and to reassure other allies in the region.

Hennessy admired the way she operated her bar. For her part, she enjoyed his conversation; he was undoubtedly more cultured than her other customers. One evening when the Carousel was quiet, she confirmed that she was from Saigon, the daughter of a general in the defeated South Vietnamese Army. An uncle, her father's brother, was a senior cadre in the North Vietnamese Army, who actually arrived in Saigon in February 1975, a few months before the tanks stormed the presidential palace. The uncle could not – or would not – prevent the execution of her father for his crimes against the people, but he would do his best for his beautiful niece, fluent in English, French and Mandarin, and insisted that she should leave. Her father also was adamant that she should leave. Pham van Mai was able to buy a seat on one of the last Cathay Pacific flights out before the fall of the city on 30 April. Mai arrived in the British Colony with few clothes but a case full of US dollars. Through his contacts, her father had obtained a US passport for her. Mai was always concerned that it was a forgery but she never encountered any problems. Her mother was actually a Hoa, Vietnamese Chinese, who had a cousin in Hong Kong.

She narrated to Hennessy how, with the help of her cousin, she had bought the bar and was in the process of replacing the local hostesses with girls from Thailand and Vietnam. The latter were being smuggled out of their detention camps in the Colony, or escaping by Mai arranging for the camp fence to be cut. Mai told the Irishman of the growing tension between Vietnam and China, which was not unexpected because there had been a long history of conflict between the two countries. The Vietnamese Chinese were being driven out, which exacerbated the discord. Finally, she disclosed that one of the reasons her communist uncle had helped her was because he was aware that the tension between the two countries – which had been deadened by the war with America – would again come to the fore, and he might have to flee in the future. Even though her mother was married to the traitor brother, he might be tarnished by the family connection, especially by his rivals, and could therefore require his niece's help in the future.

Without revealing the real source, Hennessy reported the potential conflict between the Communist allies. It was graded at a low level, being considered unlikely, though David Buchanan-Henderson, the senior Foreign Office official responsible for South East Asia and aware of the history, thought it credible and tasked SIS to collect more intelligence. Notwithstanding the Foreign Office's tasking decision, it was decided that Hennessy was not attuned to the nuanced mind of the oriental and he was posted back to London, where he was assigned to a research project. Then a trawl came in for Ulstermen. When he chose the operational name Hennessy, Godden thought it might be due to an appreciation of brandy whereas it was in honour of the bars on Hennessy Road in Hong Kong.

All the operatives were deployed, with the OC, paired with the female operative Tring, controlling the operation out on the ground, leaving Eileen Kanna and the two signallers to monitor the progress of this innovative but potentially risky operation. The two Irishmen and two others were at the chosen 'interrogation centre'. Hennessy and Pimlico had discussed, agreed and rehearsed their actions on *Trent*. Nobody else in the team would speak to *Trent*. It was to be a silent snatch. The target might think it was the IRA taking him for interrogation to ensure that he was not playing them, or possibly the Brits. The first voice he would hear would be a rough, harsh, Protestant Ulster voice and the second one an even harsher East Belfast voice. Hennessy could do both. The hope was that *Trent* would be 'scared shitless' knowing the UFF or whoever they were would have no hesitation in killing him, a traitor, and this would mean that he would agree to anything to save his life.

A team of four commanded by Tamworth were in the snatch van leaving the others on surveillance. They knew the meeting would be in the car-park of a hospital, the regular rendez-vous, or a hotel. It was the former. The meeting was following the same procedure, *Trent* going into the hospital for around twenty minutes. The opening scene of the second act was *Trent* leaving the hospital, walking towards the car of his IRA contact, *Bap* Morrin, and placing himself in the back seat, directly behind the driver's seat and diagonally opposite Morrin.

The third act was *Trent* leaving the IRA's vehicle and returning to his car. It was a tightly scripted and unchanging play. Except in tonight's performance. An additional actor, a male, entered the set and got into the back seat beside *Trent*.

The OC asked if any of the call-signs could identify the new and unexpected individual. The operative closest to the new player thought he looked like the individual that Acorn, army radio-speak for the intelligence officer, had recently tasked him to observe in *Donkey Walk*, the nickname for Londonderry. Although their communications were sophisticated and secure, they still used code-words and nicknames, an extra security fence.

All call-signs were told 'Wait'. The team members knew that there was probably a conversation between the OC and Eileen Kanna on the command net, the frequency unknown to the lesser mortals, the mere operatives.

There was movement. The new player left the vehicle and walked slowly to his own vehicle parked in the middle of the third parking row in front of Morrin's vehicle. He sat in his vehicle without switching on the engine. Although the operative felt confident it was the recent *Donkey Walk* target, he could not be certain. Braco drove out of the parking space next but one to *Trent's* car to be replaced by the snatch van. Hospital visiting hours were ongoing so the car-park remained quiet.

The exchange on the command net was terse. Kanna wanted the new player followed to confirm his identity. The OC was adamant that he did not have the assets to do *Trouser Leg*, the nickname for the snatch, and follow the possible *Donkey Walk*.

The new player switched on his engine and turned on his lights at the exact time that *Trent* left Morrin's vehicle. Synchronised. The operatives felt instinctively that it was co-incidence. *Trent* would take at least ninety seconds to reach his car. He never rushed, an ambling gait, and never took the quickest route from the IRA vehicle to his own.

On the command net, there was a further terse, even angry exchange between the OC and the SIS officer.

'Abort *Trouser leg*! Abort *Trouser leg*!'

Eileen Kanna's voice was calm but authoritative.

'Three alpha acknowledge.'

The snatch team call-sign did so. There were further orders for Braco and two other call-signs, including the OC's, to fix and follow the *Donkey Walk* man. The other call-signs, along with the interrogation team, were to return to *Power Cut*, their base.

Hennessy was also on the command net and knew of the change of plan before Tamworth and the rest of the inter-rogation team. Experience had taught him that there can always be changes to an operation. However, this decision to follow someone it was likely the unit already knew seemed illogical, particularly when they could be about to progress Op *Mythical* for the first time by recruiting a source linked to the IRA.

He was irked. He would make his view known to his superiors.

16

The debrief had been short. The decision to abort was taken for wider considerations, which of course could not be disseminated. The new player was indeed Damien McGlone, a notable and respected choirmaster, and a very surprising connection to the IRA. Eileen Kanna did not disclose her knowledge of his London trip. At some stage, *Trouser Leg* would go ahead but further enquiries would have to be made concerning the choirmaster.

The only sour and frustrating comment was by Tamworth.

'All our efforts just seem to allow you to open more personnel cards and feed the computers.'

The other operatives shared his frustration but their experiences in Northern Ireland told them it was the way of the secret world. No longer was there an expectation of tangible success. Any actionable intelligence would be passed to the SAS: it was the way of the covert world.

Left unsaid by the operatives was that Ma'am was running Op *Mythical*.

Privately, before the team debrief, the OC and Hennessy had expressed their disapproval and frustrations. The Belfast man was correct in saying that one call-sign was sufficient for following the choirmaster, especially considering that Eileen knew the individual based on the operative's tentative recognition. The snatch could have gone ahead. But it was Eileen's call and he would say no more on the matter.

Major Tim Somerville was stung by what he considered Eileen's undermining of his authority. He was responsible for operational decisions on the ground, or so he was led to believe by Arthur Godden. In military operations, there had to be a clear and recognised command and control structure. Eileen reminded him gently that *Mythical* was not a military operation, which brought a smile to Hennessy's lips though hidden behind his bushy beard. Somerville felt that he had no other option but to seek clarity on his precise role and the extent of his authority from Godden. Eileen conceded that was his right.

Alone, she sat at her desk feeling a mixture of self-doubt and anxiety. The former came from the aborting of *Trouser Leg*, in that Hennessy was right that the snatch operation could have gone ahead. But if it had and *Trent* did not play ball, the consequences might have been fatal both for the rogue policeman and *Mythical*. He might have agreed to work for them, but once he had realised it was for the Brits and that it was unlikely he would be killed, he could have thrown himself on the mercy of a Church or some left-wing organisation, eager to criticise perfidious Albion. She was sure her decision was right.

McGlone could be different. She had an instinct about the choirmaster, following Christine Latham's report and subsequent investigations. Why was he sent to meet a low grade Special Branch officer? Did this indicate, no infer, that the choirmaster had authority over *Bap* Morrin, *Trent's* usual handler? This would suggest the choirmaster held a position of authority in the IRA, even though there was no intelligence to support that and he did not fit the mould of an IRA man. She knew it was unwise to stereotype.

Apart from her superiors, none of the *Mythical* team had knowledge of Christine Latham or Peter Mayne. She mused that she felt a special bond with them because of their time at Glasgow University, though neither of them had shown any awareness of being at university at the same time as her. She pondered the matter and the options. Despite Godden's objections, Ormsby had consented to Braco approaching Mayne to confirm if he was 'still batting for the right side'. She sent for Braco.

'Yes. I remember Peter Mayne. We got on quite well together though he was senior to me. He left to join the RUC... Did he?'

Eileen nodded. Braco became slightly apprehensive.

'I did disclose him as required when I joined the team.'

'Yes you did. It's not that.'

She paused. She had consulted with Ormsby and Godden on how much she should tell Braco. Godden was adamant that it should be very little, only to be overruled by Ormsby who suggested a scenario to give to Braco, but in the end it would be down to her judgement.

'We would like you to approach Mayne and have a little chat with him.'

'Ma'am?' Inquisitive expression.

'Cut the ma'am. When it's just the two of us, it's Eileen... and you will remain Braco.'

The smile which for Braco illuminated her face.

'I like "Braco".'

She gave a skeleton outline of the relationship with Mayne, with no mention of SIS or infiltrating the RUC Special Branch. He was merely to report on the RUC in general but, in particular, their attitude towards the army which would allow the army to massage their approach to their brothers in the war against terrorism. Despite her previous experience with the army, Eileen Kanna, like others, did not understand the British Army. It was not a homogeneous body. Braco recalled his COP sergeant's description of the British Army as a confederation of tribes. And despite his intention, after seeing Murray in a Ballymena pub, of contacting him to warn him of his conduct, especially the danger of being on his own, he had been too busy to contact him. Also, Murray might have a legitimate reason to be there. With so many different specialist units in the Province, he did not want to tread on another operation. Braco knew it was a lame excuse.

'We want to know if Mayne intends to honour his agreement.'

'If he doesn't?'

'That's not a problem.'

A clucking of her tongue. He had heard it before, usually if she was conveying sly indifference and usually when the OC was making a point.

'Provided he does not reveal our agreement to any third party.'

'So no double-tap.' A smile.

Eileen laughed. 'Never thought of that. Might be the solution... No!' She raised her hands, palms facing the soldier. 'And we will both erase that thought from our minds.'

A brief period of silence.

'How do you want me to approach him?'

'I will leave that up to you. Here's details of his current station, home and also where you will be living.' She slid the A4 brown envelope across the table. 'Read it, memorise...'

'Eat?'

Met by laughter from Eileen, her face illuminated.

'Whatever suits you. No, return it to me before you go. Do you need any help? For initial surveillance, security?'

' That might be helpful... but would leave the unit short.'

'Don't worry about that. They will be on one target.'

Braco surmised the target was the choirmaster.

She continued, 'How many?'

'Two.'

She nodded. 'Tring and...'

'Tamworth.'

'Oh! You will be staying in the university area. Tring and you might pass as students... but Tamworth?'

Another clucking of her tongue.

'At your address, there will be a caretaker who will provide you with keys and make you sign for your accommodation. He will give you a briefing. If you need me as a matter of urgency, he will contact me.'

'Right. When do you want me to begin and for how long?'

'Now. Let's start with ten days. Go away, read it and return it to me. You shouldn't have any questions. The other two are not to know the nature of this task. Understood?'

'Yes ma'am.' Both smiled.

'Two other points. If you see individuals you might recognise from previous ops, ignore them. Also, I might be down for another task. I will visit you though I will not be staying in any dingy student digs. Probably the Europa. Sono un giornalista con un giornale italiano.'

'Italian?' Braco asked.

'Si. Clever boy. Speak Italian?'

'No. But I did know an Italian girl and you sounded just like her when she spoke Italian.'

'I hope so or my education and training were a waste of money... taxpayers' money.'

The ring of the door-bell brought an almost immediate opening of the door. They were shown into the living-room of the three-storey end-terrace house with a lane to the side. The broad built, middle-aged man with an even broader Belfast accent said that he would join them shortly. There was tea and digestive biscuits for them. Obviously, when their drop-off was radioed in, the caretaker was informed.

The caretaker returned and sat himself down in an armchair to the left of the square bay-window. He told them to be seated. Tamworth took the other armchair directly across from the caretaker on the opposite side of the room, while the other two shared the sofa.

'I'm Bill.' Now a much softer accent. 'House rules first.'

He explained that the house was normally rented to students but it was now the beginning of the long summer holidays and the current residents had gone. He responded to Tamworth's puzzled look.

'Yes, it's a going concern. But the rent barely covers costs. We rent only to first year students who are usually from the counties, even the Republic and England... and they don't know the big city. During the summer we sometimes rent to visiting students, even some tourists.' He shook his head. 'Bloody fools! Anyway.'

They could use the living-room to watch TV, play cards and so on. He cooked breakfast for the students and would do the same for them. Bill was willing to cook dinner and tea as well, but it was up to them. There would always be food in if they wanted to cook for themselves or get takeaways. On the first floor, there were two bedrooms for their use. Who shared with whom was again a matter for them. The devices were switched off. A smile, more a smirk. There was a boxroom which was locked and not available to them. A bathroom of course. Also, the single attic bedroom was his and out-of-bounds. If they needed him there were intercoms in the living-room and two bedrooms.

'Don't buzz me unless it's an emergency. I'll tell you the same as the students. If you abuse it, I'll rip it out.'

A grin. He expected them to keep the place clean and tidy. There were no questions.

He had no knowledge of their task and would not ask questions, nor should they ask questions of him or any visitors he received. He was well known around the area but kept himself to himself. He was a merchant seaman who had settled back in Belfast. Bill went on to say that he had no family left in Belfast. The three operatives assumed that he was an asset of one of the myriad intelligence agencies based in HQNI.

It was unlikely anyone would ask them what they were doing there. People would assume they were students, possibly even visiting lecturers. There were a surprising number of Brits living in Belfast doing different jobs. Again, it was unlikely anyone would ask them why they were there. If they did, just grunt. If anyone asked them about him, they were to grunt louder and inform him.

They should familiarise themselves with the local area. If they carried their weapons, then they must ensure they had their military ID with them. Sometimes, the police stopped and searched students and university staff. There were elements in the university who were supporters or sympathetic to the IRA.

He did not tell his three new guests that he passed titbits to a friendly police officer, though the juicy bits went to SIS. The police thought the information came from chats with students or what he overheard, and were not aware that the rooms were wired for sound. On odd occasions, a student, usually to brag, would disclose that he or she knew one of the 'boys', republican or loyalist. If it came from a female it was more likely to be true. None of it was actionable intelligence but political. Most of it was passed to MI5 as per the agreement, though the one or two percent retained by SIS was usually about an individual with business links to Europe or links to the establishment in Dublin.

A vehicle with radios fitted and spares had been provided for them, and was in a near-by lock-up. He would provide the keys both for the lock-up and the vehicle. This vehicle was not to be parked near-by or even used to drive around the area.

They followed Bill's advice about getting to know the area on foot, either solo or in pairs. Braco had been given a temporary pass as a visiting student and a library card for the University. There were searches and scanning machines on entering some of the university buildings so he did not carry his personal weapon. Several times he thought he had seen *Forth*, the female target of their work-up exercise. Making discreet enquiries, he found out that she was Christine Latham, a lecturer in English.

On one occasion, he overheard a conversation between two security guards outside the library as she walked away. Expletive-strewn remarks that she was probably on her way to raise money for the hunger strikers. The final comment he overheard was something about what a disgrace it was, a Prot helping the fucking taigs. He was certain that it was *Forth* when he followed her to her home which was close to Bill's street. Braco surmised that Eileen Kanna had anticipated that they might spot *Forth* and he decided not to inform his two comrades of *Forth*/Christine Latham. Anyway, Eileen had also said that Tring and Tamworth should be told only what was necessary.

They did drive-pasts of Mayne's home and his police station but without any sighting of the target. After dinner on their first Friday night, with Bill having gone out for a beer, the three operatives held a debrief-cum-discussion. They agreed that the threatening, even frightening atmosphere in Belfast was due to the ongoing hunger strikes. They could hear the sound of disorder each night in West Belfast. Also they agreed that Belfast was different from the rest of the Province.

'But, remember we are mostly isolated here.'

The Walsall voice as usual bringing reality into their world.

'It's like being on a cruise and we see the sights only on short excursions. We're tourists and don't meet the people. I got to know the place and people better when patrolling round the Creggan and Bogside.'

The other two ignored his breach of the rules: one was not to speak of previous tours.

'You're right,' Tring said, while Braco nodded in agreement

'We treat these people like toy soldiers. Take them out to play with for a short time then put them back in their box.' He sighed. 'Forgetting that they have a life, family, even children.'

Another sigh more a growl.

'Think I need a beer.'

'Sorry, Tam. None in,' said Tring.

They left out the 'worth' when in base. Tring and Braco both thought the soldier from the Midlands was perceptive and good at his job, even though he presented to most people an image of being slow and clumsy.

'Let's go out. There's an Indian or Middle Eastern place not far from here. Sailor Bill told me it was alright and I recced it. They have a licence.'

'I couldn't eat anything else.' Braco smiled at Tring's response.

'I'll have a small curry and a couple of beers. You can have a coke, tea.' To Braco. 'You're up for it.'

'Tempting. But better not. Anyway, need to write up my report for ma'am.'

'No bollockings for you from ma'am. In fact, I think she likes you. Doesn't she?'

This last to Tring, not for confirmation but to annoy her because he knew – or rather surmised – that she was carrying a torch for Braco.

'She's too old for him!' Said with a smile though ingrained with a brusqueness.

He resisted a cutting reply simply saying, 'I'm off to bed. Better clean my nine milli... for the third time... today.'

Tring wanted to remain with Braco but thought it was better to go. 'Good idea. Goodnight.'

'Yea, goodnight. I'll finish this and wait for Sailor Bill.' A chuckle. Tamworth had a way of producing apt nicknames. 'So he can pass it up.'

They knew he had a telephone in his room and probably other devices, because they had identified a covert antenna fitted to the chimney which would be spotted only by a trained eye.

17

On the Sunday morning, five days after arriving in Belfast, Braco decided to go for a walk. He observed the passing people, old and young, strolling singles, couples, some with children. Remembering Tamworth's remarks about their not knowing people, he was not looking for terrorists, bad people, but ordinary people. Most people appeared normal and happy, apart from a couple of screaming children. He had considered going into a church, but thought the congregation were liable to know each other and he wished to avoid a welcoming but inquisitive minister or church warden.

He bought himself a newspaper, a normal Sunday morning activity. Arriving in the Botanic Gardens just after lunch, he sat on a bench beside two elderly women and read his paper intermittently whilst observing. The lady next to him offered him a sweet from a white paper bag. He held up his left hand and muttered, 'No, thanks.' He hoped they would not detect his accent.

He noticed the couple with the child on the bench on the other side of the grass lawn, not directly opposite but diagonally to his right. He turned his attention back to the paper but focused his interest on a girl, in her early twenties and probably a student. She was attractive. Their eyes locked and she smiled, which he returned with what had once been described as his winning smile, though he felt himself becoming more alert, wondering whether he had been clocked. He was glad he was carrying a weapon. The locked smiles were disengaged by the crying, more whining, of the child of the couple on the bench to the left of the attractive girl. He realised the man, the father, was Peter Mayne.

The covert soldier considered his options. He did not want to approach Mayne while his wife –presumably – was there but he was reluctant to lose the opportunity. The decision was made for him by Mayne, now standing, lifting the child, possibly a boy between one and two, into a pushchair. The policeman sat down again. There were waves and 'byes' as Braco stood up. He took the longer route to his target by going up the path to his left, turning right onto the path dividing two grass lawns and turned down towards Mayne, who was looking towards the mother as she pushed the buggy away.

Braco inclined his head towards the girl and smiled, which was met with her moving to her left in anticipation of him sitting down. He continued on the ten or so metres to Mayne's bench.

'Hello, Peter.' Instinctively the policeman's hand slid into the left side of his leather jacket.

Braco held up his two hands close to his chest, palms towards Mayne. 'Friendly.'

'I know you. From the...'

Braco interrupted him, 'Yes. May I sit down?'

This time Mayne moved to his left. Braco thought it must be something people do when someone is going to sit down beside them. He sat on Mayne's right whilst noticing the girl on the next bench stand up, throw him a disappointed – or was it disgusted – look and walk away, her back to him

'Thanks.'

'Don't tell me this is a chance meeting.' A sneering comment.

'In fact, it is.' Braco smiled.

The sneer remained.

'You were just out for a walk. In all the gin joints...'

'I was,' said with a shake of the head and a half laugh. 'It was a coincidence but I have been looking for you for the last few days.'

'Could just have called into my station... I assume you know where I work.'

'I do, but rather not.'

'Any mates around?'

'No.'

'You have been sent to talk to me.' More a statement than a question. 'I have been expecting someone, though not an old mucker.'

Mayne looked ahead, then to his left and right, pondering the circumstances.

'Did Ormsby send you?'

It was obvious the name meant nothing to the soldier, a genuine look of ignorance.

'Godden? The patronising one?'

The same response.

'A female?'

Braco nodded.

'Bloody hell! A messenger not even from the top.'

'Look can we have a chat soon. This is not suitable.'

'I'm going back to work for a couple of hours. For a briefing. I'm meeting a colleague soon. Near here. He's giving me a lift. My wife has the car.' He thought for a moment. 'Why don't you come to my place? I assume you know where I live?'

A slight nod by Braco, whose question was anticipated by Mayne.

'My wife won't be there. She's off to her mother's for Sunday dinner. A family gathering and they like to see the grandson. She will be spending the night there.'

'Okay. That suits me.' He did not have to clear it because Eileen had left the approach to him.

'About seven?' A nod of consent from Braco.

'But no one else... and no recording.'

'Agreed.'

'I have sufficient drink in. Let me leave first.'

The other two operatives had concerns with Braco's plan, as they had with this operation. They were ignorant of the target, his employment and work-place, being there simply as driver and back-up to Braco. He was dropped off three streets away from Mayne's address and told them that he would radio or telephone for pick-up and give the pick-up point.

When they had dropped him off, Tring quipped, 'We're now model soldiers taken out of our box when needed.'

'More like mushrooms. Kept in the dark and...'

Tring completed the saying. '... fed on shit.' They both laughed.

'Do you think he and ma'am are having a secret rendezvous?'

Tring did not respond, and Tamworth knew, as intended, he had touched a raw nerve.

18

The meeting had been brief. The commanding officer of the IRA'S Northern Command did not permit long meetings. When called to a meeting, he expected his subordinates to have a grip on their responsibilities. Also, he met only one head of a section at a time, quartermaster, head of finance, and on this occasion, head of Derry intelligence. Being a Derry man, he maintained a close watch on the Derry operations; the city if not the cradle, at least the heart-beat of the Provisional IRA.

Hugh Devlin was required to update his superior on the current intelligence–gathering operations and security threats. Although the two men had known each other since childhood, the IRA's chief in the North conducted these meetings in a business-like manner: there was no small-talk, enquiries about families. Devlin was surprised that *Gaggie* McKenna was at the meeting. The explanation was simple in that Devlin was being promoted and *Gaggie* was to be his replacement, though the former was still to be confirmed in post by the Army Council.

There was not much to report, and Devlin decided against raising concerns on the loyalty of two volunteers. Investigations were ongoing, and his designated successor did not need to know of these concerns at present. Only when Devlin was almost certain of the disloyalty did he mount operations to ensnare a traitor. Thereafter, responsibility for the execution was delegated to *Gaggie* who continued to enjoy this role – though Devlin suspected *Gaggie's* enthusiasm was in order to prove his loyalty, to remove the constant fear of accusations of being a tout. It was known that the Special Branch and almost certainly the British MI5 were soaking the IRA with informers. It had to be stopped before it became a deluge. And that was even before taking into consideration the activities of the Garda Special Branch, which was dangerous because of its effectiveness.

Operations in Derry were being dialled down. Shootings at army patrols in the Creggan and Bogside had to be carefully planned to avoid the possibility of civilian casualties. In the Creggan in particular, there were few locations where the army could be engaged without risk to civilians, their supporters. In the past, it had been easy to blame the Brits, but it was becoming more difficult to do so because Derry people had their own eyes and ears. Devlin acknowledged that the Brits had become more proficient in patrolling, more alert to local sensibilities.

The practice was that the OC left the safe house first, followed by the other participant five to ten minutes later. On this occasion, it gave Devlin time for a chat with *Gaggie*.

'Who decided to use the choirmaster on that jaunt to the hospital?'

The safe house in the small Glenowen estate near to the Creggan had been 'swept' on a number of occasions: it would not have been used by the OC otherwise, and Devlin was confident that the Brits had not identified it as a safe house. The tenants were a young, professional married couple, like most of the tenants on the estate.

'I did.' A confident response.

'Why?' Devlin's tone had become chilly.

'You gave me the day-to-day running of him.'

'I don't think day-to-day running includes parading him before a fuckin' dodgy Branch man.' Tone still low, even chillier and threatening.

The swearing alarmed *Gaggie*. Devlin – once the most fluent and articulated curser in Derry if not the North – had noticeably reduced his swearing.

Gaggie stumbled. 'We need to use him,' he said with a smile in an attempt to placate his superior. 'Get our money's worth out-'

'He's not a fucking sweet shop!' Voice raised. 'We can retire you and buy you a wee shop if that's what you want.'

'Hugh, I'm sorry.' Alarm in his voice. 'It won't happen again.'

'You are right that it will not happen again.' Devlin's eyes locked onto *Gaggie's*. 'He only meets the people that I say.'

Both men heard the telephone being answered in the hall.

'Understood!' It was a command.

Head bowed, *Gaggie* was prevented from answering by a knock on the living room door with an almost simultaneous entry by the male tenant.

'Sorry, eh, but an army patrol just left piggery ridge.'

He used the local name for the army camp which perched above the Creggan estate.

'And?'

'Well, a foot patrol had just gone in and, er it's landrovers... er, gone out through the back gate.'

The three men knew that was the quickest way to the Glenowen estate.

'You go now!' An order to *Gaggie*. He turned to the other man. 'Get your wife in here. It's your tea. TV on. If they come here. No one's been here all night.'

A nod in agreement.

'If you're taken to Strand Road, say nothing.'

Another nod from the tenant.

Devlin smiled. 'You'll be okay.'

Outside, he heard the grating, loud whine of the landrovers. It was unusual because the Brits in piggery ridge normally patrolled on foot.

He gained the darkness of the living-room in time to observe the army landrovers entering the estate. The house was on the other side of the street from the safe house and three doors down. It was the home of his two closest friends: neither were in the IRA.

The rear vehicle stopped at the entrance into the estate: two of the soldiers were running towards the back of the terraced houses to cover the rear entrance. The leading landrover stopped outside the safe house. Two of the soldiers took up kneeling positions facing up and down the street, whilst the other two went to the door of the safe-house, one knocking on the door.

Devlin thought that was a good sign, in that if the soldiers had known who was in the house, they would have crashed through, or more likely cordoned it. The days of smashing in front doors were gone, well, mostly. He was almost certain that they were the normal soldiers from piggery ridge, not under-cover soldiers, and certainly not the SAS. Under the street light, he recognised the patrol commander who had stopped him on a couple of occasions in the Creggan. The soldier had always been polite, controlled, unlike some of the others who were excited by stopping a senior IRA commander, and always searched his car.

Observing, but also reflecting on how the war was developing and changing. Only a few years ago, he had taken any opportunity to engage the army, even with only a handgun; now he never carried a weapon. No one had appeared on the street to oppose the army's presence and protest at the harassment of their fellow Catholics. They would be eating their tea, watching television, simply wanting to get on with their lives. This was the reason for the safe house in the estate. Like several others, it was used only for meetings, never for storing arms or as a start point for operations. The lack of reaction to army activity – except on planned days such as the Bloody Sunday commemoration – was becoming common. Devlin mused whether the army's presence had been embroidered into Derry's tapestry, together with the poverty, the oppression and the resilience of the Derry people.

But! Someone had told the army. An informer. It must have been while they were in the house, otherwise, he deduced, it would not have been the local soldiers turning up. Their intelligence told them that the undercover soldiers were based in the Ballykelly camp outside Derry and in the RAF camp in Aldergrove Airport in County Antrim. He had not spotted any unusual vehicles in the estate. The OC, last to arrive and first to leave, would have been in a vehicle with an escort, and a scout car to check for army or police roadstops.

The two soldiers had been in the safe house for some time; no, he checked his watch, ten minutes. They would be searching but it was not a large house. The upstairs lights had not gone on.

The OC's vehicle would have been well clear before the army exited piggery ridge at speed. Even if they had been lifted, it was no great hardship to endure three or seven days in Strand Road RUC station, a bit tougher in the Castlereagh interrogation centre, the torture house. *Gaggie* and he had experienced it on several occasions.

No. Christ no! Was Gaggie carrying a weapon? He had told him that he must not carry a gun. Now, it was his brains, a chuckle, possibly a bit difficult for *Gaggie*, and his eyes and ears which he had to use. If he was, it would have meant the Maze prison for both of them, possibly even the occupiers of the safe house. Who would benefit from that? He would need to give that further consideration, and remind *Gaggie* not to carry any type of weapon.

The two soldiers came out of the house. There were amiable goodbyes from the occupiers with a 'Not a problem.' thrown in. Devlin was certain the occupiers were not touts.

The army patrol commander stood in the darkness of the middle of the street, surveying other houses. Another soldier was speaking into a small dictaphone, obviously recording vehicle numbers. The commander walked towards Devlin's refuge, and seemed to be staring at him. Devlin knew that he was being foolish; there was no reason why he should not be in the house. No need to be alarmed. He was visiting friends. Yes, there was. It would bring attention onto his two closest friends.

They would be marked for closer scrutiny by the Brits, possibly, probably spending time in Castlereagh as associates of Hugh Devlin, a senior IRA commander. Siobhan would survive it but not Liam.

The soldier stopped, speaking into the handset perched on the top of his flak jacket close to his chin. 'Okay, guys. Mount up!' The sound of the landrovers ebbed away and stillness returned.

Devlin would not return to the safe house: that could wait for another time, like his hunt for the informer. This he was dreading, because of the possible outcome. Notwithstanding, it was not the first time this particular outcome had flashed through his mind. He would stay for a drink with Liam and Siobhan, possibly even spend the night. They would not ask questions. An unsaid compromise had been reached several years ago.

The couple adhered to an old custom of leaving their front door unlocked until bed-time: it did not now have many adherents due to the present situation. Devlin had walked in, and on entering the living-room called out, 'It's me.' His friends were in the kitchen having their evening meal. Siobhan liked to linger over a meal: a custom she had picked up whilst working in Geneva.

Devlin had pronounced that their home was never to be used by the IRA.

The three had been friends from primary school, maintaining the friendship even when they went to different secondary schools. Liam and Dev – she didn't like 'Hugh' – were full of energy, and both played Gaelic – hurling and football. Siobhan played camogie, Gaelic hockey, to a high standard. She knew the boys' real passion was football. She teased them for preferring an English game. Liam's loyalty was to Arsenal whereas Dev supported Manchester United due to the Irish players of both teams. They could spend hours debating football. Siobhan's passions were literature and language, speaking Irish fluently from a young age, and French from school and university. She teased them especially on their inability to speak Irish. When she was away, she sent them postcards written in Irish, and later French. Moreover, she devoured Irish literature from Yeats to Heaney. She considered herself an Irish nationalist not of politics but culture.

She had returned home to marry Liam, a shock to most but devastating to Devlin. He knew that it was because of his involvement in the IRA, and his growing reputation as a man not to cross. She told him that was not the reason, though she disapproved of his involvement, but Liam needed her. He was sick with a wasting disease. He could barely walk, and soon would be in a wheelchair. There was no possibility of children. While she worked in a bank, Liam's and Siobhan's mothers cared for him during the day. The most wrenching part of his illness was that his brain remained active and engaged.

She was a supporter of John Hume, the local SDLP MP, agreeing with him that people were more important than land, but she would not join his party. Whilst continuing to practise her religion, she was respectful but not deferential to the clergy. She was resentful of the Church's continuing striving to subjugate women – no, she told people, it was not too strong a word. The clergy and others forgot that it was the women who maintained their community's cohesion during the many periods of poverty and oppression. Her hope was that greater involvement with Europe would free women and bring peace to Ireland.

To maintain their friendship, politics was not discussed: the *Troubles* was the forbidden apple in the Garden of Eden. Except, in one brief exchange, Siobhan told Dev that he had the talents to do much better. Still, there was much to talk about, and to laugh about, in particular their escapades when young, roaming throughout the city and beyond, even into the Protestant areas with their garish painted streets.

Devlin was married with three children; they stayed together because it was expected of them, and for their children. Apart from the children, his wife had her sisters and friends. Derry women could talk. She did not ask questions of his activities nor when he stayed overnight with Liam and Siobhan. It was not a matter of trusting him but knowing that Siobhan would not betray Liam. Understandable if she did.

Sometimes, he thought he caught a wistful look on Siobhan's face, an 'if only'. He hated himself because deep down in that hidden pit of his mind, he wanted his friend to die, freeing Siobhan for himself. He should confess it but, he never went to confession; attended Mass but no longer listened. The reduction in his swearing and curbing other aspects of his behaviour was due to Siobhan. He craved Siobhan's approval for what he was doing for Ireland, no, Derry. Even that was not right. Simply, he craved Siobhan's approval and company. He pondered how far he was prepared to go for Siobhan, as far as betrayal... ?

– 19 –

Braco assured Mayne that his radio did not contain a recording device but that he needed it for pick-up or an emergency. It was a dedicated frequency and other radio traffic would not be on it.

'Not made any food. Hope you have eaten. Just crisps and nuts. Sit down.'

The room was large but sparse, with a worn sofa, two armchairs, an oval coffee table and a TV. Despite a two – bar electric fire being on, the room was cold. The sofa was against the wall facing the window. The armchairs were together facing the fire with the table between the chairs and fire. The TV was in the corner by the window.

Braco sat on the sofa so he could observe the door to his right and the window. 'Well-trained,' muttered Mayne.

There was a bottle of Bushmills whiskey and two tumblers, not crystal, on the table.

'Drink? A wee Black Bush?' Braco detected a slight Irish accent.

'No thanks. Take a lager if you have it.'

Mayne went out of the room, returning shortly after with four bottles of Harp Lager which he placed on the table, opened one and gave it to Braco.

'Glass?'

'Yes, please.' Mayne passed a glass to him.

'Just help yourself. Have as many as you want. More in the fridge.'

' A couple will do.'

'If I recall you weren't much of a drinker.' Braco nodded. 'I drink too much. Especially of this.' He held up an almost full glass of straight Irish whiskey. 'But in the morning I'll remember everything I said.'

A grin.

'What do I call you, no, I'll not use a name. Maybe the messenger. You can call me Peter or Pete as the peelers do.' He took a mouthful of Blackbush. 'Don't worry. I won't ask you any questions. I know the script.'

They discussed their time in their regiment, incidents and personalities.

'You know Murray is over here?'

'Yes.'

'You were in COP with him?' Mayne knew the answer.

'Yes.'

'How did you get on with him?' Mayne snorted. 'How does anyone get on with him.'

'At least you knew where you stood with him. Have you seen him?'

Mayne nodded. 'Last saw him a couple of months ago. We had a session here. He crashed on the sofa.'

'How is he?'

'The same. He hates his job.'

Mayne was having an internal debate before speaking.

'He saw you. In a pub. Said he left when he saw you. Didn't tell me where or when. But that's him. Probably the tightest guy I know.'

'He wasn't very communicative.'

There was a silent interlude whilst both men sipped their drinks, Mayne's more a gulp. The policeman leaned towards the soldier. 'Sure Ormsby or Godden didn't send you?'

'Never heard those names.' He resisted the temptation to quip, 'unless they are our two signallers.'

'So it was the delectable Eileen Kanna.' Mayne held up his left hand. 'Don't answer.'

He brought his hand down to his side at the same time as taking another swig of whiskey. A melancholic scan of the room. He decided against quoting *Ricki Tarr*'s opening words to *George Smiley* from *Tinker Tailor Soldier Spy,* which had recently been turned into a BBC television series, so instead said, 'Let me tell you how *you* ended up sitting on my sofa.'

Without looking at the other man, he began with his trip to England for the lecture, his lunch with Godden, the meeting with Ormsby in the Waterloo house, the pitch to leave the army and join the RUC – which he was already considering – and the openness of them being SIS.

'Godden. Condescending. Well, being ex-colonial police, what do you expect. Gawd knows how he got into the Service. Well he was sponsored by Ormsby – to be his factotum...' He turned to Braco and with a grin said, 'Actually more like a platoon runner.'

'Peter, you should not be telling me this.'

Mayne paused for another drink of the Irish whiskey, his face humourless, not looking at Braco. 'It's my tale. You're the messenger so you can tell them what you think relevant.'

Braco knew that he should leave but he was fascinated by an insight, even if whiskey-driven, into the secret world. Others thought special forces were part of the secret world but they were only instruments, like those a surgeon used.

Mayne continued.

'Ormsby. You haven't met him. No. He wouldn't soil his hands mixing with the lower orders. He's a blue-blood. The type Murray used to mock.'

Braco nodded, having been accused of being a blue-blood by his former sergeant.

'Unlike the officers in the battalion, Ormsby is an authentic, top of the range, sixty-four carat blue-blood.' He turned to Braco, 'Can you get sixty-four carat?'

Braco shrugged.

'His weakness is that he thinks lesser beings do not have the intelligence to analyse complex situations. Often they are complex only in his mind.'

He refilled his glass and encouraged Braco to have a second bottle of Harp, which he did.

'So I decided to leave the army. I had met a girl here, now my wife, and she didn't want to leave here.' His voice was full of derision. 'Who can blame her!'

'People were surprised and even shocked at you leaving. You were the star, especially after the shooting at Tirkane. I heard senior ranks saying you were almost certainly going to be RSM.'

Mayne grunted then asked, 'Did you ever hear Murray saying that?'

' No.'

Another period of silence before Mayne continued. He had to attend a course and was welcomed by Eileen Kanna. He had thought it was a test, so pretended that he did not know her, but he had recognised her immediately from Glasgow University.

'There's a clever and wilful girl.'

Braco decided to followed his host's example and not react.

Mayne continued talking. The police training had been easy. He had married Jo and had a boy. Initially it had not been a conscious decision not to do Ormsby's bidding: life was just so busy, with duty, sleeping and of course drinking. He got on well with his new comrades. But on duty, out on the ground, it was so intense, especially in Belfast. He knew some Special Branch officers and most seemed committed. He did not try for Branch. Probably, he would have got in, but might have found himself in a regional headquarters basically as a collator without access to real intelligence.

It was unlikely for the first few years that he would be out recruiting sources. Special Branch HQ through its regional officers was imposing its grip on covert operations. No longer were there the independent, sometimes maverick Branch officers of the earlier years, who could decide which unit they would task for a covert operation.

'Anyway from the start, I was not impressed by Ormsby with his talk of – what was it? Yes. We want to solve the Irish problem. If we can reveal to the British public that Branch are conducting an internecine war, not for the...'

He paused, scrambling in his memory for the words.

'... Not acting for the good of the Province's people, then we might be able to convince the British public to demand withdrawal. Or words to that effect.'

He laughed, shaking his head as he replayed the meeting in his mind.

'Wanted me to find Branch collusion whether with the IRA or the Loyalists. Huh! If they wanted to find collusion they should look at some of the army intelligence people.'

Braco again did not respond though he had heard rumours of the army colluding with loyalist terrorists.

'What Ormsby conveniently forgot was America and NATO. Despite the support over there for the IRA, the American government doesn't want the North becoming part of the neutral South. Need here to protect the sea lanes for NATO reinforcement.' A smug smile. 'So much for Ormsby being the Brit Henry Kissinger... A *master strategist* ! Huh, a fucking sixty-four carat numpty.'

This time it was a sip of whiskey before turning to Braco.

'You know, his colleagues want him to fail. Screw up his chances of becoming C... you know who C is?'

'No,' said Braco with a shake of the head.

'Head of SIS. Ormsby wants that, but not just that. With his philosophy of cross-fertilisation, he wants to run the whole damn charabanc, MI5, Special Branch, customs, the lot.'

Braco thought the other man was befuddled by the whiskey though it did not show in his face. He recalled that in the army, Mayne was not known as a blow-hard. The serving soldier no longer could resist asking, 'How do you know all this?' A blend of irritation and scepticism in his tone.

'Well I am part of an intelligence organisation.' He smiled. 'It's called the Mayne family.'

Another pause and a self-satisfied smile.

'We have sources in politics, the intelligence services, academia, the establishment... Not bad for an old Anglo-Irish Catholic family. Also, careful reading of the Telegraph.'

He extended his left arm in a gesture which said 'don't believe me if you don't want to.' He looked at Braco. 'I don't know your present outfit, though I know the unit you left the battalion for. But now, if you are working for Eileen Kanna, then you are working for the Secret Intelligence Service. Not the army.'

It had never crossed his mind. Braco thought Kanna was Intelligence Corps.

'Can I use your toilet?'

'Yea. Upstairs straight in front of you.'

When Braco got to the living-room door, Mayne quipped, 'No bugs.' A sheepish grin from the covert soldier.

With Braco back on the sofa, Mayne said, 'Look at the present fuck-up. Should have prevented this way back. Stopped the blanket protest.'

'How?'

'Wine, women and song!'

The policeman saw the bewilderment on the other man's face.

'When they went into the Maze, we should have given them drink and women to make them soft. So when they got out, they would be reluctant to sit in ditches waiting for an army patrol. Instead... we adopted a hard-line regime. Take yourself. You can do your job because you did a tough, relentless course. Being on the blanket has the same effect. Fucking fools!'

Braco knew the policeman was referring to the British Government. Mayne took another swallow of whiskey and shook his head, his eyes staring ahead.

'Did you tell Murray your opinion of the prison regime?' asked Braco.

'Of course, and he agreed with me... think he was disappointed that he hadn't thought of it. And you should hear his views on the Hunger Strike. He thinks the government shouldn't have allowed any of them to die.'

'How can they prevent it if they are willing to die.'

'Murray thinks the critical point was the decision on medical treatment when Sands or Frankie Hughes became unconscious. The decision should not have been left to the relatives. It was illogical... illogical... that the government would decide what clothes they wore, but not when they required medical treatment. We're responsible for the prisoners.'

'Interesting. Never thought of that. Suppose it raises moral questions.'

'Huh! It's not about morality for Murray. It's about winning.'

'And I suppose he expressed his opinion to others.'

'Of course, and it caused arguments with the guys in his present unit.'

'That won't bother him.' A grin shared by the other.

'No. But he thinks it will lead to support for Sinn Féin from some of the Catholic middle-class who mostly are SDLP voters... He speaks to middle-class taigs, especially female ones.'

Braco knew that he had probably witnessed Murray speaking to middle-class taigs. He looked at his watch. 'Time for me to go.'

'Right.'

'Better phone my taxi. Be about ten minutes.' He reached into the bag at the side of the sofa and sent the signal for pick-up by using the pressel switch. 'Not outside. Need to walk there.'

'Thanks.'

He stood up, as did Mayne. The soldier had forgotten how tall the policeman was, and he himself was not small.

'I don't care what you tell them. I'm not batting for them... but I'm still batting for the right side.'

Braco recalled that Eileen had used the same cricketing expression. At the time, he had thought it was not a Kanna expression and now surmised it had come from Ormsby of the Secret Service.

'And I don't think there'll be consequences for me.'

'Okay. It was good to see you again.'

'Absolutely.' He grasped the soldier's extended hand. 'We should do this again.'

'Unlikely. Take care.'

Braco refrained from saying 'I'll go in to bat for you.'

20

Eileen Kanna arranged to meet Christine Latham in the latter's house in Belfast. The university lecturer did not want to go to London or any other place; she was fed up with being transformed into different people by the Service make-up artist – usually as a dowdy, old academic. Now there was no need for make-up because she considered herself to be one.

Godden had been reluctant to allow his female subordinate to meet with Christine. In some ways, it was understandable, in that Christine Latham had been the first and only source that Godden had ever recruited in a solo capacity. Handlers felt they had proprietary rights in respect of a source, especially one who produced useful political intelligence. However, Christine Latham was now a registered agent, designated *Mighty Midget*, and Ormsby felt it right that Eileen Kanna had a one-to-one with Christine. She had observed Christine during meetings with Godden. The SIS officers knew Christine was close to breaking-point and Ormsby reasoned that she might be more willing to continue with Eileen's prompting. It had been Eileen's instinct to pursue Damien McGlone when Latham provided his name. Now he was a subject of interest and Eileen would prepare the ground for the operation. The university lecturer might be the keystone of the operation.

An Italian journalist visiting her house would not raise suspicion, even if anyone noticed. Christine Latham was well-known as a supporter of the Republican cause. Her home was a mid-terraced house, but smaller than the near-by SIS safe house. Her living-room doubled as a study where occasionally she gave tutorials to groups of 2 to 3 students, but never used it for political purposes. Her second bedroom upstairs was for her parents, though their visits from England were becoming fewer. On odd occasions, visiting lecturers stayed with her. Her boxroom stored books and papers.

Christine visibly relaxed when she saw that the journalist was a woman and not Godden. She could not envisage Godden as an Italian journalist. The assumed Italian journalist said the agreed words which confirmed her as a colleague of Godden's. Unlike Mayne, she did not have to pretend that she did not recognise Eileen Kanna from Glasgow University. She did not.

Coffee and biscuits were provided. The new handler told the agent to leave the curtains open so that any enquiring passer-by would see a well-dressed female sitting in an armchair facing the window with a notebook in hand. If the individual peered closely, they would spot a pocket memo on the coffee table. The home-owner sat with her back to the window in another armchair. Eileen spent some time fumbling in her large canvas bag, first to switch on the scanner to check for listening devices, then to take out the pocket memo and place it carefully on the table. She then dived back into her bag to switch off the scanner, which would have emitted a sound and left a red light on permanently if the room was bugged. She switched on a more powerful recorder and took out a notebook which she flipped open on her lap, a pen in her right hand.

'Tell me about life as a lecturer?'

It was a genuine question because Eileen had a hankering for teaching. She listened carefully, sometimes making notes as Christine described her working day, the initial enthusiasm but now the frustration.

'I really need to move across to the mainland to progress.' The words said academic career but her eyes said to escape. 'I have applied for a couple of positions.'

'I understand,' nodded Eileen. She enquired about her personal life, which rather shook Christine because Godden never did.

'Relationships? Sure there are attractive lecturers in Queen's?'

Initially the other female was shocked. 'Er, no... not at present.'

'Me neither.'

'Not much time these days... and I'm getting older.'

'I am much older than you and still not married. Though I keep looking. But, he needs to be rich and pliable, subservient.'

Christine laughed, more a nervous giggle.

'So, no great romances?'

Christine shook her head but she did not want this woman to think that she had no experience of men.

'Well, when I was in Glasgow, at university, there was someone, a local boy.'

She was conjuring up the memory of her fellow student.

'Ian. He was brilliant at English literature. Even better than me.'

She looked at Eileen and smiled, a sheepish smile, signalling the comment did not reflect the way she had been raised.

'He could remember whole chunks of Shakespeare and other pieces.'

'What happened?'

'Oh! Politics and er... he was so intense.'

She did not tell Eileen that she had seen Ian Barclay in London and that Godden was intending to recruit him. She had never asked Godden whether he had recruited the intense Glaswegian, and rather hoped that he had not, fearing that probably her first boyfriend was not suited to this world.

Eileen gave a faint smile, hiding her thoughts. It was time to move onto business.

'Bring me up-to-date.'

Christine was now a member of Sinn Féin. Initially, SIS had not wanted her to join, but after her involvement in the campaign for the hunger striker Bobby Sands in the Fermanagh and South Tyrone by-election, it was a natural progression and both sides would have found it odd for her not to join Sinn Féin, considering her excellent campaign skills. She had enjoyed the election campaign because campaigning and advocacy were in her blood. Godden had been unhappy about the extent of her involvement and wondered whether she had gone back over to the other side. Ormsby was more sanguine, telling him that she was young and in the overall scheme of things, her contribution would not make much difference but it would reinforce her cover. She had assuaged her feelings of guilt by the hope that the election of the hunger striker might resolve the issue. The British Prime Minister was not for compromise.

Subsequently, Christine was sent to new branches of Sinn Féin, North and South, to advise them on campaigning and in effect run tutorials for new and mostly young members. She was able to step back from involvement with the approval of Sinn Féin as the exam season approached, when she had to prepare her students. Also, there were elements in both the leadership and among the new recruits who were suspicious of her, because of her Protestant and half-Brit background. Generally, she had found the people out in the counties more friendly and less suspicious of her. She had put the former attitude down to the ghettoising of Belfast.

She narrated who had influence: the decision-makers, those on the up and those going in the opposite direction. This was all from memory because she had been instructed for her own protection never to write anything down in the Province. There were random and snap checks when an IRA security team would turn over a house, search a car, looking for possible British touts. Christine had a prodigious memory.

Eileen thanked her for her excellent work.

'One final point. Have you seen or spoken to Damien McGlone recently?'

The other woman's surprised showed in her expression.

'You know whom I mean. The...'

'Yes, yes.'

Christine leaned forward towards her inquisitor, assuming that she must be aware of the meeting, which implied that she was being followed. She believed that Damien McGlone, the Derry music teacher and choirmaster, was not involved unless he was a British agent like her. Godden had told her that she was not alone and that there were other assets, which she suspected. Sinn Féin and the whole Republican movement were paranoid about British informers. This British intelligence officer had been open and friendly. Did her open approach cause her to be careless! She knew she had to be honest.

Eileen Kanna sat patiently waiting for an answer.

'Well, in fact, I did meet him a couple of months ago... and also, two or three weeks ago.'

'And?'

'We didn't discuss politics. Only music. You want to know?'

Eileen nodded her head.

Christine had been in Dublin, giving advice to a group of Sinn Féin workers. She was spending the Friday night in Dublin. At the end of the workshop, one of the female members said that there was a choral concert in her church after the 6 p m

Mass. The concert was free apart from a few pennies for the collection. The guest conductor was Damien McGlone.

Afterwards they had gone for a drink. McGlone and the choir's usual conductor turned up in the same pub. Where was the pub and its name? Christine said it was on Grafton Street or nearby. She did not know the name. Might have been the Black Horse because it had a large black metal horse above the open fire. McGlone spotted her. No she was sure that it was coincidental. He came over.

'You get around. It's er..don't tell me... Christine.'

'Yes. Christine Latham.'

'Right. What are you doing here?'

He was also spending the night in Dublin and in a hotel close to Christine's. When the others drifted away to go home or on somewhere else, they remained for another hour or so. They talked music and literature.

'Are you sure?' asked Eileen.

"Well, he did ask me if I was not fed up with politics.'

'Your reply?'

'I ignored it. Anyway, I didn't want to talk politics.'

'Then?'

'Nothing. We walked back to our separate hotels.' A pause. 'He gave me a lift back to Belfast.'

'Why?'

'He said that he was going to Belfast to see his brother. It was better than the train which is often delayed or cancelled by bombs, mostly hoaxes on the tracks.'

'Left by your people.' She saw Christine was stung. 'Only teasing you.'

'Oh. Okay.'

'What happened when he dropped you off? Did he come in?'

'Yes. Just for a tea. Said he prefers tea in the morning.'

'In here?'

Eileen gestured to indicate the room they were sitting in. 'Yes.'

'Not upstairs?'

'No!'

'Fine. You said that you saw him a couple of weeks ago.'

Christine emitted a sigh of frustration and irritation.

'He had told me that he was going down to Dublin again. He was helping a choir prepare for a competition. He was spending Friday and Saturday with the choir. And on the Saturday they were doing a sort of dress rehearsal for the competition. Family and friends were invited. It was free and he was sure that there would be no problem if I went.'

She ran her right hand through her straight, white blond hair. She was nervous and still irritated.

'He said that with the expenses for the work, and as he didn't usually spend a lot, he intended to treat himself to the Gresham Hotel.'

'Expensive. Did he offer to pay for you?'

'Not directly. Anyway.' Her voice became stronger. 'I told him that I might not be able to make it. And if I did I would pay for my own hotel.'

'Did you go?'

' I was reluctant.'

'Because of your age difference? Or what he wanted? Or both?'

She was again shocked by the directness and the lack of finesse. 'I thought you people had good breeding, were polite and circumspect.'

'I'm not from that background. Well?'

'I decided to go. I liked their programme of music.'

'So you went?'

'Yes.'

'And stayed in the Gresham?'

'My own room and I paid for it.' Then, tartly. 'I don't spend much either.'

Eileen was aware of the trip but there had been no mention of a particularly close relationship between the choirmaster and a female. After the rehearsal, McGlone and a few others, male and female, went for a meal. The report had estimated about ten. After the meal, he returned to the bar in the Gresham. By the time they had eyes and ears in the bar, the subject was in conversation with six others of varying ages seated at a table.

Hennessy, suited and booted for a Saturday evening in the Gresham, enquired of one of the bar staff if he knew who McGlone was, because he seemed familiar. He didn't, but he thought they all came from the North, and probably would be the last to leave. After trying to ear-wig the conversation, Hennessy decided there was no more to be gained by hanging around. The report had been clear in that apart from the choir-master, none of the others were recognisable as subjects of interest.

Eileen thought to herself that Hennessy and Pimlico had joined after the work-up training, so of course they would not have recognised Christine Latham as target *Forth*.'

'Go to the concert?'

'Yes. It was very good but they didn't win the competition if that is helpful to you.' A curt tone from the agent.

'What happened after the concert?'

'He went for a meal with some of the choir and their friends.'

'What did you do?'

'I went back to the hotel.'

'Have a drink in the bar?'

'No. I went to my room and ordered room service.'

'Did you meet later for a drink or...'

'No. I told you I went to my room.'

She was aware that McGlone had met a few people from Belfast, including a couple whom he knew slightly through his brother. Christine felt certain that the bar had been under observation but her presence was not reported because she was not there.

Sometimes, Godden in his debrief, unwittingly gave away some morsels of information. It was an aspect of source-handling which was emphasised to all agent handlers and agents, probably in all intelligence services. The handler should never reveal any information from other sources or tradecraft techniques. Similarly, the agent should refrain from using language, even individual words, which might link them to the intelligence agency. In Ireland, members of the national-ist community were unlikely to say that they had been stopped at an army vehicle check point or VCP. The use of Brit terms and expressions was an indication of a link to the Security Forces which could, and mostly did, lead to a visit from an IRA security team. Often it was innocent, but at times could lead to the individual being alone, face down on a Border road.

'When was the next time that you saw him? At breakfast?'

Now a pleasant smile on Eileen's face. She was worried about losing her. Another very important element in this relationship was not to lose control of the debrief.

Christine's previous inner satisfaction receded slightly. She knew that the watchers would have reported that he had had breakfast on his own and left the hotel almost immediately to drive back to Derry. They hadn't. Hennessy had decided not to begin shepherding him in the busy centre of Dublin in case they lost him, deciding instead to pick him up north of Dublin and take the chance of missing him. Hennessy, as an SIS officer and not a soldier, felt able to make these decisions. They did pick him up, and once across the Border handed the choirmaster over to waiting *Mythical* call-signs who shepherded him to his pen in Derry. Hennessy had decided, because of the choir-master's more frequent travel, to recommend to Eileen Kanna that a tracking device be attached to the subject's car.

'No. He came to my room. '

'Was this planned?' Eileen was trying to remain calm.

'No.'

'Go on.'

Christine explained that they had arranged to meet in the bar later, but when McGlone encountered the people from Belfast he thought it would be better if she did not join them. She agreed. Later, just after ten, he telephoned and asked if he could come up. He would bring a bottle of wine. Christine insisted to her handler that she had been reluctant, but she did want to talk about the choir, which had been excellent. They had a couple of glasses of wine. McGlone was a little drunk, though not loud or aggressive.

'No politics? No mention of the upsurge in support for the Republican cause?'

Abruptly. 'No! We discussed the concert.'

'What time did he leave at?'

'Not sure.'

'Did you go to bed?'

'What! It's nothing...'

'Did you have sex?'

There was no response. Christine's eyes were down. Eileen knew it could go two ways, with the worst option being Christine telling her to leave and that she would speak only to Godden. She could see that the younger woman was uncomfortable.

'It just happened. I was... we both were...'

'That's fine. I am not a moral arbiter.'

Although Eileen's response was calm, the realisation that

one of their agents had had a sexual encounter, albeit brief, and probably more of a clumsy fumble, with someone with a growing connection to the IRA, raised possibilities. But that was for a later time, and to be considered in a cold, detached manner.

'Excuse me.'

When Christine returned, she had composed herself.

'Just a few more questions. Fine with that?'

'Yes.'

'What happened next?'

Christine had not returned with him because she was treating herself to another night in Dublin and had brought some essays to mark – much more comfortable at The Gresham than her dreary home in Belfast. Yes, they intended to meet again but had made no firm arrangements. It was better that he telephone her.

He had telephoned once, briefly a few days ago, said he was as busy as he was sure she was, but he would get back to her. She confessed that she thought it was a 'thanks but goodbye' call. Though she didn't think he was like that. Possibly it was the age difference or her involvement in Sinn Féin.

'You could be right. But if he does call again, for example to go to a concert, accept.' A pause accompanied by a smile. 'And of course tell us... before the concert.'

Christine shook her head. 'Why are you interested in him? I'm certain that he's not involved. He only went to the meeting in London because of his sister. Music is his life. Not politics. '

Eileen hoped, for her agent's safety, that none of her Sinn Féin friends saw her as a Brit spy though only said, 'You are probably right but when a Catholic, no matter how respectable, from Derry takes an interest in one of our people, it's best that we take precautions.'

'I understand. And thanks.'

'Anything else?'

Christine's eyes were cast downwards, her hands clasped together in her lap.

'I was rather hoping... when it was a different person, a female... that you were here to tell me that it was over.'

Eileen did not respond. Christine rose from her chair and stood in front of the fireplace, looking at the old, mahogany clock on the mantelpiece.

'I'm not sure I can continue. I have applied for a couple of posts across the water.'

Eileen remained silent.

'To be honest, I am terrified every time I leave here and leave the university. The worst part is walking there and back. Just waiting... expecting a loyalist gunman to appear.' She turned towards Eileen. 'I'm at the stage when walking to Queen's or home, I am constructing a discursive essay in my mind... not 'Is Hamlet mad?' but...'

Now talking to the clock.

'Better to be shot from the front than the back. Discuss.' Her eyes were filling up. 'I start with the back. You don't see your killer... It's sudden. No time to think.'

A pause.

'Then there is the chance that it's a car back-firing or... selfishly and ethically reprehensible, the gunman shoots someone else by mistake.'

Eileen remained silent whilst banishing the thought that some consider spying – especially the betrayal of family, friends and colleagues – as morally reprehensible.

Christine continued: 'On the other hand, if I see the gunman, I might be able to run away... to disarm him... Even talk him out of it. Appeal to his better nature. Tell him that being a murderer would devastate his mother. I would drop to my knees and beg him... telling him that I am a British agent and we are on the same side.'

She dabbed her eyes with a small handkerchief.

'Then the same image comes into my mind. He, the gunman, smiles and says, "We know." or sometimes "Confession is good for the soul." '

21

After submitting her report, Eileen knew that she had been crass in her meeting with Christine. It was vital that Christine continued in place though, hopefully, it would not be for much longer. Her report did emphasise the agent's emotional frailties and expressed concerns that she might crack and bolt, which was likely to reveal her role as a British intelligence agent. Operationally it was Ormsby's decision whether to leave her in place.

The following night, sitting in her bedroom in the Europa Hotel, with a large glass of Chablis in her hand, her thoughts turned to *Mighty Midget*, Latham's code-name, and the choirmaster. They were an odd couple, though she preferred the term anomalous. What attracted them? What was the spark? Music? Probably it was on Christine's part. Was he looking just for sex? Why was he not married? He had appeared from almost nowhere, but seemed to be everywhere now. Surveillance did not indicate that he might be homosexual. She believed Christine that they never discussed politics: he knew that she was active in Sinn Féin. Had he been directed by the IRA to get close to Christine to test her loyalty and find out whether she was really a Brit informer? That was preposterous. They could find out by using people in Belfast.

She had taken only one sip of her wine. She put the glass on the table. She wanted to think this through with a clear head. One glass of wine would not have made a difference but she did not want to write her thoughts down. After further musing, she concluded that it was loneliness which brought the anomalous pair together, as both were leading secret lives which neither could declare to the other. Music was the balm which allowed them to continue. To McGlone, she was not a British agent and to Christine, he was not active in the IRA.

Initially, after the first check of the choirmaster, he had been written up and put in the pending tray, not a person of immediate interest. Thankfully at the *Trent* seize operation, an operative had recognised him and she had overruled the team's OC by ordering that the choirmaster be followed, thus aborting the seizure of *Trent*, which she had considered foolhardy. Despite her Service training, the most important training had come from an 'aunt', actually a friend of her mother's, who had served in the Special Operations Executive during the Second World War, and had told her that it was the unexpected, the unforeseen which often produced the best outcomes.

The team had observed the choirmaster throughout Northern Ireland and in the Republic, mostly Dublin. The reasons for the visits were assisting a church or school choir – now always Roman Catholic – or attending a concert, which provided ideal cover for meeting people. He was never observed meeting any senior figures, only individuals on the periphery, the outer ring of the IRA. Nor was he seen going into premises with links, associations with the terrorist group. He had been observed going to a house in the Coshquin area of Derry which was owned by a sister of a senior IRA figure, but the team could not get too close because the house was isolated. It was decided not to put a static OP on the target's home, not only because the IRA were surveillance-aware, but also in case of any encounter with other special forces or the local army unit. The problems arose from being a deep-cover force.

In her hotel bedroom in Belfast, Eileen had decided that it was time to emerge from the depths. The same conclusion had been reached that morning in London.

22

The message relayed through Bill was that Braco's debrief on his meeting with Mayne could wait, and the three operatives were to remain in the house. Braco felt the other two were being distant and rather chilly towards him. He was under strict instructions not to disclose the nature of the task, and Tring and Tamworth should know that was the nature of their work: the need to know. Nevertheless, he felt that he should have been able to give them some feedback on the task. But where would he start?

He had spoken to a serving RUC officer, an ex-soldier from his battalion, with whom he had served. This former comrade had been recruited by the Secret Intelligence Service to join the RUC in order to spy on the latter. Now he wasn't playing ball. And by the way, Eileen Kanna is actually a member of SIS, and it is likely that we are working for them, not the army and not even the Group. Also, this ex-soldier, now a policeman, thinks IRA prisoners who murdered soldiers, police officers and innocent civilians should be able to drink and have sex. And there is another member of my battalion – in fact he was my platoon sergeant and a sort of mentor to me – who is on a posting here, and who thinks the government's policy towards the hunger strikers is wrong. Moreover, he socialises with middle-class Catholics who are now supporting Sinn Féin which is really the IRA.

He could hear Tamworth's voice.

'Remind us again which battalion you were in? Second battalion the IRA!'

No, better to put up with the chilliness.

Their instructions arrived: Tring and Tamworth were to return to base location but Braco was to remain for another couple of days. Once the other two had left, Bill informed Braco that the next evening at six, he was to collect the lady from the Europa Hotel. He should wear a jacket and tie, clean shaven. Yes, he told Bill, he did have a jacket and tie. He always took one because sometimes the nature of an operation could change and smarter dress was required. He was to make sure that he had his army ID card. He asked Bill to relay to the lady that it was not a good idea for him to enter the Europa. Apart from journalists, it was always full of special forces and intelligence people. Someone might recognise him so it would be better if he waited in the car-park.

The SIS officer was waiting for him when he entered the car-park five minutes early. She told him to drive to the Army Headquarters in North Ireland in Lisburn – a visit instigated by her meeting with Christine Latham in Belfast. She told Braco she would debrief him there. It was a silent twenty-minute journey.

They walked up the stairs to the second floor of the main building and turned to the left. As it was after normal working hours the building was empty, apart from those personnel on duty and conscientious officers or those tasked to produce briefs for the commanders for the next morning. Eileen produced a pass and they were allowed through the metal gate. He did not need to produce his ID, leading him to conclude that they were expected. Braco knew this was the inner sanctum of the British Army's intelligence and covert forces network. There were doors, most of them closed, on either side of the long corridor. Halfway down there was another metal gate through which Eileen's pass gained entry. Just inside the gate on the left was a door opening into a small waiting-room, furnished with six chairs and a coffee table on which were two neat piles of magazines. Eileen told him to wait in there and she would fetch him. She closed the door behind her.

He had been in the corridor once before, albeit before the second metal gate, when he had had an interview with his OC who told him that he was being seconded to another unit of the Group. Even the OC of the unit which probably produced the army's best intelligence and results did not merit an office in the inner sanctum. He recalled that at the interview there had been no mention of the SIS, probably because his OC did not know. The covert soldier thought the area beyond the second gate must be the holy of holies.

Braco had been in the waiting room just under ten minutes when Eileen returned. She closed the door and sat down on the chair next to the soldier.

'One question. Is our friend willing to cooperate?'

'No.'

'Think there might be any wavering? Another visit be useful?'

'No.' A pronounced shake of his head, his lips pursed and his face stern to emphasise the negative response.

'Right. Do you think he'll stay quiet?'

'Yes.' A firm nod, then he said, 'If he's left alone. I think.'

'Have you written a report?'

'No.'

'Good. No report.'

At that moment there was a knock on the door and a man came in. Braco stood up with the names 'Godden' and 'Ormsby' in his head.

'Well?' This was to Eileen.

'No.'

'Has he put it on paper?' To Eileen, as if Braco was not present.

'No, sir. I have not.' Braco was irritated.

Godden looked at him for the first time and said, 'Good. Nothing on paper. No mention to anyone else. It did not take place. Understood?'

'Yes sir.' Hint of disdain in his voice.

'Meeting starts in five minutes.' To Eileen and then he left the room.

'Don't worry about him.'

Braco shrugged his shoulders.

'Right. You can go back to Bill's for the night. Pick me up from the hotel about eleven. We are going back to base. Likely there will be some changes. However, we'll stop for lunch in the Dunadry Hotel. Do you know where it is?'

'Yes, I think so. Near Aldergrove?' He had been in it once during his tour with the Group. 'Transport?'

'What you are driving.'

'Thought that was a loan. Just for here.'

'Yes, but I'm requisitioning it. Unless there are any changes from this meeting, I will see you in the morning.'

− 23 −

The conference room was rectangular with a single table dominating the space between the door and the window. The chair at the window was unoccupied, reserved for the Intelligence Co-ordinator's use. Two men in pin-striped suits sat in the chairs on the left of the door, at the Co-ordinator's right. The two SIS officers sat in the chairs on the opposite side of the table. The female officer did not know either of the two men.

'If there is no objection, I will chair the meeting and record the Minutes.'

There were no objections.

'Good. There will be three copies only: one for the Co-ordinator and one for C and the head of my service.' With a smile, he said, 'Of course, the senior officer from each unit will have sight of them before I sign them off. Acceptable?'

It was to the other three present.

'For the Minutes, I will ask each attendee to state their name and position which I will note.' Another glance to the others for any expression of dissent.

'Good. I am Nigel Colville, assistant to the Co-ordinator.'

Colville had been head of the Security Service station in Northern Ireland until his designation was changed when the Prime Minister appointed Maurice Oldfield, the former spy chief, to the newly created post of Intelligence Co-ordinator. There had been opposition to Oldfield's appointment because although he had an intelligence background, some, especially in the Foreign and Commonwealth Office, felt that he was a little too set in his ways. The FCO had pushed for a diplomat coming to the end of his service, Sir David Buchanan-Henderson, to be appointed to the post. Although he had no formal intelligence background, he was considered astute with no ties to any of the intelligence agencies. A fresh perspective might be what the Province needed. He had had a 'good war' when serving in the Guards. His lack of connection to the Security Service might find favour with the RUC Special Branch. He was a gentleman, unlike some of the Englishmen who could speak out of both sides of their mouths at the same time. There was support for him, until someone whispered into the PM's ear of concerns that Buchanan-Henderson was not a fully paid-up member of the Britain's Glorious Imperial Past club, and on one occasion had argued that Hong Kong should have been handed back to Communist China. The PM decided that he was not 'one of us' and turned to the old spy, though his appointment was terminated after a year.

'Colonel Angus Struthers. Senior Military Intelligence Officer in the Province.'

'Arthur Godden. The Secret Intelligence Service. Senior liaison officer to the Security Service in Northern Ireland.'

'Eileen Kanna.' Though she longed to quip 'from the real spies', she followed Godden's example. 'The Secret Intelligence Service. Controller of Operation *Mythical*.' The designation had been agreed with Godden beforehand.

'Good. Now we know who and what we are, we can press on.' Another smile.

Eileen thought, 'And we know who will be held responsible if there is a disaster.'

Colville placed his pen to the right of the A4 lined paper. He removed his spectacles and positioned them, lenses away from him, on the paper, then clasped his hands on the edge of the table as if he was going to say a prayer. He looked at each of the other three in turn before saying, 'As you know the heads of our respective Services, Arthur's and mine...' For clarification. '... have decided to run *Mythical* as a joint operation. As it were... to bring it in from the cold.'

A smile. No one's expression changed, no acknowledgement of the reference to a novel by a former intelligence officer.

'Could you just remind each of us of the aim of *Mythical*.'

'Certainly. The aim of *Mythical* is to place an agent or agents close to the leadership of the Army Council of the IRA.'

Godden did not catch Colonel Struthers's fleeting expression of surprise, but his fellow officer did.

'Now. This is political intelligence, not military. Our customer is the Prime Minister. Although the IRA uses violence, terrorism, Irish unity is a political not a military aim.' He paused. As instructed from London, there was to be no reference to rogue Special Branch officers apart from *Dee* being identified in the course of surveillance. 'We think we have identified a potential individual whom we believe to be a courier but at a high level.' Godden paused. 'High level' was a bit of burnishing.

Colonel Struthers took the opportunity to ask a question. 'So *Mythical* was, is a SIS operation?'

'Yes.' From Godden.

'The Hereford boys involved?'

'No.'

Struthers wanted more information. 'Who undertook the surveillance?'

Godden provided the answer. 'A small team of special forces trained soldiers, supported by my Service.'

'Undeclared to me or the RUC? It could have been a disaster if any of the other covert agencies, army or police, had come across them. A bloody disaster if it had been the Hereford boys.'

Colville moved to placate him.

'It was declared to the Prime Minister who gave it her approval. There is some understandable disquiet but we are where we are.'

'If the RUC learn of this, there will be hell to pay. They were reluctant to accept an intelligence co-ordinator.' The colonel stared accusingly at Colville. 'And this private enterprise happened on the Co-ordinator's watch. The one thing he was brought in to avoid happening. Did he know?'

The Co-ordinator's assistant shook his head. 'I was not aware of it till yesterday. But, I understand the current Co-ordinator was informed recently.'

Colonel Struthers turned away from Colville as if dismissing him, to fix on Godden. He had been given a short, vague summary on the potential source without naming him.

'You think he is an important courier?'

'Yes,' said by Godden without hesitation.

'You have been following this individual without following the normal protocols.'

'Approved by the *top*,' Godden said quietly.

'Even so, there could have been a disaster by disregarding... I don't want to know any more.'

'That's why we wish to formalise it. Look to the future.' Colville wished to bring the meeting back under his control. He inclined his head to his right catching the colonel's eye.

'Angus, let me remind you that due to the aim and nature of our operations we do not require the permission of the RUC Special Branch. I am confident that they, despite the mandatory protocols... they are not disclosing all their sources and information. No doubt there are still one or two mavericks among them.'

The two SIS officers and the colonel recognised Colville's message that with regard to Northern Ireland, the Security Service was in control.

'Nigel, I am not sure why I am here.'

'We will come to that.' Then. 'Arthur.'

'We are not ready to approach, no, he is not ready to be approached.'

'How do you intend to do that?' Struthers again.

'We have an asset who is close to him.'

'Is this *Mighty Midget*?' asked Colville.

'Yes. However, she is not aware of the real reason for our interest in him.'

'Is this an SIS source?' An irritated Struthers.

Colville answered, 'Yes but it was agreed between our two services at the time she was recruited.' Not totally accurate, but Colville was not aware of the full history of Christine Latham's recruitment.

'So is this operation to be coordinated with Special Branch?'

Colville was firm. 'No, Angus. Knowing the intentions of the IRA leadership is our responsibility.'

He looked across at the senior SIS officer. 'Arthur, please continue.'

'If you don't mind, I am going to hand over to Miss Kanna. Eileen.'

'*Mighty Midget* has been in place for some time. She has produced valuable political intelligence especially on the developing political side. What they call 'The Armalite and Ballot Box' strategy. And as we all know, they have settled in for the long war.'

She paused, looking down at her highlighted points though she had no need to be reminded.

'She has wanted out for some time. She is at the end of her tether, frightened, especially of being targeted by the loyalists.'

'Most Republicans have to live with that.'

'Yes, Colonel, but she feels more exposed and threatened by being a Protestant. A traitor to her people and religion.'

'Yes, quite. Being a traitor is not a healthy pastime here.'

'No. Though essential for our trade.'

Struthers smiled to acknowledge Eileen's retort.

She continued, 'Her relationship with this individual is why we want to keep her in place.'

'What glues the relationship?' Struthers asked.

'Music,' answered Eileen.

'And loneliness,' said Godden, which had been in Eileen's report of her recent meeting with *Mighty Midget*.

'How can I help?'

'Angus, we really need the loyalists to keep away from her so she can remain in place. Eileen... we have concerns that she might just up sticks. We need her at least until we make our approach.'

'When will that be? Patience is the foundation of our game. We all know that it may take years before we are able to recruit a source.'

'Yes. But we are hoping to accelerate it.' Godden tried to sound convincing though he did not reveal that exploiting *Mighty Midget* was the means of acceleration. He suspected Colonel Struthers and Colville would understand the intention.

'So, you want me to keep our loyalist murderers away from her. It will be difficult for two reasons. First we can give only hints, suggestions that she is the subject of something ongoing. But that can be only for a limited time. Three months possibly, six months at the most, but they will come back and ask what is happening. Secondly, they are not as disciplined as the IRA.

Nigel talked of mavericks earlier. Let me assure you that the loyalist gangs have their own fair share of mavericks. Frankly, I think some are beyond control.'

Struthers paused to look at each of the other participants in order to hammer home his message about rogue loyalists.

'A final point. If we reveal in any way that she was, is our agent then it will get back to the IRA. Be assured that they have sources into the loyalists.'

Another pause to look at each of the others.

'They are actively and constantly trying to improve their intelligence networks. No one should be fooled that they have not infiltrated the army. However, I will do my best.'

'Thank you,' said Godden.

'Angus, you will confirm when the message has filtered down to Her Majesty's loyal subjects.' Not trying to hide the disdain.

'Yes, Nigel.'

'Good. No need to detain you any further. Just a few operational protocols to agree.'

'Right. Good day.' The colonel stood up, glad to be escaping the insulated world of the civilian intelligence officers.

The protocols and new SOPs were imposed rather than being agreed. Agreement had been reached earlier between the heads of the respective Services. Further, it was decided that Major Somerville, if he agreed, would remain the nominal OC, but his role would be restricted to commanding the ground surveillance part of the *Mythical* operation. Godden was tasked with telephoning him to obtain his agreement. It was anticipated that Somerville would be more receptive to Godden rather than the female SIS officer.

24

In the car the next morning, Eileen Kanna briefed Braco on the new operational control. There was no business discussed during the lunch at the Dunadry Hotel which was used by individuals from the UK and the Republic on brief business visits, both to be near to the airport and to enjoy some luxury. It was also used for assignations away from the prying, village eyes of Belfast and Dublin.

They had selected a table suited to their physical security and to avoid inquisitive neighbours. Their conversation was of farming, of which Eileen was totally ignorant, and the sights of Paris and Rome, of which Braco had a limited knowledge. Any listener would not have been able to connect their conversation to the security forces or even an interest in the present situation.

However, any intruder into her mind would have discovered that Eileen had decided that Braco would now be her aide, her factotum, and she would be his mentor. In the Service this was not unusual. It was well known that Ormsby had been Godden's mentor, though perhaps more of a patron, otherwise the former colonial policeman would not have advanced. Eileen liked Braco, whom she found intelligent, tough and humble. She intended that as one of his duties he would protect Christine

Latham, despite the refusal of both Colville and Godden to grant her request. Furthermore, she would inform Christine, as it had been decided that Eileen would now be Christine's handler with Godden taking on more unspecified duties. She suspected, indeed was sure, that he wanted to distance himself from the potential loss of an agent, his agent, and an officer manoeuvring to avoid blame was another characteristic of the Service. She had already secured sailor Bill's silence on Braco spending time in his home. She gambled, no, assessed that Godden was not sailor Bill's type. This would be her last operation: Rome, Madrid or even ramshackle Lisbon was more appealing than Belfast.

Eileen's briefing to the team was short and concise. The choir-master was *Mythical's* sole target. No military personnel were to cross the Border. Hennessy and Pimlico were to be based in Dublin to cover the target when he went south, and if required, would be augmented by Embassy assets. The target's home telephone would be monitored, as would his house and vehicle. This was now an HQNI operation involving other covert agencies as and when required. Braco would be detached from the team in order to undertake other duties specific to the operation. A knowing smile from Tamworth to Tring.

'Any questions? Suggestions?'

The first contribution by Hennessy. 'Should we be bugging his car and house?'

'That was your proposal.'

'I know, Eileen. However, as Keynes said: when the facts change, my opinion changes.'

He was not sure if his quote was totally accurate, but he was confident that few in the room would know the quote or even have heard of John Maynard Keynes.

'If this guy is becoming a figure of importance, then no doubt they will sweep his house and car at some stage, probably more than once.'

'I think Hennessy may have a point,' said Major Somerville, the nominal OC. He had agreed to his new role during the telephone conversation despite finding Godden needlessly abrupt.

'Also, *ma'am*.' An intended emphasis verging on impudence. 'If he is *so important*... there is a good chance that he might spot us for two reasons.' Tring's tone now bordering on insolence

'Go on,' said the SIS officer ignoring the other woman's tone.

'First, if we follow all his movements, then we do not have enough people and vehicles to ring the changes. And if he is important, then he is going to be given anti-surveillance training.'

'I agree,' asserted Tamworth.

Eileen looked at the major and Hennessy both nodding in agreement with Tring.

Hennessy said, 'I don't think it will be a problem in Dublin.'

'So we have to be selective,' stated Eileen.

'We don't have to follow him to the *Trent* meets. I assume that we are continuing to monitor him?' The major continued, 'His telephone calls should give us some sort of steer on his movements – sometimes.'

Eileen stated, 'We need to proceed on the basis of speculative and random lingering in and around Londonderry.'

The special forces soldiers were appalled. Speculative and random were not hallmarks of covert operations.

The three non-military individuals sensed the uneasy, almost dispiriting attitude of the soldiers.

'Let me' said Hennessy, ' make a quick trip to Dublin. I might have a solution.'

25

Over the next two months, the *Mythical* team put together a fuller picture of Damien McGlone, the choirmaster, the IRA courier, which allowed them to predict with almost complete certainty their target's movements out of Londonderry, thanks to a number of factors.

The seconded SIS officer had called in a favour from a friend in the CIA station in Dublin. For extracting him from a potentially career-ending situation in South East Asia, the CIA officer supplied Hennessy with sophisticated bugging equipment which had not yet been shared with friendly intelligence agencies, but for a period of four weeks only. If it was discovered, the British security and intelligence organisations could truthfully declare that they had not requested the equipment. The CIA officer was confident that the IRA did not have the necessary means to locate the bug. The intention was to attach the bugging device to the choirmaster's car during the night, when it was parked outside or near his home. However, in a timely stroke of good-luck, Eileen learned from Christine Latham that the choirmaster was going to Dublin for a concert and no, Christine was not going. Hennessy and Pimlico, in the convincing guise of Dublin down-and-outs, attached the device in the car-park of the church venue of the concert while the CIA officer sat in his car to confirm it was working.

The team now knew when the target was on the move and put him in their shepherding box once he was outside his home city. There were trips to Belfast and Dublin as well as to Armagh and Enniskillen. There was a further useful aid. Braco recalled that his COP sergeant had lampooned intelligence operatives who paid for information which was often to be found in the local newspapers, especially those read by people with republican or nationalist leanings. Eileen Kanna took up the suggestion Braco made to her, and established that the choirmaster's forthcoming appearances at churches or other venues in Belfast and other places were usually contained in notices in the local newspapers. It became apparent over the four week bugging period that, except on one occasion, the choirmaster left Londonderry only for these commitments.

The telephones belonging to both the target and Christine were tapped and provided further information to help create a picture of the former's routine. On the telephone, the choirmaster told Christine when he was intending to go to a concert. Although she had been instructed by her handler not to accept any invitations at present, this was not a problem because of her present university workload, at which their target did not demur.

Even after the removal of the bug on the car, the newspaper notices gave the team early warning of his movement except in Derry, though there were one or two notices in the Derry Journal of him leading choirs or being a judge at church or school competitions. However after reviewing the surveillance reports, it was assessed by Eileen, with Godden's concurrence, the choirmaster acted as a courier only when participating in musical events.

If the British intelligence officers had been able to meet Hugh Devlin, one of their IRA counterparts, and now the most senior leader of the IRA's Intelligence team for their Northern Command, he would have confirmed that the choirmaster acted as a courier only under the cover of his musical activities. Further, he did not carry instructions on military operations, only messages in respect of what the Brits would call political intelligence, and also on finance.

Devlin had told his courier that even if he was stopped by the Brits, it was unlikely that the average squaddie or peeler would attach any significance to the notes in his musical folder. With his chilling grin, he had told the choirmaster that the Brits would only know the meaning of the messages if he told them, and he would face the consequence. There was only one. His message to the choirmaster was that no one was above suspicion. Devlin told him that without prior warning, people would check his home and car to make sure that, knowingly or unknowingly, he did not have any Brit equipment. He should hope, pray, that Devlin's team after investigation did not establish it to be the former.

He should alert *Gaggie* McKenna if he saw anyone acting strangely around his car, but not to challenge the individual, or if he felt someone had been in his car or house. He was to report any strange or unusual telephone calls, or workmen or unknown people calling at his home, even if they claimed it was by mistake. It could be Brit intelligence or the Special Branch trying to recruit him as an informer. Once more he was given a reminder on the fate of informers. If a policeman or squaddie during a road stop or on the street in Derry engaged him in lengthy conversation, that should be reported. The choirmaster confessed that it happened quite often when he was stopped by the soldiers though seldom by a policeman. When they saw his musical instruments or just the music sheets and songbooks, most of the soldiers were keen to talk to him, although usually once he mentioned church or classical music they were not so keen to prolong the conversation.

'Yes. Suppose some of them would be.' The amiable grin again. 'They are bored and lonely. Most of them don't fucking... sorry.'

Unlike *Gaggie* McKenna, Devlin tried not to swear in front of the choirmaster.

'Almost all the soldiers don't know why they are here and probably don't care. Probably be happier shooting Argies or ragheads.'

Devlin laughed but Damien McGlone did not show his irritation.

'It's the unionists supported by the generals and MI5 in Stormont and London who are keeping this going. Also the Tories with that bloody woman. Some of their MPs are in hock to rich unionists here. Yes, the upper-class unionists here through the Orange Order keep the ordinary Prots in check by peddling the fear of a united Ireland and control by the Roman Catholic hierarchy. It's bollocks!'

This time a mocking laugh and no apology.

'The bishops can't even control us.'

He looked at McGlone anticipating a reaction in defence of his Holy Mother Church but none came. The reality was that McGlone was terrified of the IRA man.

'Then, of course there's big Ian stirring it with his bigotry... and supported by his sycophants. I know what I would do with Paisley if I got my way.' The IRA man paused with no trace of a smile just a callous, enraged face. 'Mind you, Labour aren't much better. Especially when that wee shite Mason was here. Also helped by Newman.'

The IRA leader assumed that his companion would know Roy Mason had been a Labour Secretary of State for the

North and Ken Newman a former RUC Chief Constable. The choirmaster, like most people in the North, knew the personalities.

'Funny,' said the tall Devlin, 'both were wee men. Tells you something about wee men.' A chuckle.

He resumed his account.

'We can rely on two things. The stupidity of the loyalists in calling their strike in seventy-seven even though it was a failure. But... but it reminded our people, especially the nationalists, the SDLP people, of the reality of the Protestant ascendancy. Probably better to leave Paisley alone. And the hunger strike was another gift from the Brits. We had to control it for publicity reasons. We're now in the political game and we are not getting out of it.'

His voice dropped almost into a whisper. 'Pity a couple more died than probably had to.'

He paused briefly to regain his train of thought.

'And the second thing?' He was looking at McGlone though not expecting or wanting an answer.

'Our fifth column, the good old naive British liberals. Squeamish about Mason's and Newman's torture tactics. Upholding the decency of British justice. Mind you, many of their families did well out of the empire, getting rich by theft. And of course the anti-establishment lefties including some MPs. They support everything the Church abhors such as abortion and homosexuality but that doesn't matter if we are giving the Brits a good kicking.'

McGlone refrained from pointing out the Church abhorred everything the IRA did and that even the Pope had condemned the IRA, though not by name. And there were some bishops and priests supportive of the IRA. The Church, like the Island, was divided.

Later, sitting at home after his tea and not, as was his wont, listening to music, McGlone pondered the encounter with Devlin. He was afraid of him because he knew that his threats were real. He determined that he would be more on his guard against surveillance by the security forces and any possible approach to him. But, he was certain that in his encounters with the soldiers or the police, no one had attempted to approach him. He would not talk to the soldiers but blank them as others did. Again, Devlin had told him that being natural, being himself was his best protection. Be natural but be alert to surveillance. He felt incarcerated by his secret role. Though that was better than a bullet in the back of the head and being dumped on a lonely road in South Armagh.

Although he feared Devlin, he was slightly in awe of him. He was not just a man of violence but one who seemed to know and understand what is called 'the big picture'. Devlin was willing to use anything or anyone, including British MPs, to further the cause. He was intrigued by the comment of not getting out of politics. He could imagine him speaking at a political meeting. Derry might be too limiting for Devlin. The one disconcerting note was his comment on a couple of the young hunger strikers probably not needing to die. Damien McGlone felt the deaths of all the hunger strikers, and the other young men and sometimes women, were needless. He did recognise his dilemma of helping an organisation which was willing, encouraging its young to lay down their lives for a cause. The cause of a united Ireland on which he was an agnostic.

He had no one to turn to for guidance on how to resolve his moral dilemma: not even his priests because some of them might report him, not to their hierarchy, but to the other one. In their own way both hierarchies, but also the Orange Order, had warped the minds of the people of Ireland. He could not even share his predicament with Christine who supported the republican cause. With her background, he mused on what warped her mind. But he could forgive her because of their shared love, even passion, for music.

26

Godden was adamant. Braco would not provide personal protection for *Mighty Midget*. He did not care if Eileen Kanna had a tame history professor in Queen's University who would employ Braco as an assistant on the professor's research into colonialism in Africa, even if Braco's Kenyan background provided natural cover. Anyway, she should not have approached the professor: a hands-off notice had been circulated. She had ventured well out of her remit. Ormsby and Colville would need to be informed. Godden was not interested if the soldier was taken off surveillance duties to act as her driver and valet.

Eileen had ignored the intended belittling remark. She would circulate her newly – drafted memo repeating her previous warning on their agent's mental state. Of course, Colville would receive a copy as required by the new protocols.

Godden's response had been angry. 'I will not yield to moral blackmail.'

'We are hoping, counting on the choirmaster, to do so.'

'We are acting in the best interests of our Service and our country.'

Eileen could not disguise her contempt.

'Sanctimonious piffle!'

'That is quite enough, Miss Kanna. You are not indispensable to this operation.'

An immediate retort.

'Christine is!' She spoke quietly, 'All I am proposing is some attempt to keep her safe till we are ready to approach the choirmaster. You heard Colonel Struthers saying some of the loyalists are beyond control.'

Her superior was quiet, and she knew that it was better not to say anything further, while he calculated the best way to approach his superiors to ask them to change their decision.

'I'll get back to you.'

Godden telephoned her after dinner. He did not say that he had consulted Ormsby and Colville; she knew that he had. Limited protection could be provided from the safe house near the university, but under no circumstances was the soldier to use the cover of a research assistant. It was unsustainable. It had come to their attention that the soldier had been in the Province almost continuously since the beginning of 1979. Someone, especially in the security forces, might recognise him and blab. Later, when she told him, Braco was relieved because he shared the senior officer's assessment. As an additional measure, new and better alarms would be installed by MI5's technical wing in the agent's home.

Once more, Eileen went beyond her remit by taking Braco into Christine Latham's house three days after the decision on protection. She impressed upon him that he must never reveal his knowledge of the agent to anyone in the team – especially Tamworth – on pain of being sent to Siberia. The soldier was not surprised by her specifying Tamworth because it was obvious that he, or possibly just his accent, niggled her. He promised himself that one day he would tell the intelligence officer that Tamworth was the one he trusted the most out of all the *Mythical* team.

Christine recognised him from his time around the university though she did not say so, and Braco knew that she had recognised him. The new alarms had been installed the previous day by electricians in red overalls. As instructed, Christine had left her key with an elderly neighbour so she could let the workmen in, which would allow Christine to go to work. The neighbour reported that someone would call round later just to check that she was happy with the work – to brief her on the alarms.

Eileen explained to Christine that her colleague would be around to keep an eye on her but it would not be all the time. That was not possible. Anyway she probably would not notice him.

'Oh, a chameleon,' said Christine, exchanging a fleeting, knowing look with Braco which Eileen did not observe.

Braco gave Christine a short briefing on how to react to certain scenarios. When Braco was finished, Eileen suggested that he have a cup of tea in the kitchen. Braco agreed, knowing that his ears were out of bounds to the secrets, the exchanges of the intelligence world. Only his eyes would focus on the resulting product.

'You have got him well-trained.'

Eileen saw her opportunity. 'Have you got *your man* well-trained?'

'He's not my man.' Christine was irritated. 'He's a friend. Anyway, he's quite a bit older than me.'

A smile flashed across the intelligence officer's face.

'Prince Charles married a younger model.'

'The aristocracy do that.'

'Why should they have all the fun.'

'Who said it was fun. To answer your real question. I haven't seen him for a while though we have spoken on the telephone a few times.'

Eileen knew how often they had spoken on the telephone and the content of their conversations.

'Any intention of seeing him?'

'Thought he was off-limits?'

'We do not think he is a problem, a threat to you.'

She paused, not wanting to be too encouraging. Not wanting to plant the seed in Christine's mind that they could be interested in Damien McGlone. This thought was concurrent with another one, that Christine's long involvement with the Service would mean her knowing that the Service takes an interest in everyone. She was accurate in regard to Christine's thinking, which also included her considering another motivation for this interest: McGlone comes from the Bogside, the home, even the womb of present-day republicanism. Eileen had wanted to tell the agent that the aim was to recruit the choirmaster without giving any reason, but that had been vetoed. It was best that she did not know.

Eileen had protested to her superiors. 'She's a university lecturer in English literature. She has spent years studying and teaching deception and disloyalty. What do you think Shakespeare is!' She was frustrated. 'You think, really think that she has not worked out what is going on!'

'I have applied for two jobs, one in Glasgow the other in Southampton. Don't worry, they would not be until the start of next year... the academic one.' The clarification for Eileen's benefit. 'That's if I even get an interview.'

'Which one would you prefer? Glasgow? You did your undergraduate there.'

Christine almost asked how she knew that but recalled that they knew everything about her.

' I quite liked Glasgow. Well the university, not so much the people.'

'Thought you are all Celtic cousins?'

'You're forgetting I'm half English.' Christine's tone had a tinge of condescension.

Eileen changed tack by asking, 'Have you told Damien? What does he think?' Though she knew the answer.

'Yes.'

She did not answer the second question. Eileen knew the answer. He had suggested that if she got an interview, he would go over and they could take in some concerts. They had agreed that there were often good concerts in Glasgow City Halls. Also, if she had an interview in Southampton, he would go over to London and they could take in a concert there. She had told him that it was likely that she would fly over and back on the day of the interview. But she had ended the discussion of interviews with 'We'll see...' thereby indicating that it was something she might consider if circumstances allowed.

The SIS officer decided not to press the issue of Christine's relationship with the choirmaster. Christine provided some titbits of information on Sinn Féin personalities and activities but of no real significance. To Eileen, it felt like one of the role-plays she did on training and refresher courses. Information was being passed because that was what agent and handler did.

Eileen was worried, slightly alarmed when she left the agent's house. Later in the nearby safe house, in response to Eileen's question, Braco said that there was nothing in the agent's demeanour that he had found alarming or disconcerting. But that was the first time he had actually met and spoken to her. Previously she had been one of the opposition. Braco did not disclose to Eileen that he had been intrigued by Christine. Though not all that pretty, there was something appealing about her. He understood why the choirmaster might find her attractive. If he did reveal his thoughts he was certain that he would be on his way back to Fermanagh and back on surveillance duties which he now found tiresome.

The covert soldier realised that this was the first time that he had met an agent, a source. In briefings, mention would be made of a source or sources, but to the operatives, these were distant, unknown figures, almost like teapots who poured information into the Branch or army intelligence officer's cup. Sometimes the tea was hot, but most of the time it was lukewarm, sometimes cold. Christine was a real source, flesh and blood. He was struck by her equanimity. There was an indefinable quality to her. Was it due to her ash blonde hair? It made her look older but captivating. Of course, she was older than him by a few years just as the choirmaster was older than her. An inner smile. Christine was being bracketed by the choirmaster and him.

Eileen remained slightly disturbed by her agent. She would need to consider the matter, reviewing the signs and reports in the way which had first brought her to the attention of the Secret Intelligence Service, when she was a colonial civil servant. One of the periodical whole-team debriefs was coming up when the floor was open to all. Each would give an assessment of what they had seen and heard. There was discussion and debate. She was not greatly in favour of this type of session but she knew sometimes they produced an odd nugget or idea. They needed something concrete.

This time, her instinct told her that *Mighty Midget* was planning to bolt!

27

On this occasion, the debrief was conducted by the team OC, rather than Eileen who wished to concentrate on what each operative said and make any relevant notes. This free-for-all type of session had been alien when she first encountered it. She had been more accustomed to the hierarchical conclaves of the colonial civil service, in which one was forbidden to step outside one's parish, and to the boardroom-style meetings of SIS, where each sat at their designated place at the table, but only the experienced or anointed ones could speak beyond their remit. She understood from the OC that the practice had emanated from the SAS in which the major had also served. Eileen could not imagine him being a proponent of such an 'equal opportunities' practice.

There was unanimity amongst the operatives that the choirmaster was batting for the other side, though one of them suggested it was more fielding than batting, which brought an appreciative chuckle from the OC accompanied by, 'Probably more exact.' Eileen concurred and made a note of it which she would include in her report to Godden. Tamworth felt rather miffed that he had not thought of it.

Several of the operatives felt they should look more closely at his movements in Londonderry, especially his visits to the house in Coshquin. The house telephone intercepts had not revealed anything of use and the listening had been discontinued. There were so many other targets. One operative suggested bugging the Coshquin house, but this was rejected for the same reason as not bugging the choirmaster's: that it was likely to be swept by the IRA's security team.

That assumption was wrong.

Gaggie McKenna's sister, Ciara, had been firm that she would not allow his boys to trample over her home. And she would bloody well tell Martin McGuinness the same. Their da murdered by the UVF or UFF or UDR: the initials didn't matter, they were all the same. And their father had never been involved in anything. It had broken their mother's heart and she was gone barely a year after her husband.

Their young brother on the blanket: she had used all her powers of persuasion to keep him from going on the hunger strike in 1980 by telling him that it would break his niece's heart because she saw him as a brother. And what had he done: carry a couple of guns from one house to another, barely a hundred yards away, when he was stopped and searched by the Brits. Ciara was told that a couple of soldiers were going to shoot him till a sergeant or corporal stopped them. And he only stopped it, she was told, because people had come out of their houses onto the street. And the man who got her brother to do it was not brave enough to do it himself. Even her brother *Gaggie* was surprised that the guns had been moved during the day and while the army were around. Unless, they were undercover soldiers which meant they knew about the move and were waiting. *Gaggie* would look into it. But he did not have the clout then and was told it would be taken care of. And what about her husband's brother, shot by the Paras on Bloody Sunday, thankfully not killed.

Hadn't their family given enough for Ireland?

The two from what was now called 'the Dublin outstation' were not present. They were keen to remain there to enjoy Dublin's attractions, away from the depressing North: both remembered the reason why they had left their homeland. Nevertheless, Hennessy had dispatched a signal which Eileen did not share with the others. Hennessy agreed that the choirmaster was rotten but possibly not yet to the core. To Eileen, this resonated with the 'fielding' comparison. Furthermore, the SIS officer considered him potential fertile ground for turning. He would like to get him and Miss Latham to Dublin again and into the same bedroom. He was confident that with the assistance of his CIA friend, and even some help from the Garda Special Branch, they could catch them *in flagrante delicto*, both sight and sound. He had added helpfully, though unnecessarily, that the Latin term was a euphemism for individuals being caught whilst indulging in sexual activity. Obviously Hennessy believed the female officer was prim and proper; Eileen thought he was trying to be too clever by half.

Tamworth reported on the telephone records. He and Tring had been assigned to monitor the telephones. Eileen had decided rather than rotating the listeners, she wanted continuity. Tamworth and Tring did not mind because it gave him more time to watch football and other sports on television, and her more space to pursue a new interest, reading Jane Austen novels. Tamworth, despite his gruff, simple manner, was excellent at honing in on words or behaviour that the others would not consider unusual, such as a slight, almost imperceptible, change in tone of voice or movement. When this was considered again, it sometimes made the others reconsider what they thought that they had heard or seen.

Tamworth opened with, 'Think I now have a music degree. God, all they talk about is music and listen to it sometimes. Their telephone bills must be enormous.'

He shared some of the knowledge he had gained. Mozart was a child genius. He started composing when he was five. Should have been out playing football. *Contralto* was the lowest of the ranges of female voices and *soprano* the highest, though he thought he knew that. The *William Tell* opera was written by Rossini, an Italian – not for the telly series that he used to watch as a kid. A Mazurka was a Polish dance in three-quarter time – whatever that meant. They would both like to attend a concert in the Wigmore Hall.

'That's in London.' Looking at Tring he said, 'She told me that. She's clever.'

He ended with, ' Did you know that Catherine Wilson is a soprano. She's Scottish. I thought Andy Stewart was the only Scottish singer.'

There was a brief hiatus. A lightening of the atmosphere, making Eileen hope that people would now speak freely and offer opinions and suggestions.

But Tamworth was not finished.

'They are the queerest couple I have ever known. They're in a relationship?' he asked Eileen Kanna.

'We're not sure.'

Apart from herself and Braco, none of those present knew that *Forth*, the code-word for Christine, was a British agent. She was the only one in the room who knew what had taken place in the Dublin hotel room.

'Now, she's an active supporter of Sinn Féin and we believe, know, that he is involved. Maybe only a fielder out on the boundary.'

A turn and a nod towards the operative who had first used

the fielder metaphor, though Tamworth was pleased that he could make it more precise.

'She is not so active at present,' stated Eileen.

'Still, both have been mentioned in the newspapers.' Tamworth, having taken on board Braco's suggestions, had read the local press, the Newsletter, the Irish News, the Belfast Telegraph and the Derry Journal, even back copies. 'But, I, we, have never heard any mention of politics, the bombings and shootings, even the Dropping Well pub bomb with so many casualties.' He paused, then smiled. 'Maybe they only read the New Musical Express.'

'Not their type of music,' interjected Tring. That newspaper, commonly called the NME, was for followers of pop music.

'We know they listen to the radio because they discuss concerts which have been on or are due to be broadcast. They sometimes listen to parts of concerts when they are on the phone. Do they switch off when the news comes on?!'

Another longer pause.

'They are freaks.'

Eileen turned to Tring to ask if she wanted to add anything, but she said that her colleague had covered it all. Tring admired her colleague, though no *Mr Darcy* he, more of a *Mr Bingley*. And she knew that Tamworth was not finished.

'There's another thing. Part of my music degree. *Fantasia*. Might not be using it in its strict musical term but I think they live in a fantasy world.'

'Thank you. Never a dry briefing,' said the OC whilst Eileen jotted down 'fantasy world'.

They took a short break.

When they reconvened, the OC said that this was now the time for discussion, opinions and options. Tring opened the discussion.

'Surely, the IRA must be aware of their relationship? Probably better described as a connection. Would they be happy about it?'

'What do you think? You normally have an opinion.' The OC was looking directly at Braco who had decided to say nothing, rather than say anything which, even inadvertently, would disclose or hint at his new knowledge.

'Well, I...'

Tamworth came to his rescue. 'He's good at sitting in bushes but has no knowledge of intimate relationships... especially when there's a big age gap.'

A chuckle from the speaker met with a grin from a nodding Braco while most of the others sniggered. Tring glanced at Eileen for a reaction. None came. Her face was impassive. Over the years, Eileen had honed this skill to perfection.

The intelligence officer quietly said, 'They probably are aware of it but do not see it as posing a threat.'

'Probably, they think they are bloody strange. Oops. Sorry.'

Tamworth knew that the OC did not like any foul language even the mildest during formal sessions.'

The OC smiled and said, 'You are forgiven but only because you may be right.'

Eileen was nodding in agreement while making another note.

The assessment, more supposition, was right. Christine had informed what might be considered her Sinn Féin line-manager of her meetings with Damien McGlone; they shared a love of music. Later she was told that there was no problem; though he might not be 'one of us', he wasn't playing for the Brits. Even if he was, which he wasn't, it could be helpful.

Similarly, Damien McGlone told his 'line-manger', *Gaggie* McKenna. He would get back to him. *Gaggie* took the matter to Hugh Devlin.

'Imagine, the holy choirmaster is riding a Belfast girl and a Proddy to boot. Hear Belfast Proddy girls are good rides.'

'Don't be so crude.'

A few years ago, Devlin would have participated in similar risqué craic with *Gaggie* and others. Now there was a new image to cultivate: he was nearer to the ballot box than the Armalite. Several days later, Devlin told *Gaggie* there was not a problem. The choirmaster was not committing a mortal sin. Their passion was music. Actually they were bampots, but harmless and not a threat.

'It was alright at the start but now I don't like having Proddies involved. They're not the same as us,' said *Gaggie*. 'Sure we can trust that wee Belfast girl?'

There was no reply.

$-$ 28 $-$

The surveillance of the choirmaster continued, but at a lei-
surely pace and on an irregular basis in order to confirm that
his pattern remained unchanged – which it did. To both the
professional intelligence officers and the covert operatives, a
set pattern was an anathema. The Security Service's Colville,
now firmly in charge of the operational side of *Mythical* in
the Province, insisted on light surveillance that lessened the
chances of the target or possible IRA minders spotting the
surveillance. The use of any type of tracking or listening device
on the target's car was firmly vetoed. Colville maintained that
what was bound to happen was that the opposition would
decide to search the choirmaster's car the day after the devices
had been inserted. It had happened on other operations. It had
just been bad luck.

At C's direction, Simon Ormsby made a rare visit to Lisburn.
The SIS chief wanted to make certain that the *Mythical* coordi-
nation between the two services was on a firm footing, and that
there was no misunderstanding over the mission. He did not
have complete faith in Arthur Godden's ability to ensure this,
especially when dealing with Colville, a wily operator.
  Ormsby did not like visiting the Province: Washington, Paris

and even dull Bonn were much more attractive places to visit on duty. He had come to think of the Province as a dismal, divided corner of what should be an unimportant island.

Another reason for Ormsby's dislike of going there was that he was required to travel by RAF, usually in a Hercules transport plane which was noisy and uncomfortable. At RAF Aldergrove, he travelled to Lisburn by helicopter, but on one occasion he had been driven through the bleak and barren countryside to the reasonably pretty town of Lisburn.

On this visit, he was in the ugly transport aircraft which had few passengers and mainly cargo. He ignored his fellow passengers, and in the uncomfortable seat, he closed his eyes and let his mind drift in an effort to make the short journey bearable.

He mused that the IRA were doing Britain a favour by trying to eject us. If not for the Americans insisting the Province remained under NATO control in the event of a war with the Soviets. That was absurd, because any attack would go nuclear within days, before the arrival of any reinforcements. And if NATO activated the plans to send reinforcements as tension rose, this would only exacerbate the crisis. Had they not heard of the spiral of insecurity propagated by one of their own academics, Robert Jervis? Forgotten the history of the lead-up to the first world war? Even more salient, did they not remember the words of their own George Kennan on Russia's foreign policy? What drove it was their sense of insecurity with flat open ground to the west of Moscow.

Even more irritating of the Americans was the way that they could straddle the divide, insisting this god-forsaken piece of land remain under British sovereignty, but permitting vast amounts of money to flow across the pond to finance terrorism, and at times provide a safe haven for terrorists. Some of

their politicians obliquely supported the ending of partition –
though it was more to do with appeasing their Irish-American
voters. Even our own generals did not help: needing a war
in order to train their commanders and soldiers, despite the
fact that as a war it barely registered on the Richter-scale, or
whatever its war equivalence was. More disheartening was the
attitude of the Dublin diplomatic and intelligence establishment which did not favour unification, though left it unsaid
because they could not argue against their constitution. They,
and probably the majority of the Dublin establishment, did
not want the thin Northern Ireland gruel ladled into their
dish: they did not have the necessary cutlery to deal with a
disaffected unionist minority, including organised, well-armed
groups. De Valera was probably wise to refuse Churchill's offer
of unification in 1940 or 41, notwithstanding that it was most
likely not a genuine offer. Then there were the Unionists with
their ridiculous Orange Order and the Lambeg drum. Also, he
had never felt at ease in the foreign climes of Scotland, Wales
and even Manchester.

Time for a scuttle, though he hated using the word and
forbade its use by his staff. England should declare independence and seal their borders. Let the Celtic tribes stew and
resolve their own problems. But the cries would go up that they
are our kith and kin. That we cannot abandon them, though
the establishment and senior Tories would not wish to desert
the estates which provided shooting and fishing. And Labour
relied on Wales and Scotland to have any chance at all of
forming a government. Of course, it was the European project,
with its clarion call by some that our future lies within Europe.
They had not read their history and had forgotten that the
narrow stretch of water had created a much greater chasm. He
was being dishonest. It was his heart speaking, not his mind. A
Scottish colleague called it the disassociation of the heart and

head. The colleague claimed it had plagued the Scots since the Act of Union. His own mind insisted he support the idea of a closer Europe and he could not abide the little Englanders who seem to infest not just the Tory Party and even the Bennite left, but also the military, the police and the Security Service. Was it Trollope who had said, 'One is patriotic only because one is too small and weak to be cosmopolitan.'?

Their arrival at RAF Aldergrove was announced over the tannoy. Ormsby was pleased that he had not felt the bump of landing. 'Possibly it was a better pilot this morning.'

On arrival at HQNI for the meeting with his staff and Colville, Ormsby endorsed Colville's decision on light surveillance, and asserted that it was no longer where he went, but what the choirmaster carried which was important. But no opportunity had presented itself to approach the choirmaster. Their agent *Mighty Midget* remained the conduit, but as Ormsby described, 'One awkward fumble in a Dublin hotel bedroom is not substantial enough for my liking.' The 'liking' was the approach to the target in order to recruit him by fair or foul means. Since Dublin, their agent and their target had met only once and briefly at a concert in Belfast, because the latter was accompanied by his brother and sister-in-law. Nevertheless, they spoke regularly on the telephone with their conversation following the same pattern, one subject, music.

Eileen Kanna expressed the view that she thought they might flee either together or singly, and rendezvous somewhere like Milan. Godden, when his superiors were present, adopted his normal abrupt manner towards his subordinate, enquiring dismissively, 'On what do you base that hypothesis?'

'On Tamworth's comment about them living in a fantasy world. It's all in the report, Arthur.'

She adopted her demure approach with a smile. She knew that it irritated Godden. It did.

'He's the bloody clown.' Rarely did Godden swear even in its mildest form.

'He might not be to everyone's taste. Doesn't play cricket.'

Major Somerville came to Eileen's aid.

'But he is intelligent and perceptive.' He smiled. 'Actually he does play cricket. According to his reports he's a bloody good one.' A mild but rare expletive. 'In the Ian Botham mould. And unfortunately, I can't convince him to extend because he wants to go back to his parent unit for stability – and to play cricket.'

The major felt slightly guilty because he, not Godden, had mentioned cricket. But the SIS officer now tended to irritate him, whereas previously it had been the female officer.

Godden ignored the army officer and stated, 'There's still no real basis to support your theory of them fleeing.' A pause. 'Feminine intuition.'

An unworthy comment intertwined with a conceited sneer.

'Now, now, Arthur. You know that I place great faith in feminine intuition. Especially Eileen's.'

Turning his gaze away from Godden and with a slight incline of his head towards Eileen, smiled. An intended chivalrous gesture which was acknowledged by a slight nod of the head in gratitude, though scornful on the inside.

Nigel Colville had remained silent, amused by the contretemps between the two officers of MI5's sister – or was it brother – service? He could never be sure. Even more he did not understand why individuals joined them. Yes, sometimes their postings were good, even exotic, but they engaged in meaningless talk caused by a lack of candour and of course their hallmark, prevarication. He considered it a service of envy and impotence. Now it was time to conclude.

'So where do we go from here?'

'Well, sir, it is possible our two might go to a concert in Belfast in a few weeks...'

Colville now determined to exert control, interrupted, 'Where did you get that from?'

'It came from last night's telephone. I received it just before the meeting.'

Godden's intervention was pre-empted by Colville's raised left hand. 'Go on, Eileen.'

'They didn't mention a date but Tamworth...'

'That's the cricketer?'

Smiling, Eileen said, 'Yes sir. He did some digging and there is a concert in the cathedral on Friday sixteenth. Two weeks tomorrow. But, there was no commitment by either.'

'Can we encourage her to go?' asked Ormsby.

'It would reveal to her that we are listening. I know that she probably thinks we are but why confirm it?'

Colville agreed. 'You are right.' He turned to his counterpart. 'What do you think?'

'I would prefer Dublin but we need to seize any opportunity.'

Ormsby meant 'I'. He was under pressure in that he knew the three year time-scale decreed by the PM was nearing its end. He was confident that he would be granted a short extension, but substantial progress would likely increase the extension.

'Ideally, they spend the night together.'

'What is it with you people and sex!' It was not a question and he did not wait for a response. 'We begin planning for them going to the concert.' He turned to the major. 'Tim, do the necessary recces around the location both inside and out.'

'Yes sir.'

'Once you are done, come back to me with your proposals. Direct to me. Understood?'

'Sir.'

'We might need to encourage *Mighty Midget* to go with him. Who's handling her at the moment?'

'Eileen,' said Ormsby.

'Good. I don't want to go down this path but be prepared.'

'Yes sir.'

'We might need to engineer something to keep him in Belfast.' Colville was thinking aloud.

'We can use some things which have worked in the past.'

'But no rough stuff.' Colville paused, smiled and said to the major, 'I forgot. You are not the Hereford Hussars.'

He paused to write something in his small, black notebook before turning back to the others. 'And no more 'choirmaster' in reports. It is *Danube*.'

His eyes perused the room for the confirmatory nods.

'Good. Any other points? Questions? And I don't want any words or warnings of doom. We know that the majority of our operations end in... not failure... let's say end inconclusively. Thank you.'

He stood up, an additional signal that the meeting was at an end. The others gathered their folders and prepared to leave.

'Simon. Please remain. I have ordered up some lunch.'

29

The operation on the Friday went ahead. On the Wednesday before the concert, the choirmaster confirmed in a telephone conversation with the university lecturer that he was attending. No arrangements were made to meet, just that he would see her there. The operation report, *Op Mythical 118/2*, was short but concise. It began with the date and time and the short distribution list. It read:

1. The subject *Danube* was collected on the Craigavon Bridge in Londonderry. He stopped for petrol between Ballymena and Belfast. There were no eyes inside the shop but he was inside for sufficient time only to pay. There was no indication that he communicated with anyone or that he was aware of the shepherds.

2. He parked his car on Hill Street, a two minute walk to the cathedral. Inside, he spoke to several individuals including a clergyman. All appeared to know him, and according to the shepherds inside, the discussions were friendly.

3. The second subject, *Mighty Midget* arrived after *Danube*. She spoke briefly to two people whom she seemed to know,

then took her seat. There was no interaction between the two subjects. *Danube* sat on the other side of the aisle from *Mighty Midget* and three rows in front.

4. On leaving in the midst of the departing audience, *Mighty Midget* followed the other subject, keeping four or five paces behind, to his car. She paused, a few metres away, while he got into his vehicle. Once *Danube* was in, and had half opened the front passenger door, the other subject walked quickly and entered the vehicle.

5. They drove to *Mighty Midget's* street and parked several doors down on the opposite side.

6. They walked together to a Lebanese Restaurant on Botanic Avenue. They did not try to conceal in any way that they were together. Entry was not made into the restaurant but did two walk pasts. Each subject had a glass of wine. There was not a bottle on the table.

7. They left the restaurant. They walked back to *Mighty Midget's* home. No holding of hands or any signs of affection.

8. *Danube* could not start his vehicle. Due to our intervention. Now 2245 hrs. We did not have eyes close but *Danube* did seem apologetic and rather embarrassed. The other subject appeared reluctant to invite *Danube* in. They eventually entered together.

9. The light in the downstairs lounge was on from entry to 0345 hrs. The upstairs bedroom light came on at 0255 and off at 0310. Curtains of both rooms remained closed.

10. At 0800, *Danube* exited the house and tried to start his vehicle. A middle-aged male, out for a morning stroll, assisted him to restart the vehicle. *Danube* did make a comment about having had recent problems with his vehicle. A stroke of luck.

11. The shepherding and penning of *Danube* was completed without any mishaps or detours.

12. At no time did the subjects either singly or together engage in any obvious anti-surveillance drills. They did not walk arm in arm, hold hands or display any signs of affection.

The team OC, following instructions, did not disclose that the local passer-by was a friendly. Once back in base location, he told Eileen Kanna that it was now over to her.

Eileen knew the importance of debriefing the source as quickly as possible while her recall was fresh. Especially in this case where their target had been in their agent's company for almost 12 hours, possibly even in her bed. Godden was in agreement during their discussion on the secure telephone on the Saturday that arrangements would be put in place for a meet within the next 24 hours, but just required clearance from Colville and Ormsby. A formality.

The team were buoyant during their late lunch. Although they had not been informed officially that the mission was to recruit the choirmaster, they could presume this by the nature of their operation. The choirmaster was not a ruthless, active terrorist so they were not prepping him for the SAS. He was a courier, so ideal source material. Most had become rather bored with the operation, and either wanted a return to other special duties or their parent units. Tamworth was the only one who had actually asked for a return to his parent unit.

However, it would be worth the long and boring hours, if there was some tangible result.

Just after lunch, Eileen was called to the secure line.

Godden was terse. His instruction was to sit tight.

'Why?' she demanded.

'From our masters.'

She could sense the disappointment, bafflement in his voice.

'This goes against everything we have been taught, our training, and what we know from experience. We need to speak to her as a matter of urgency.'

'The decision has been made.'

'I will come up to...'

'Eileen, no. Stay there as... for your own good.' His voice was low, plaintive,

She paused, reflecting before asking, 'Anything else?'

'Braco is to stay in place. You can send up a couple of others to assist him. They can stay in Bill's. Otherwise, everything else is to stop. No surveillance. No listening. The team is to sit tight. You can work out something with Tim so some can go on leave for a few days.'

He paused before saying, 'And Eileen, no going off piste. That's from Simon. Understand?'

'Yes. Capisco. The guys won't be happy.'

'We are all in the same club on this one.'

'Is there any time frame?'

'No. I will get back to you as soon as I hear. Goodbye.'

He had ended the call before she could respond. She thought that it might be the first time she and Godden were singing from the same hymn sheet. A slight smile at the music analogy.

She briefed the OC before the team, and she was right – the team were not happy. She had to repeat three or four times that on this occasion she was not keeping anything back. In his languid way, Tamworth said that in the same way they had mutual support on surveillance or even with interlocking arcs of fire, possibly there was mutual support, though their wise masters had chosen not to reveal it. Eileen surmised but did not say that, possibly, Tamworth had again provided the answer. Instead of preparing for Christine's debrief, she would give thought to this possibility. Also, in consultation with the OC, she decided that Tamworth and Tring would be despatched to assist Braco. They had already been to the location and knew Bill. The two were not to be told of Christine Latham's real status but Eileen knew that Tamworth and Tring were perceptive enough to realise that they were engaged in source protection.

The original *Mythical* briefing on their mission to identify rogue, even treacherous Special Branch officers now seemed a long time ago and irrelevant. The consensus, though never said as a group but emerging in brief chats between two or three operatives, usually when doing their physical exercises, was that the creation of a special team and the excessive secrecy was over-kill. The task could have been done by the Group which had experience in source protection and recruitment. It was quite obvious Miss Kanna was not Intelligence Corps, probably Five. The modern hi-tech surveillance and communications equipment which they had used could have been put to better use in catching active and dangerous terrorists.

Lives could have been saved.

30

The early morning flight to London Heathrow was on time, which pleased Christine Latham. She was relying on everything going smoothly; the tube to Waterloo train station and then another train to Southampton for the beginning of the interview process. There would be an introduction to the department and a tour of the campus, with the formal interview board taking place the next morning. She knew that she should really have taken the flight on the previous night, but she wanted to finish the marking of essays so that she could return them to her post-graduate class before leaving for her interview at Southampton University.

When she had not been contacted after her evening with Damien McGlone, which she thought her handlers would know about, she used the emergency, telephone contact procedure. Like the *Mythical* team, she was told to sit tight. She also informed the listener, Godden, of the dates of her upcoming interview at Southampton. She was informed that instructions would follow, which they duly did. She was told to book her return flight for the Sunday, not the Friday night after the interview. She would receive further instructions in Southampton.

The Sinn Féin activist was stopped by Special Branch at

Heathrow. When they checked Christine's status, she had been placed in the category of a person of little interest, reflecting her reduced involvement in republican activities, and to be detained only if something was specifically suspicious. There were now so many people on their watch list that the Special Branch officers were content to let her pass.

Tamworth and Tring were on the same flight to shepherd her to Southampton. Braco had flown over the day before on a RAF aircraft carrying his and the other two's personal 9mm Brownings. He did not see the need for the weapons: the covert soldier was not expecting a contact with an IRA ASU in Southampton or at Waterloo station. The man waiting for Braco at RAF Lynham reminded him of Sailor Bill. He was the caretaker of *Mythical's* London base. Braco was to take his car. He provided Braco with a thick, well-sealed brown manila envelope and asked to be dropped off at Swindon station to allow him to catch the train back to London. Braco waited for the pair in the Southampton hotel into which the three operatives had been booked.

He unsealed the envelope once he was in his hotel room. Inside, together with his orders, was a sealed envelope addressed to Christine Latham and instructions to deliver the envelope by leaving it at the main reception desk of the university. He decided that Tring would do that.

The instructions to Christine were brief. She was not to contact Damien McGlone by any means during her visit. She had been booked into a hotel for Friday and Saturday nights. Saturday lunch has been booked for her at 1 pm under the name 'Dunlop' in an Italian restaurant. As he left, a 'Mr Allan' would recognise her as an old friend and she would accept his invitation to go for a quick drink. The details of hotel and restaurant were provided.

Arthur Godden and Eileen Kanna were waiting for her in the Waterloo *Mythical* house. The interview had gone well, though she was not sure whether she wanted to live in Southampton and would prefer Glasgow. However, that interview was now not for another six weeks due to an internal problem. If she was offered the Southampton job then she would have a difficult decision to make. The three SIS officers, including Ormsby in another room monitoring the meet, reflected that she had a difficult decision to make now.

In response to not being contacted by them after her recent meeting with Damien, Godden smiled and said that there was an internal hitch, though he did not admit that he did not know the nature of the problem.

'Did you enjoy the cathedral concert?' asked Eileen Kanna.

'I am sure that you are not interested in that,' came the terse reply.

Godden thought this was the Christine Latham he had re-cruited, a combination of brittleness and obduracy.

'Yes, you are right. Just tell us what happened.' Godden's voice was low and fatherly. 'From when you invited him into your house.'

'Because his car wouldn't start. Was that your doing?' A confirmatory nod by Godden. 'I can't remember everything. It was a few weeks ago.'

'Did he say anything political this time?' Eileen asked.

'Yes.' She shook her head, trying to declutter her mind and put her thoughts into some kind of order.

'Take your time, Christine.'

The continuing fatherly tone from Godden.

'I made some coffee. We sat for a while talking about the concert. It wasn't that good. Anyway, he asked me if I was not troubled or something like that, by working for Sinn Féin. I was taken aback. It was the first time he had ever mentioned

Sinn Féin or the Troubles. He didn't wait for my answer but launched into a monologue. Did I know Irish history? Again not waiting for or even wanting an answer. He said that he had some sympathy for the IRA because he had been brought up, no, immersed in Irish history. One knew of the perfidy of the English. He sort of laughed, well, chuckled really, saying something about we always blame the English but many of the unionists had come from Scotland.'

She stopped, looking at, almost challenging her handlers before saying, 'Why am I telling you this? You know it. You have it on tape.'

Neither handler responded for a moment till Godden said, 'Yes. We have.' Instructed by Ormsby through the earpiece in Godden's right ear. On this occasion, Eileen did not follow her aunt's advice of never showing any reaction.

'You didn't know. Not conductor and leader.' She smirked. 'Just first violinists.'

'It was for your protection.' Godden relayed Ormsby's explanation.

'No. You still don't trust me even after all these years.' She shook her head. 'I suppose mistrust – or is it distrust – is the music of your profession. Not sure if that's the right description. That's why we didn't go to bed.' Another pause. 'That's for you, Eileen. I know that you have a keen interest in my sex life.'

'Time for a break,' said Godden on Ormsby's orders. The two intelligence officers stood up.

'Coffee?'

A shake of her head was Christine's reply to Eileen's offer. As Godden opened the door for his female colleague, Christine in a low voice said, 'Hell is empty and all the devils are here.'

Godden turned to face Christine. 'Sorry?'

'Shakespeare. *The Tempest.* You can always rely on him to provide the appropriate words, no matter the situation.'

'We won't be long.' Though Godden did not know how long.

'Take your time. I trust that when you come back you will all have the same sheet of music.'

'Why didn't you tell us?'

'Arthur, please. No sham moral indignation,' came Ormsby's smoothing tone. 'She made both of you look a little foolish. It happens.'

'Could have told us of the tape. When did that happen? The alarms?'

'We thought that it might provide a little insurance.'

'Didn't we tell her that we would not bug her?' Eileen had read it in Latham's file when she became her source-handler.

'We wanted to ensure that she was telling the truth. You, Eileen, had concerns that she was going to ... what was it... *up sticks?*'

He paused, still smiling.

'I'm glad that we brought her here. She is relaxed and at ease, her confident self again. Agree?'

'Yes sir,' replied Eileen, while Godden nodded, though a little reluctantly.

'On the table,' Ormsby indicated with his left hand, 'there are two transcripts. Only need the highlighted part on the second page. Then back in and obtain her reaction to what he said. And you know the rest of the script.'

The two handlers read the highlighted portion of the transcript of Christine's evening with the choirmaster:

Aren't you troubled by working for Sinn Féin. Does your conscience bother you? Have you read any Irish history? I have some sympathy for the IRA... the cause. Of course I have. I was brought up... no, immersed in Irish history. We knew of the perfidy of the English. Ha. We always blame the English but many, most of the unionists, the Protestants came from Scotland. Yes, we Catholics have suffered discrimination here in the North, but shooting policemen and soldiers is not the way to end it. We are different from the South. You must have seen that. Up here many Catholics have prospered. They know their lifestyles would not be as good in a united Ireland. They want a united Ireland but like Saint Augustine – not just yet. They know the South is not a land of milk and honey. We have got patriotism and nationalism mixed up. Now people see them as the same thing. They are not – but I won't bore you.

(Sound of drinking. Tea/coffee? The mug being put back on a table?)

You know my father served in the Royal Navy during the War. But the contribution of people from the South and the number of Catholics who fought for the Brits in both wars is conveniently airbrushed out of history. It is as if World War two did not happen. I understand why young men... and women join, want to fight for the cause. And the Brits don't help with the murders on Bloody Sunday. Young Catholics being beaten up if they're lucky... killed if they are not. Why? Because they live in the Creggan or the Bogside. They mouth off at soldiers who are also young and don't want to be here so... what is it called... being macho. Then the hunger strikes. Why let young men die over the colour of their clothes! Did you know that at the same time as the British government was trying to get the Church to use its influence to end the hunger strikes, it was trying to close the two remaining Catholic teacher-training colleges? Mrs Thatcher might well become in history a figure hated as much as Oliver Cromwell... by the Catholics. Ha.

But both sides are equally to blame. Asking young men to starve themselves to death, even allowing them to do so when agreement was possible with the Brits. (Pause.) It's immoral... and against the Church's teachings. But that's another thing. The Church. I think someone once said (pause) the relationship between the Irish Republican Army and the Catholic Church is similar to the

'Prince and the Showgirl'... You know that picture? Despite having nothing in common they have a relationship. Ha. But there is even division among the bishops. So what hope is there for the ordinary person if the Church can't speak with one voice? Ha. How can you, a Protestant, support them. You are a minority within Sinn Féin. Haha.

This is all about being a minority. Catholics are a minority in the North. Protestants are a minority in the Free State even if there is a united Ireland. We, you and me, are a minority because we like classical music. It all comes down to my minority is more oppressed than yours. My father and my brother knew violence wasn't a solution. I did as well. The more intelligent IRA men realised that in the sixties. But the civil rights and the RUC's, especially the B Specials', reaction alienated many Catholics. The violence in Belfast and burning people out of their homes. What did they say IRA stood for 'I ran away'. You've heard that. Yes. (Female voice barely audible).

And the army didn't help smashing up houses. Though I have never had any problems with them. Now, you don't hear so many stories about army brutality. Sorry. I'm being a soloist tonight. That's alright. I don't mind. (Female voice still barely audible.) But shooting and bombing won't bring a solution. Violence isn't the way to end injustices. It simply breeds more. It is constitutional means as my brother argues. It was constitutional politics which brought emancipation and land reform. Ha. I know that's in the past. Even some in the IRA favour the ballot box. You must know that. (Inaudible.) I just don't know what to do. How can I go to my confessor when he might be... well... I'm sorry. I'll stop now. (short silence)

Any chance of another coffee?

(His voice and tone fluctuated and at times it conveyed him being under stress. Confused.)

The two handlers finished reading the highlighted portion at the same time and turned to their superior.

'Now get back in there and get her reaction to what he said. There's nothing on the transcript. She did not respond. And no more vacillation or procrastination. She has to be left in no doubt what our aim is and her role in it.'

'Yes sir.' Both handlers in harmony.

Normally, Godden called his superior, Simon, but knew that he, like most of the Service's senior officers, enjoyed the odd 'sir', and this was one such occasion.

'And if she plays her part, I will release her... to Southampton or to whatever dreary place she wants to go.'

'Do we tell her?'

'Yes, Arthur, if you think it is *appropriate*.'

'That's a firm commitment?' asked a hesitant Eileen.

'I am an Englishman.'

'I didn't know what to think. I was stunned. I could feel his angst, his despair. He had never mentioned that he was involved but... is he?'

'Yes,' confirmed Godden. 'But at a low level.'

'He's not active... not on the armed side,' said Eileen to reassure Christine.

'What does he do?'

'Courier,' replied Godden.

'His trips to Belfast and Dublin for his music commitments?'

'Yes.' Again from the male officer.

'So he has been using me.' It was a statement.

The two handlers exchanged glances and Godden nodded slightly to indicate that Eileen should reply.

'We don't think so. It was you who alerted us to him after your meeting in London.'

'I had forgotten about that.'

'Anyway, we had a look and assessed him as low level.' She was not going to rehearse the choirmaster surveillance. 'We became concerned when he began to see more of you. That he was vetting you.'

'That's preposterous. Damien... a hitman. Plenty of people in Belfast could have done it.'

' Yes.' Eileen agreed although she knew that sometimes the IRA did not use a local discipline team to eliminate a security problem. 'And I'm not important.'

'Don't underestimate your contribution, Christine.' Godden in his paternal voice. 'And we have a duty to protect you.'

'Is that why you have that handsome young man looking after me.'

Godden was surprised and alarmed that Christine had spotted Braco. So much for him being an excellent operative, the team's best. But this was not the time to pursue it. Which relieved Eileen who had not disclosed to Godden that she had introduced the covert soldier to their agent, who no doubt would exploit it.

'We don't think that he is a threat to you. But please go on about your reaction.'

She did not reply immediately having to reorder her thoughts.

'As I said, it was the despair, the conflict, the angst. I could see it in his face. He was torturing himself.'

A sigh.

'At university, when I was a student, I saw a student... Ian Barclay. We went out a few times. He was constantly torturing himself over fears of rejection by females... even not getting his essays in on time. In fact you people tried to recruit him.'

Puzzled expressions from both handlers.

She looked directly at Godden. 'At the St Ermin's Hotel before one of our meetings, you were going to interview him.'

'I don't remember, Christine,' replied Godden.

The agent smiled.

'Liar.' In a jocular tone. She turned to Eileen. 'I was usually transformed into a dowdy, middle-aged, spinister academic in tweeds. By your make-up artists.' She laughed. 'Though it was more comfortable there than here.'

She looked around the room.

'Tory cuts. I wonder what happened to him. If I get the job in Glasgow I might look him up. Can you find out for me?'

'I'll see what I can do,' said Godden. 'Please. Back to Damien?'

'Damien's torture was three times more even than Ian's. I did not know what to say. How to respond. I was... think he didn't want me to respond. He was confessing but... you understand the Roman Catholic practice. Confessing and forgiveness of sins?'

The handlers nodded. The strengths and weaknesses of religions were taught in the basic training course. Eileen recalled her 'aunt' telling her that watching a man in church, especially a Roman Catholic, could reveal much about the individual. When considering an individual as a possible agent, religion or lack of it was a factor to be considered as well as the usual gambling and sex.

'He didn't want me to give him absolution.'

'Anything else?'

'Well, I did briefly at the beginning think that it was me he was concerned about, especially when he said something about me being a Protestant and my conscience bothering me. But I dismissed it and realised that he was talking about himself. I kept telling myself that he wasn't involved. He couldn't be but the more he... Is he? Are you certain?'

'Yes,' said Godden.

'That's the first time that he has ever mentioned politics, the situation... Why and why to me? Surely, he must know that I am duty bound to report him for expressing doubts about the cause.'

'We think that he likes you. He sees you as... what do they

call it now... a soul mate.' Godden said the last word with a trace of scorn.

'Maybe he sees you as his salvation,' Eileen said.

Christine mulled over the remark then said, 'No, no.' She waved her right-hand towards her handlers. 'I am not going to...'

'We are not asking you to approach him. In fact, we do not want you to say anything to him which gives even the slightest indication that you are working for us.'

Immediately Eileen followed Godden and said, 'But we do want you to continue to see him. However, for completeness can you just tell us the rest till he left in the morning?'

'You know.'

'Christine, we don't. We have not been able to read the full transcript.'

She smiled. 'I think Sinn Féin is more competent than British Intelligence.'

Eileen retorted, 'Their dismissal procedure is more severe than ours.'

'Ladies, please,' said the male. To Christine. 'Just keep to the point.'

There was not much more to tell. She went to bed upstairs and he slept on the sofa, Christine having provided him with a blanket. She was concerned about getting his car started in the morning but Damien had told her that his car was temperamental, like an opera diva, and he was sure it would start in the morning. No, she had not thought that he had engineered the breakdown, but she was worried about having to call out mechanics and having Damien hanging about outside her house.

The car would not start in the morning and Damien was getting a bit panicky. Thankfully, a local, middle-aged man, out for his morning stroll, sorted out the problem. Something had come loose, which could easily happen in an older vehicle, especially if Damien had bumped the pavement when parking. Damien did not seem suspicious about the car break-down. No, she did not know the good Samaritan, but had seen him around. He lived close-by and he sometimes took in students. She knew this because on several occasions when walking home with students, they had pointed him out, saying that he was their landlord. He had been a merchant sailor and his house rules were quite strict, but he was friendly.

'Good. Thank you,' said Godden. 'Have you any more concerts coming up?'

'Nothing planned. There is one coming up in London in the Wigmore Hall in a couple of weeks which we discussed attending... Though you know that.' She saw Godden's frustrated expression. 'Sorry. You haven't read that part.'

'What about Dublin? Be better.'

'There is one in Dublin. I think it's exactly two weeks later.'

'When is your Glasgow interview?' Eileen asked.

In a slightly frustrated tone, Christine replied, 'In six weeks.'

Godden took control. 'No changes. Act as normal. If he brings up his doubts, listen but tell him that you would rather not discuss it. We will remove the stuff from your house but leave the alarms.'

'Are you sure?'

Godden was not going to give his word as a gentleman. Many of his SIS colleagues would not consider him a 'gentleman', as he had not attended the right schools and universities.

'We are not going to follow him. Go to London. Enjoy it. Book a good hotel. I know that you can afford one.' A smile. 'But we will pay for it.' Another smile. 'A good one, not five star. Then go to Dublin. We will give you final instructions on Dublin a couple of days before you go. Eileen will do that. Any questions?'

'No.'

'Good. Just relax. We will not ask you to do anything that you are uncomfortable with.' Godden's fatherly tone had returned.

'After Dublin,' said Eileen, 'a successful interview in Glasgow and you will be free.'

31

A faint and unexpected knock on the door.

She had not ordered room service, and she had agreed with Damien that they would meet outside the Wigmore. She had bought the tickets, a treat for him. He was visiting his sister but not staying with her because her children were just a little too boisterous. Instead he had selected a small guest-house off Euston Road, close to Christine's hotel. Before he set off for his sister's, the pair lunched together in an Italian restaurant. Italian food and music was an unbeatable duet. There was a silent understanding that he would return to her hotel after the concert.

On opening the door, Christine was surprised to be confronted by Eileen Kanna who glided past her followed by her handsome protector. Possibly he was actually Eileen's protector. Braco closed and locked the door, standing with his back to it.

'Change of plan, Christine.'

The intelligence officer sat in the one soft armchair in the room.

'Have a seat and I will explain.'

Impulsively, Christine was going to refuse but decided to sit on the edge of the bed looking at Braco rather than her handler.

'Damien, can't make the concert. Another appointment. But

you can still go.' Eileen smiled. 'And you have the choice of me or... tonight, he can be Ian.' She looked up at Braco. 'Happy with that?' The soldier nodded.

'You lying bitch! You knew all along that...'

'Remember you said yourself that I was not a leader or conductor but a first violinist.'

A cluck of her tongue. Eileen had not known until two days before but she was not going to reveal that to the agent.

'And using "Ian".' She was shaking her head, a mixture of anger and despondency, resisting the tears. 'You really are a scheming, conniving bitch!'

'Don't give me the sham moral outrage.'

She had remembered Ormsby's words to Godden and her.

'You have been in this game long enough. Who was scheming and conniving when deceiving your Sinn Féin friends... your comrades in the struggle!'

'What have you done to Damien?'

'Don't worry. He won't be harmed.'

She thought, not by us at least. Depending on how he responds.

'He is a gentle soul. He can't cope with stress. You know that he can't. I thought that I was going to talk to him. In Dublin.'

Eileen did not respond, musing on the fact that Christine remained the same Glasgow student, always fighting for a cause. This time Damien McGlone was her cause.

She smiled, her expression becoming friendlier and said, 'You have ten minutes to sort yourself out and then we will go and enjoy some Italian music. I love Italian music.'

Eileen did not disclose her time in Italy when she had attended concerts, usually paid for by an embassy colleague in the forlorn hope of getting her into his bed, or accompanied a target at the Service's expense. The target usually had more chance of her ending up in his bed.

Apart from Braco, this was a joint SIS and MI5 mission. After the formal debrief of the Christine Latham meeting in the Waterloo house, in private, Godden had sought clarification from Eileen on how their agent knew Braco. Her disclosure of introducing the soldier to Christine dismayed and angered Godden. He stated that he had no choice but to report her unwarranted action to Ormsby. Eileen did not care because she had written her letter of resignation. She wanted to return to the real world. Since her time in 'intelligence', using her hands to convey the inverted commas, the only honest people, individuals with any integrity that she had met were soldiers – Sergeant Knight, and Gordon Buchanan-Henderson in Shala, and now Braco, even the perceived clown Tamworth.

Ormsby said that he had picked up the agent's remark but he was not sure to whom Christine was referring. He had intended to pursue it but it was not his highest priority at present. He thanked Godden for bringing it to his attention. Of course, Miss Kanna would be required to face disciplinary proceedings; nevertheless, the soldier could be useful for the upcoming London operation in that he could hold Christine's hand. And if she, Christine, made trouble, squealed about unfair treatment, went public, then it was a problem for the military.

The choirmaster, now as per Colville's directive, identified only as *Danube* in all transmissions and reports, had been picked up by a MI5's surveillance team on his arrival in London. Unlike its army equivalents, it was not made up entirely of fit young men and women, but consisted of a range of ages and types.

Hennessy had been brought over from Dublin to execute the lift and conduct the conditioning before the offer. In Dublin, the now clean-shaven SIS officer had made an impression by securing good links with the Republic's intelligence service and the Garda Siochána Special Branch. Consequently, having been fully rehabilitated, he was now a permanent member of the Dublin office. Ormsby, with C's blessing, had suggested that his next step on the ladder could be the proposed Service's coordinator of Europe-wide operations against terrorist groups. Of course, this would be dependent on getting *Danube* up and running, and handling him at least for the first year. His time with the soldiers on *Mythical* had been enjoyable, refreshing and interesting – a bit like a three week scout camp or a holiday in Costa del Sol without the sun. It was time to return to the arena of real intelligence with its challenges and perplexities. And he had reverted to his own name, Daniel Irwin.

32

Damien McGlone was on his way to the tube station. He was in good time to get to the Wigmore Hall. It was the twilight of the day. As he went to cross the street, he realised that the two men on the opposite corner were fighting, both obviously the worse for drink. A third man was shouting at them to stop amidst a flow of obscenities. Damien did not want to get involved and turned right into the side-street. It was a short detour down the street, then a left turn round the block and back onto the main road. He saw the elderly lady with her shopping trolley leaning forward towards the open window of the car. The younger woman in the front passenger seat was speaking to the elderly pedestrian, probably asking for directions. Behind the car was a dark-coloured van, too dirty to know the colour. He thought the area itself was dirty and depressed-looking – and here were English journalists writing of Derry as being rundown and depressed. A man in coveralls and woolly hat came from a shop doorway to the van and opened the sliding door on the side. As Damien drew level with the elderly lady, he paused, as her trolley was sticking out at an angle across the pavement. 'Sorry, son.' He was not sure if her accent was Irish or Scottish. There was another barking voice from behind. McGlone half-turned and realised that it was the 'peace-keeper' who was shouting after him, calling his name. There were four uniformed police officers surrounding the drunks. The elderly woman was advising him, 'Ignore them, son. They're always causing trouble.' He was past her, still looking back, but aware of the tall, broad man in coveralls stepping back to allow him to pass, and another man, similarly dressed, coming from round the back of the van.

His arms were pinned violently to his sides and someone hit the back of his knees with what felt like a metal bar. His thoughts turned to the elderly woman, as he was pushed and pulled into the van with a hood placed over his head.

He was being held down on what he thought was a mattress. The side door was closed but not with a loud bang. He felt the van was doing a u-turn in the street.

'Keep fucking still, McGlone!'

The voice was harsh Belfast but could not be sure if it was Catholic or Protestant. Outsiders laughed at the idea, but it was true that most of the time one could tell the religion.

'We going furra wee trip.'

There was a softer, Derry voice. 'Leave him be. He's not going to be seeing his wee Belfast girl tonight.'

The Belfast voice again but both coming from above him.

'He might not be fucking seeing his Belfast tart again. She's fucking next. Look he's pissing himself.' Definitely Protestant Belfast.

'That's enough. Remember what *Gaggie* said.'

The van seemed to be making right and left turns. It stopped several times and on two occasions the door was opened. He prayed that each time he would be taken out of the van. He was not only disorientated but confused. He had thought that he had been seized by loyalists, even the hated Brit intelligence, but *Gaggie*. There could not be a loyalist *Gaggie*.

If it was the loyalists it would be a slow painful death. Like the Shankhill butchers. He realised that he had wet himself, and it was only the second time that he had worn this suit. He had brought it over especially for the concert with Christine. But she would do something when he didn't turn up. But what could she do? All the time saying his prayers, mostly acts of contrition before he was killed, and Hail Marys, but they were for Christine. Why kill her? She has done nothing wrong. Maybe a bit foolish. But if they were from *Gaggie* then she would be okay. Maybe it was just a test as they had said that they would do a security check on him, but why in London? They could be arrested. Possibly the policemen at the corner saw him being dragged into the van and they were now looking for the van. No, they wouldn't see it, being too busy with the aggressive drunks. How did that person know his name. He would not be a friend of his sister.

The van had stopped. The side door was opened and he was aware of people getting out and the door being closed again. There was silence. He realised that his arms were not bound. He could move them. It must have been the terror that immobilised his arms. Should he try to remove the hood on his face and sit up? He was sure that he could hear breathing. There was still someone in the van. Maybe he was waiting for him to move. No, he would not give them an excuse.

The silence ended by the door being opened. *Danube* was grabbed and hoisted out. Without talking, the two MI5 officers manoeuvred *Danube* up into the same room where Christine Latham had sat two weeks before. It was now more Spartan with just a table, four hard-backed chairs and a small wall lamp shining onto the table. They had dragged *Danube* up in silence, seated him on the chair with its back to the window and placed a hand on each shoulder to restrain him. The interrogator was standing behind the empty chair looking down at the still hooded suspect.

The interrogator was, if not the Security Service's best, certainly the most unconventional. He was a graduate of the Joint Interrogation Wing in the home of the Intelligence Corps. His background in the Royal Air Force was training and conditioning aircrew in the event of capture. Eventually he had been tapped up by the Security Service on the advice of one of its officer, a former RAF pilot.

The interrogator's policy was to refuse to read the file offered to him by the case officer. The Service worked on the principle of need-to-know. He did not need to know, requiring only a synopsis of the suspect's actual or alleged misdeeds, potential weak points and a list of questions, but he would also improvise depending on the response, if any. He preferred not to have irrelevant clutter in his mind. Too much information could be detrimental to the effectiveness of the initial interrogation. He worked on the premise that once the suspect reached him that he or, sometimes she, was an outlaw. If the individual was not, then he would tell the case officer not to waste his time and that they needed to get new informants.

Also, he was not a policeman requiring to obtain personal information, so there would be no prelude. On one occasion, however, the wrong man had been placed in front of him, the brother of the badman. The excuse offered was that he was a rag-head and they all sounded and looked the same. The professionalism had improved since that occasion. He would have preferred to have the suspect in his own fort rather than a terraced house in Waterloo. His instructing officers were not from his Service but clogheads from the other fort, though the troopers were his unit.

'Now listen carefully. I am going to have your hood removed. When it is removed, blink your eyes a few times to get used to the light. Don't get off your chair or make any sudden movements. Do not look around. Drink the water in front of you. If you do not comply then there will be some pain for you – and you will remain seated, bound and hooded. And it could be for some time. Do you understand my instructions?'

A muffled sound.

'Take your time. I need to hear you say "Yes. I understand." Take a deep breath. Good. I will ask you again. 'Do you understand my instructions?'

'Yes.'

'No. You must say, "Yes. I understand."'

'Yes. I understand.' Damien McGlone felt slightly relieved though he was not sure why, that it was an English voice, accentless, not harsh but authoritative. He was probably a good singer.

With a raising of his two open hands, the interrogator told the guards to remove the hood.

McGlone complied with the instructions, too terrified not to.

'Good.'

He grasped the plastic beaker with two hands, devoured the water and placed the yellow plastic beaker on the table. The interrogator, his hands upright, palms facing the suspect and guards, extended arms to indicate to the guards that they should move back to sit on the chairs which framed the window. Once they were seated, the interrogator sat down facing the suspect. His hands clasped, lightly touching the edge of the table he asked, 'Why are you in London?'

'Where am I?' Hesitant, fearful but the natural first response.

'No. This is simple. You are off the reservation. This is not a powwow. I ask the questions and you answer them. Why are you in London?'

'To attend a concert.'

'No. That is your cover. You are on a scouting mission?'

The interrogator preferred 'scouting' to 'recce', reflecting his love of Western movies, especially the ones with John Wayne against the Comanche Indians, though his favourite cowboy was Jimmy Stewart.

McGlone was shaking his head in more confusion. 'No, no... what...'

'What was your target? The Wigmore?'

'No.'

'Euston or St Pancras?'

'No. I'm...'

'That's why you're camping off Euston Road.'

McGlone was shaking his head all the time trying to deny the accusations.

'Or is it another go at the BT Tower?'

'I'm here to... for a conc...'

'Just as well the cavalry captured you.'

'No. I ... cavalry... that's...'

Was this a joke? Was he the victim of a prank? What was it... the TV show which... No, they had threatened to kill him in the van. The Belfast and Derry voices.

'You are here to prepare a bombing attack.' The voice was more authoritative, cruel and accusatorial.

'No. No.' The head shaking continued.

'Is *Gaggie* McKenna leading the gang on the raid?' A hard stare. 'You will give him the targets when you are back on the reservation.'

'No, no. This is ludicrous. I'm...'

'Ludicrous!' His voice raised for the first time.

Springing to his feet, he towered over McGlone. ' Ludicrous! To send your braves – by canoe even – over here to kill women and children. And you...' His right hand extended, the index finger close to McGlone's face. '... will be responsible for the murders.'

'I wouldn't ...'

His head down facing the floor, tears forming. Maybe 'ludicrous' was the wrong choice. But it was ridiculous to paint him as an IRA commander.

'Maybe *Gaggie* and his raiding party are paddling their way here just now. Or maybe they are in a tepee. Putting on their warpaint. Waiting for their chief.'

A pause.

'What will they do when they realise their chief, *you*, has been captured by the dog soldiers?'

It wasn't ludicrous now. It was madness. Had he been brought into a lunatic asylum?

'I don't tell *Gaggie* what to do.'

There were smiles and nods to each other in the next room.

'So this two-bit cowpoke tells you what to do.'

McGlone had not taken in the change in metaphor from 'brave' to a 'cowpoke'. The interrogator was seated with his face leaning close to McGlone's.

'No. Our scouts have seen you and *Gaggie* having powwows. Didn't you trust him to do the scouting. No?'

The interrogator leaned back in his chair and in a lowered voice said, 'And who can blame you.'

McGlone was looking directly at his tormentor, this fantasy indulger, his eyes pleading. 'This is...'

'Ludicrous? Will you still think it's ludicrous when you are in front of the judge, charged with possession of explosives. Yes. We know where they are stashed in Camden.'

It was not improvisation because a cache was under surveillance, the connection had been suggested by Daniel Irwin who had provided the intelligence on the cache, well, relayed it from Garda Siochána.

'We were hoping that we would capture *Gaggie* and the whole raiding party when they went to pick up the dynamite. But *Gaggie* will be safe back on the reservation.'

A 'so be it' shrug of his shoulders.

'You will have to do. Especially when we have your finger-prints on the sticks.'

The man was mad. McGlone knew that he would be waking up soon. His trousers were still damp. Despair was enveloping him once more.

'I have never touched dynamite, explosives... why would I be charged?'

'Well. Never mind. Might not get to the judge. Dangerous territory, badlands, between here and the courthouse.'

Once more, fear gripped McGlone. It was not even a subtle threat. 'I have done nothing wrong.'

His interrogator ignored him.

'*Gaggie* is likely to be happy. You in the stockade. If you get there. He could be chief.'

'No. No. It's a... please believe... I don't have anything to do with bombs.'

'You are an active member of the Irish Republican Army!'

More shakes of the head by *Danube*.

'You run an Active Service Unit.'

'No, no.' Tears now sliding down his cheeks.

'You plan the operations. You tell *Gaggie* to carry them out.'

'No, no. I don't tell *Gaggie* anything. He doesn't run an ASU. I don't think so.'

'He tells you what to do?' Question asked in an astonished tone with a similarly surprised facial expression.

'Sometimes. But nothing to do with bombs or guns.'

Tears in full flow, his head still shaking but now in his hands.

'I wouldn't... I couldn't do that... harm anyone... it was a mistake... impulse.'

Trying to recall why and how he got involved.

'What do you do for *Gaggie*?' The question posed quickly and sharply so as not to give McGlone time to regroup.

'Sometimes I deliver messages.'

'The Pony Express!'

Ormsby and Godden congratulated the interrogator on an excellent job. Irwin, having changed out of his coveralls was now dressed like the other two SIS officers in dark suit and tie, office dress. He refrained from adding his 'Well done. Excellent'. The interrogator stated that it was fairly straightforward. It was not false modesty on his part. Some interrogatees, after the initial fear, are sometimes able to manufacture emotional distress in order to deflect or slow the questioning, but he was fairly sure that unless he was an outstanding actor, this individual's emotional distress was real. There was no way that he was an active terrorist. He would be reluctant even to use him in a minor role. He wished them good luck and good night. He left unsaid that such effort and time seemed disproportionate for a minor figure.

33

Christine Latham wanted to return to the hotel. They, the agent and the soldier, had just returned to their seats at the end of the interval when she decided that she wanted to leave. She whispered that she was not enjoying it. There were apologies to the people in the row as they made their way from the middle of the row to the aisle.

Eileen Kanna had already left to return to the Waterloo house, having been informed that Five's team was on station. On return to their base, the four uniformed police officers had changed into mufti and made their way to the Wigmore Hall. Now positioned around the hall, two in the Cortina and the other two on foot, they were a precaution in the event of Christine bolting.

In the hotel room, she did not want to watch television nor have a drink, alcoholic or hot. She sat in the armchair staring at the window, on occasions glancing at Braco out of the corner of her right eye. The soldier stood at the door. She had protested when he tried to move the cushioned stool at the dressing-table. She might need it. He could discuss with Christine the concert, favourite songs and food but not anything connected to the operation and certainly not *Danube*. He was slightly pissed off by these instructions but Eileen apologised, informing him that her orders had come from the top, not Godden. She did not mention Ormsby's name. Mere soldiers who risked their lives were not of the necessary status to be told such a hallowed name.

When Christine went to the bathroom, he told her not to lock the door. He moved from his position to place his foot in the bathroom door to prevent her from locking it, though his eyes remained in the direction of the bedroom.

'I thought that you were different.' The words spat out with contempt.

When she came out, she said, 'There you can have the chair. I'm going to bed. And no, I'm not undressing.'

She lay in the centre of the double bed, stashing the pillows high up behind her back. He moved the armchair to beside the door and sat down. The agent resumed her silence.

McGlone had been given more water but otherwise sat in silence, not daring to look round at the guards behind him. He folded his arms, scrunching his shoulders for warmth and comfort. Was this the end of his ordeal? Christine flashed into his mind. He felt guilty, ashamed that he had not thought of her. He tried to convince himself that he had expelled Christine from his mind to protect her from this hell. He would need to confess this lie. His concern was exclusively for himself. His flesh was weak: now ashamed rather than contrite. Why did his tormentor think that *Gaggie* McKenna was an important figure? It was ludicrous to think that he himself was a senior IRA commander, though he thought the fantasist did not believe that. His target was clearly *Gaggie*. Was *Gaggie* a more senior figure than he thought and was led to believe? *Gaggie* was a bit dim. Initially he had thought *Gaggie* was higher up. Then he realised that *Gaggie* was not in the same league as Hugh Devlin. Devlin had not been mentioned, and in an odd way he was pleased. Devlin would be too smart for the Brits.

The voice of the ex-chief petty officer, the house janitor, was the next thing that McGlone heard.

'Good evening, sir. You are probably ready for some hot food.'

The voice was warm and welcoming.

'Not much choice tonight. Lasagne or fish pie? We always offer fish on a Friday. What will it be sir?'

McGlone just wanted to leave, to end the nightmare. He couldn't eat but he thought that co-operating might be in his interest. He wanted a coffee.

'The fish... er... please and...' His voice was weak and still quavery.

'Tea or coffee?'

'Coffee please.'

'Yessir. Coming up. But in the meantime – and there is not a choice here. There is a change of clothing for you. Up here. Including footwear.'

He was pointing at the wall facing McGlone.

'If needed, my colleagues here will assist you.'

A mild but explicit warning that he would change his clothes either with or without aid.

'There is a bag for your clothes. We will return them to you. Laundered, of course.' The friendly voice had returned.

By the time the janitor had returned, McGlone was dressed in blue, heavy coveralls and carpet slippers. The janitor's colleagues had made clear without speaking that all his clothes had to be removed. McGlone undressed and dressed unaided, accompanied only by embarrassment and shame. The tray was placed on the table. It was a take-away meal with plastic cutlery and two paper serviettes as well as coffee in a green plastic beaker. The janitor removed the yellow beaker which had contained the water.

'Enjoy, sir.'

McGlone did not respond.

When the janitor was at the open door, McGlone slightly emboldened asked, 'How long are you going to keep me here?'

The janitor turned and replied, 'That's not something that I would know, sir.' A regretful tone. 'I expect that the gentlemen will be with you soon.'

McGlone wished to make a comment about a complete lack of gentlemen here, but he was not that emboldened.

Irwin confirmed that 'the seize and bring' part had gone smoothly. The MI5 boys and girls certainly knew their stuff. If it went as planned tonight, would it not be possible for the Five team to do the next part. Ormsby agreed that it would be a good idea but Five had so many tasks and like everyone else, limited resources. Godden insisted that he felt the team across the water were more than capable and in fact were currently recceing RVs on the Belfast and Armagh routes.

'Let's not get ahead of ourselves.' Ormsby ended the discussion. 'We have further work to do tonight.'

He paused for the others to refocus on the task at hand.

'So. Arthur. Still Eileen and you in first.'

'Yes.'

'And if we need a bit more firepower then we send in Daniel.'

'Yes.'

'But no matter how it pans out, Daniel has the last session to do.'

All were agreed.

'Good.'

He looked at his watch.

'Another fifteen minutes, so you can do what you need. Straighten your ties, brush your hair. Make sure your flies are zipped.' A smile. 'Not you, Eileen.'

He was trying to relax the troops before they crossed the start-line.

'Sir, the telephone call to Braco as agreed?'

'Braco?'

'The soldier minding *Mighty Midget*.'

'Yes. Of course. – Remember apart from he's alright, no information release. Except that you will speak to her tomorrow and put her in the picture.'

'I'm sure that will cheer her up. Don't think I am on her Christmas card list. I'm a bitch.'

'Good. Agents should not be pandered to or appeased. Controlled.'

The three other SIS officers smiled, not in appreciation of his wise counsel but being aware of the office totem (the Service's undocumented cardinal belief) that Simon Ormsby had never recruited or run an agent throughout his long career.

'Don't answer it. Please.'

Braco moved to the side of the bed and picked up the receiver of the telephone on the bedside table.

'Yes.' Followed by three more at short intervals. Thankfully there was a pen and note-pad on the table so he could note down the number. Another 'Yes.' Finally 'Right. Good.'

He ripped the sheet off the pad and slipped it into his right side jacket pocket. He returned to his chair. Christine pulled herself up so her back was against the raised pillows, an inquisitive and expectant look at Braco.

'He's safe and well.'

'Damien?'

'Yes.'

'Where is he?'

'Don't know.'

'Who is with him?'

'Don't know.'

'When can I see him?'

'Don't know.'

'You don't know much. Obviously you are not even in the chorus. Just a stage-hand.'

Now it was the soldier's turn for an enquiring expression.

'I do know that my boss will be coming to speak to you, probably tomorrow.'

A muttered response of, 'That bitch.'

'And if you want to go out to eat...'

'With you.' A nod from Braco. 'No thanks.'

'Or I can order a takeaway.'

She slid down the bed and turned away from him.

The room was fully lit though the window shutters were still closed. The two guards were not required, though remained on station outside the door. Eileen sat in a chair beside the door and Godden sat in the interrogator's chair. The tray and traces of the meal had been removed. McGlone realised that it was not a cell, and with the right furniture to complement the wallpaper, could be made into a pleasant and comfortable room.

'How are you feeling... er sorry. Stupid question. But I am sorry that you missed the concert.'

On impulse, he was going to ask about Christine but bit back the question. They would know that she was a member of Sinn Féin. It was because of her that he was here. No, you fool. It's because of *Gaggie* McKenna that I'm here. Where ever 'here' is.

'Introductions first. I am Peter and my colleague, Mary.'

Godden extended his left arm back to indicate Eileen Kanna who nodded towards McGlone.

He thought, 'Am I supposed to be Paul?' It was surprising what an appetising fish pie and hot coffee could do to re-energise one's spirit. Surely the Brits weren't so stupid to use the names of a folk singing trio. Or was it a pathetic nod to his profession? If so, they could have come up with a more relevant name such as Johann.

'May I call you Damien?'

McGlone did not respond. He remembered the limited training which was in fact just advice that if arrested, to try not to say anything for as long as possible. By their dress and especially the man's voice, he knew that they were not the feared but 'cute' Special Branch men that he had been warned about by *Gaggie* and Hugh Devlin.

'We are British intelligence officers.'

No response.

'You have admitted that you are a member of the Irish – Republican – Army.'

No response.

The intelligence officer, Peter, was wrong. He had never been sworn into the IRA, merely being a part-time helper. He could explain his limited involvement.

'Also, your membership is corroborated by your failure to respond, answer questions. Your silence is a recognised hall-mark, indicator of an IRA member. Membership is a criminal offence and you could receive a custodial sentence.'

McGlone was to an extent heartened by this because there was no mention of possession of explosives. Obviously the first guy's task had been to frighten him: he had absolutely terrified him. His confidence was ebbing back but slowly. This interrogator was not in the same league as his predecessor.

'However, you can avoid a custodial sentence by assisting us.'

He had expected this, having been warned by Devlin, although he was surprised that it had come so early. But he would not become a tout, an informer. A prison term was more attractive than a lonely road in South Armagh which did not have a release date.

'I am aware that you have been told not to speak to the Brits. And you are following your instructions... confirming your membership. But listen to the offer.'

He looked at McGlone trying to engage his eyes but the prisoner was looking down.

'I think... I know that you are a sensitive, compassionate man. A man like you with a love, no, a passion for music, real music, must be disturbed, troubled by some of the acts of your comrades – the bombings and the murder of innocent civilians. Many of them Roman Catholics.'

He paused to allow McGlone time to think though he did not raise his head.

'I know that sometimes individual soldiers or police officers over-react. Their conduct well below the standards expected of ...'

'Wh... What about Bloody Sunday! That wasn't individual soldiers! It was a British government decision to massacre... thirteen innocent people.'

The two SIS officers could see the anger flare in McGlone's eyes as he stared at Godden.

'Bloody Friday, eleven dead and one hundred and thirty injured; the Birmingham pub bombings – twenty one dead and one thousand two hundred injured... We could go on swapping statistics but to what end?'

Godden paused. McGlone, feeling tired and drowsy, realised that he needed the toilet. The fear of wetting himself again gripped him.

Godden was saying, 'But we want to stop these atrocities and end the violence totally and for good. We think that you as a good Christian also want the same as me. And we can do it together.'

Weakly, feeling embarrassed McGlone said, 'I need to go to the bathroom. Please.'

'Alright.' Godden glanced quickly behind at his colleague and gave her the pre-arranged signal. She knocked on the door, then switched off the large light and turned on the intense wall-light, bringing back the gloomy atmosphere. McGlone was so distracted by the sudden intensity of the spotlight that he did not hear or realise that another man had entered the room.

'I think you also need a rest before we resume our chat. It will give you time to consider my offer.'

The MI5 officer was now behind *Danube*.

'What you need to keep in mind is that this is a one-time only offer. I am not a second hand car salesman. This is your only opportunity. Rest and think about it.'

Godden gave a slight nod. The hood was quickly placed over McGlone's head and he was pulled to his feet, then propelled towards the door which had been opened by Eileen.

– 34 –

Christine decided that she was hungry but preferred to eat in her room. The number that Braco had noted was the Security Service's operations desk for *Mythical*. Eileen's instructions were to place any food order or other request via them. On telephoning his order, he was told that one of their guys would bring it up, give three short knocks and leave their order outside. In addition, with the order, there would be an envelope containing further instructions for him, and the man on the line expressed surprise that he did not have one of their radios.

The 'controlled' agent enjoyed her food, observing that it did not taste like typical take-away. It wasn't. It came from a top Chinese restaurant in Soho's Chinatown. Braco read his new instructions and again placed the paper in his right jacket pocket.

'Does it say anything about Damien?' He shook his head.

'Of course, I forgot. You are not important enough to be told such things.'

She decided to have a bottle of wine from the fridge. 'Might as well. You're paying for it.'

She turned on the television using the remote, flicked through the few channels and switched it off. She sat looking at herself in the mirror of the dressing-table. She laughed, and without turning because she could see her guardian, or gaoler, in the mirror said, 'You know, Arthur Godden sat at my dressing table in my bedroom when he was recruiting me. All those years ago.'

She caught the expression of surprise on the gaoler's face.

'In my bedroom.' She laughed. 'Don't worry, Arthur is a gentleman. Anyway my father was downstairs.'

The surprise had not completely left his face.

'Oh, you are surprised that I know his real name. No codes... false names.' She laughed. 'Arthur and I are old friends. We have been in a relationship for many years. No, not that type. He's older than Damien. I think.'

Braco could not hide the look of disapproval on his face.

'You are obviously new to this game. How long have you been in the *secret service*?' she asked with disdain.

She decided to have another bottle of wine: they were small ones. She returned to the bed, placing the plastic bottle and glass on the bedside table, bunching the pillows high on the headboard and then lying back.

'Which one do you prefer. Eileen or Arthur?'

He finally spoke. 'I do not know the gentleman that you are talking about.'

'Of course, you do.' She smiled. 'I have long experience in spotting facial expressions. Not trained by your lot. I'm a teacher. I need to know what my students are thinking. Whether what I have said has gone in? Students often don't like admitting that they don't understand. So that's why I need to be focused and spot if anyone is having a problem. Easier in a tutorial group than a lecture.'

A sigh followed by several head shakes. She took a sip of wine and replaced the glass on the bedside table.

'I wish my lecturers at Glasgow had been like that. They

ambled in, gave their lecture at the speed of an express train, seldom took questions and rushed out. Sometimes the tutorials were a bit, just a bit better. Suppose it was better when you were at university.'

Another pause for reflection.

'Mind you, sometimes the tutorials could be fun when... depending who was in the group. Students I mean. There was a posh English guy who... think he was the black sheep of the family. His brothers and sisters had all gone to Oxford or Cambridge. Think his family owned half of England, well Manchester at least. He was funny but disruptive. Peter Mayne. I wonder what happened to him.'

Braco was relieved that she was not looking at him. No doubt she would have caught his look of surprise.

'Peter and Bernadette, Bernie. Mayne used to call her 'Belfast Bernie'. It amused Bernie because she was not from Belfast. She used to call him... em... that's right, the big galoot. They had some ding-dong arguments. But...' She looked at Braco before continuing, 'I think he had a thing for her. Though I am pretty sure that it was unrequited.'

Another sip of wine.

'Of course, at the time, I didn't find it funny. I was much too serious. Involved in civil rights here. Bernie used to mock me, gently, for helping the down-trodden taigs. You know what taig means?'

Braco nodded.

'Bernie was... is a Roman Catholic. I saw her a few weeks ago. She brought some of her pupils on a familiarisation visit to the university. She teaches in a small market town. We had a quick chat. Funny, I never thought of asking her about the big galoot.'

More time spent staring, reflecting before she said, 'Mind you, if I was serious, Ian Barclay had a PhD in it. That's why the charming Eileen said to call you 'Ian'. She was trying to be cute. Needling me.'

Braco resisted the impulse to defend Eileen.

'Godden tried to recruit Ian once. In fact, I compared Damien to Ian... but you probably know that.'

Again, no response from Braco.

'You're going to be good at this. Though you do have to communicate with your agent sometimes.' A smile. 'I'm teasing you.'

Both knew the wine was affecting her a little.

'At least tell me what university you went to?'

' I didn't.'

'I thought that you had to go public school and then Oxbridge before you could join.'

Braco shrugged, 'Maybe.'

' You are not in SIS ?'

He saw no point in denying it. 'No.'

'Oh! I'm intrigued. The plot thickens.'

She swung her legs onto the floor on the opposite side from the dressing table. She looked closely at him. 'Well?'

He knew he was breaking the rules, in particular the rules of the 'secret or undercover soldier' world but he was becoming dissatisfied with that world. He had been warned of the dangers of remaining too long in it.

'I am a soldier.'

She did not respond immediately. Of course, there were always stories in the press and the street craic of the undercover soldiers especially when someone was shot. Usually, the SAS were held responsible.

'Are you in the infamous SAS? The Brit's secret assassination squad.'

'No.'

He regretted the impulsive negative reaction, fearing that

she would conclude he agreed with the 'assassination squad' description. In the army, there was criticism of the SAS sometimes called the 'Hereford Hooligans'. He had worked with some SAS troopers and they were professional. There had been a couple of ex-SAS soldiers in his battalion and they were tough, good soldiers, certainly not hooligans. Indeed, the captain of his COP had gone to the SAS after their Londonderry tour. He was a good, decent officer.

With a smile she said, 'You are the first undercover soldier I have ever met.'

Without thinking he replied, 'You are the first secret agent I have ever met.'

The agent laughed, joined by the soldier.

'I am glad that you are not one of them.'

McGlone had slept on the bed used by Peter Mayne during his training, though the third floor room now had only the bed, a small bedside table and a chair in which a Security Service officer sat. The window was shuttered and the light remained on. McGlone wanted to think and plan a response, like organising a choir so that the singers were in the right position. Constructing a choir was not simply placing people in rows. But, it was hopeless, he was too drowsy and feared that he had been drugged. *Gaggie* had mentioned the possibility but not Hugh Devlin, and he must make sure that he did not mention the latter's name.

He was being shaken with a voice saying, 'Time to get up. You've slept too long.'

Two men were lifting him up from the bed, replacing the hood and dragging him downstairs. Placed in his usual chair. The other two of the trio were in the same positions and after the door closed, the main light was switched on.

'Take your time. Get comfortable. Well as best as you can on these chairs.' Godden smiled. 'At least, there is equality in the seating.'

McGlone was too tired to respond.

'Before I ask for your answer on my offer, I think it's only fair to you to clarify it. The terms of our contract. We are asking you to provide us with a first sight of your messages, your post before you deliver them.'

A pause to allow McGlone to take it in.

'We will not give you a camera. Or any of the trappings of the spy movie. Which is for your safety.'

An ingratiating smile to McGlone who was now looking at his soft interrogator. From police shows and films, he was aware of the bad/good cop approach and *Gaggie* had warned him of the Special Branch using it. But on television, they were in the room at the same time.

'And your safety is our first concern. We will protect you.'

Another short period of silence not broken by the Derryman, albeit he was finding it more difficult to remain silent. Anxiety was infecting him: he needed to explain his limited actions. There was no point in denying his minor involvement.

'All that is required is you stop somewhere on route, leave your vehicle for a few minutes and we will do the rest. We would not do it for all of your deliveries.'

Eileen and Daniel Irwin had expressed doubts about disclosing any of the operational methods no matter how insignificant, but Ormsby said that it was Arthur's call on the 'bowling'.

'Of course, you will be told where to stop. But that is for later. What do you think?'

No response.

'Oh, I am not sure if I have already said.' Godden leaned forward conspiratorially closer to McGlone. 'We would not use any of your information to arrest anyone unless...'

In the control room, Irwin muttered, 'Bloody hell,' earning a disapproving glance from Ormsby.

'... unless it was to stop people from being killed. And I would trust that you would warn us if you knew of any such action.' Edging slightly closer. 'However, I know that you are not involved in the military side.'

McGlone had returned his eyes to the floor. An anti-interrogation technique – not to look at your inquisitor which was taught by most intelligence and security organisations.

'Well, Damien. What do you think? A fair offer. Take your time but I do need an answer.'

Silence. McGlone was looking around, anguishing in his mind. The four SIS officers, the two interrogators and the two in the control room, individually but at different points in the silence thought that McGlone was going to accept. He was tormenting himself, angst gripping him though Eileen thought that was his normal state.

'Damien?'

He was shaking his head, fear had returned to his mind and body.

'I can't. I can't. They... you don't understand.' The vigorous head-shaking continued. 'No, no.'

'Oh well. That is disappointing . Think you need some more rest. It will allow us to contact London's finest and arrange your hand-over.' A pause. 'We will have a brief chat before you leave us. To say our goodbyes.' No smile.

A knock on the door and the wall-light on.

As McGlone was being hooded, Godden said, 'Their food is not as good as ours. But you will renew your acquaintance with your cowboy friend.' Godden did not know why he said it. Improvisation.

'Please, may I explain. If I could...' It was muffled due to the hood.

'Really no point. Be a waste of our time.'

'Please, sir. I beg you. Just so I can explain.' Desperation.

Godden nodded to the Security Service officers flanking McGlone. A rewind of the actions followed.

'What do you want to explain?' A curt tone.

'I can't help... you don't understand... they would...'

'Kill you.' Eileen completed the sentence.

He looked at the female officer.

'And Christine. She... they would suspect her.'

'Undoubtedly.' Godden's tone had softened slightly.

'And there would be no more nights in a Dublin hotel.' Sounded smug.

McGlone was stunned by their knowledge but also angered by the female's comment.

'That's not a crime.'

'No. But a sin. Sex outside of marriage ... with a Protestant... and you a good Catholic. Confessed it?'

Revulsion creased McGlone's face.

Internally, Godden was unhappy. Whilst discussing their tactics, he had wanted to avoid mentioning Christine Latham in the hope that the agent could remain in place. Eileen and Irwin believed that was a forlorn hope, in view of the fact that Christine wanted out. Keeping an agent in place when he or she was at the end of their tether and producing material which could be obtained from another source was a cardinal sin. Ormsby had sided with his two younger officers: Godden had a touch of old-fashioned morality. The two younger officers did not play with a straight bat. He rather wished that he had encountered Irwin earlier in the latter's career. Godden's fall-back position, no exploitation of Christine being one of their agents, was opposed by the other two. Ormsby's decision was to wait to see if the bowling needed to change because of the pitch. He would leave that decision to Eileen's feminine intuition.

Godden tried to re-assert his control. 'What do you want to explain?'

Other advice from Devlin or *Gaggie*, now not sure which of them, was if he had to talk, to minimise his involvement.

'Look. I admit that I sometimes carry messages. I don't know what's in them. They are not important.'

'How do you know that they are not important if you don't know what's in them?'

Straight away, he realised the instruction not to talk was the best course to take, but in his desperation felt that he had to continue. 'I don't know what's in them. Please you have to believe me.'

The interrogators were not aware that on a few occasions, McGlone had carried verbal messages though he did not know their meaning or import.

'But it's only... not to important people.'

Eileen's next intervention. 'You have been meeting some senior IRA commanders recently.'

McGlone cobbled together an answer, again in desperation. 'I don't know who they are... what they are.'

Godden smiled and quipped, 'You are now going to tell me that *Gaggie* McKenna is not in the IRA's discipline squad. What do they call it? Yes, the nutting squad. When you meet, he's actually auditioning for the church choir.'

One of the pit-falls of interrogation was disclosing intelligence to the suspect which could be reported back in his debrief. However, *Gaggie's* role in Londonderry was common knowledge

'*Gaggie*. The choir boy.'

Her comment made McGlone look at her. He was beginning to fear this lady: she was cute. He did not mean in looks but smart. He had been warned of 'cute' Special Branch men but not females.

'And no doubt you believe that Martin McGuinness is still a butcher.' A Godden smile.

Eileen added, 'Well, I suppose he still is. But now his butcher trade is not animals but innocent human beings.'

'Please go on with your explanation, Damien.'

A shake of the head.

'Damien, we are listening.'

Another shake of the head and a slow, deliberate act of turning his head away from Godden and facing downwards.

'Ah. I think he has retaken his vow of silence.'

McGlone had decided that he would revert to the tactic of silence. Talking created problems. These people could twist his words and they were not interested in his explanation. He was not a terrorist. He was not responsible for people's deaths. He would go to prison. Membership he thought only carried a short sentence. It would be hard and probably he would not cope. But he could not, would not betray anyone.

The bowling had to change. Following Eileen's knock on the door, McGlone was hooded and held in his chair by two guards. When the hood was removed, the guards had gone. There was a return to the gloomier atmosphere with the small light still on, and the trio had changed with Eileen replacing Godden and Irwin in Eileen's position.

'So. You have decided to go to prison.'

McGlone did not respond. He sensed, though he could not see the person in the corner, the male and female had swapped positions.

'Not willing to inform on your friends, your comrades. Very noble.'

' He'll still fucking end up in South Armagh hooded and with a bullet in the back of his head!' The van man's Belfast voice.

'Oh, Jesus, Mary and Joseph' was his inner prayer. He felt crushed and empty. He could feel the shaking spreading up from his feet. 'Mary, Mother of God. Hail Mary, full of...' He couldn't continue with his silent prayer due to the van's Derry voice. '*Gaggie* will be upset. Especially as he's his boy. He might be...'

'He'll be fucking shitting himself.' The Belfast voice.

'You know *Gaggie* might have gave him up... tae protect himself.' The Derry voice.

'Naw! It wis that wee Belfast proddy. It wis hur!'

'No. She's one of us. Are you sure?' The Derry voice.

'Fucking right I'm sure. It wis defanetly the wee Proddy wummin!'

It was to be 'whore' but it was thought after the rehearsal that it might be a word too far. Irwin had restrained himself from laughing at Ormsby's description of the word as being 'a little too insensitive'.

McGlone was desolate and abandoned. McGlone broke his vow of silence. 'No, no... no way.'

'*It is true!*' said Eileen. 'Christine works for us.'

'No! An informer?' He shook his head. 'No! She's too committed...'

'The best fucking type for a tout!' The last contribution from the van's Belfast voice.

Eileen said coldly, 'So your prison sentence will not be a reprieve, merely... a stay of execution.'

'What will happen to Christine? They will... er.' He did not want say or admit that the IRA would shoot her.

'We will save her.'

'And we can save you,' said the voice in the corner.

McGlone thought it sounded Irish but certainly not Belfast or Derry.

'No. You can't. They are all caught and killed.' He looked at Eileen and then towards the corner. 'You said so yourself.'

The response came from the corner.

'No. Most are not discovered. The ones caught are because they had been stupid. They don't listen. They make mistakes. Also, the IRA leaders are not as clever as they believe.'

Followed by Eileen's lines:

'We know that you have doubts about what's happening. The violence.' She leaned forward. 'And *I* think that in a hidden corner of your mind, *you wrestle* with the terrifying thought that what you are doing, *even if* it is only a small part, might lead to deaths.' She was unsure why she had improvised, but was confident that she was right.

For McGlone, it confirmed that she *was* cute, and she was right.

She returned to the script. 'My colleague was being honest when he said that he wanted to end all the violence and that you could help.'

'I couldn't.'

'You could contribute towards ending the violence.'

Ormsby had suggested the line. 'You could be a peacemaker. Blessed are the peacemakers.' Irwin thought it was crass and McGlone might think that we were mocking his religion. Ormsby bowed to the younger officer's knowledge.

'And pursuing a united Ireland is a legitimate political aspiration.'

Eileen in her extensive research on taking up the role in the *Mythical* team had become empathetic to Irish unity, though once she was involved in the day-to-day operations, consideration of the argument for ending Partition slipped from her mind. Again, it was Irwin who had suggested the united Ireland comment but both officers had missed or ignored McGlone's downplaying of a united Ireland during his monologue in Christine's house.

McGlone did not respond. He had never been a fervent supporter of ending partition. It was the murders on Bloody Sunday and the harassment and ill-treatment of Catholics, especially the young ones, which had caused his involvement, even though by the time he had arrived at the Coshquin farmhouse he had hoped that the IRA had forgotten his offer. He had been sickened by the IRA's actions after Bloody Sunday and he had witnessed two soldiers being shot on Magazine Street. He had agreed to help because he was frightened of *Gaggie* McKenna and of Hugh Devlin in particular, as well as having a misplaced sense of obligation which had made him offer his assistance. In his despair, he was seeking a way out.

These Brits would understand, after all they were intelligent and educated, not like the rough and ready soldiers who patrolled the Derry Streets, taunted by Derry's young: a mirror image. With his cooperation, he might receive a lighter sentence, maybe not even prison. He had no previous convictions. Subsequently, he would explain to *Gaggie*, no, Devlin that he had not betrayed anyone – which was true, because the Brits knew about *Gaggie* and he had not mentioned Devlin's name. He would stop carrying messages. Anyway, the Brits knew so they would be stopping and searching him all the time; and he would not mention Christine.

The cocktail of stress, fear, loneliness and desperation produced a mindset of dangerous delusion.

'Can I explain why... how I got involved? I'm sure that you will understand.'

'Certainly. Go ahead,' said Eileen

Beginning with the events of Bloody Sunday in January 1972, *Danube* narrated his involvement in the IRA, emphasising the pivotal meeting with *Gaggie* McKenna in the Coshquin farmhouse. Eileen made a mental note of the need to check with the legal experts whether not being sworn in as an IRA member was a defence against the membership charge. According to McGlone, his progress was incremental and he remained reluctant. He did deliver messages but he did not know the people, especially those in Belfast. He avoided reading newspaper reports or watching the television news on

The Troubles. Eileen made another mental note that it was probably true based on their intercepts. He could not leave because he had obligations to his choirs and pupils. This was a last minute thought. Simply, there was no way out for him. He did not mention Hugh Devlin.

'Anything else, Damien?' asked Eileen.

'No. I hope that you now understand my position. I had no choice.'

Neither SIS officer spoke for a short period.

Irwin moved his chair beside Eileen who, once her colleague was settled, said, ' I do understand your predicament but it will not prevent the outcome for you. If anything, by baring your soul to British Intelligence, it removes the slightest chance of a reprieve.'

'Why? You won't tell them?' Torment dominating his voice.

'Of course not. However, to lighten your sentence – which I assume is why you told us of your involvement – your lawyer will have to tell the court of your cooperation.'

'I'll plead not guilty.'

'That's your right. But we will have to give evidence of you making a statement and play the recording of this interview.'

The two officers knew that it was a bluff because the recording would be inadmissible, and a competent defence barrister would depict his treatment as torture.

'Damien,' Irwin interjected, 'your only way out is cooperating with us.'

He leaned closer to McGlone.

'And I promise you that I will do everything within my capabilities to protect you.'

Irwin was sincere in his promise. He considered himself a first-rate and conscientious officer.

'I will tell you what to do and guide you at each stage.'

'Also, as we said before, we will not stop you every time.' She paused then dismissively said, 'We can't spend any more time on you. We have others to speak to.'

McGlone wondered if *Gaggie* was one of the others and he might cooperate. It had been decided that there would only ever be one offer to McGlone.

Eileen's voice was solemn. 'This is your final opportunity. Yes?'

Once more, Irwin leaned towards McGlone in a friendly manner.

'Com'on, Damien. We, you and me, we will make a great team. What do you say?'

Weakly, McGlone nodded.

'I need you to say yes,' Eileen said.

'Yes.'

McGlone was allowed a shower and given clean trousers and a shirt. His suit was not quite ready. After a meal, he was allowed a few hours sleep. Eileen and Irwin took the opportunity for some sleep. Ormsby and Godden returned to Century House.

Irwin confirmed with McGlone that he had not made any arrangements to visit his sister again. For the rest of the time before he caught his flight back to Belfast, he was closeted with Irwin, being taught rudimentary tradecraft.

In their final session, Irwin pointed out to him places on the map which would be his stopping points. McGlone knew most of them and he promised that he would check out the other ones. However, in the next two weeks if he was given messages to deliver there would be no attempt to copy them, but he should stop at one or two of the spots just to familiarise himself. He was not informed that he would be photographed at the stops, simply as a precaution, insurance. He was still to go to Dublin. Irwin did not know if Christine would be going because it was not his decision. There would be more discussions in Dublin which Irwin would arrange. He could still stay in The Gresham if he wished. McGlone must not change any of his routines in Dublin or anywhere.

He had a final brief meeting with Eileen, who thanked him but warned him against resiling on the contract. A troubling conscience leading to the confession of his guilty deed would not bring forgiveness from either side. Cooperation was reprieve. Yes, he understood the meaning of resiling.

– 36 –

The MI5 officer expected her but she still showed her identity card. Christine was sleeping with a cover pulled over her but had not undressed. Braco had removed the empty wine bottles and the debris of their meal.

Eileen's voice was gentle. 'Christine, wake up. You need to wake up.'

She resisted the urge to shake her or touch her in any way. She stood beside the minder who had replaced Braco at 1 am. The letter delivered with the meal had informed him that a MI5 officer would take over. A room had been booked for him in the hotel, so he should collect the keys from reception. He was not required any further and was not to inform the subject of the change-over. He was to go on leave; his hotel costs, though nothing above 3 star, would be covered. A flight was booked for the following Wednesday evening: he would be collected from Aldergrove, and enjoy his time with his brother.

Braco had told Eileen that his brother was spending a week in London arriving on the Sunday and he was pleased that she had taken it on board, especially when she had been engaged in preparing for the operation, although he was aware only of the 'minding Christine' part. The only downside was being unable to wish Christine well for the future, though he thought that the protective role in Belfast might continue.

Christine woke up slowly and on seeing Eileen muttered, 'Oh. It's you.'

She did not notice her minder had changed. Realising the disgusting, invasive taste in her mouth was due to the alcohol, she rushed to the bathroom, locking the door. Eileen did not object, counting on the fact that her agent was woozy so not able to think clearly.

'Who is he? Where's? Doesn't matter.'

Almost throwing herself on the bed, said, 'Well?' A sarcastic tone.

Eileen told the minder to wait outside and replaced him in the armchair.

'He has cooperated.'

'Blackmailed! Intimidated. I know your ways.'

'You brought him to us.' A tactical lie.

'Am I supposed to be appeased by that. You couldn't even let us have a weekend together.'

Her handler did not respond.

'What happened to Dublin?'

'I know that you will not believe me. But I was only told a few days ago.'

The haze clearing, a smiling Christine said, 'Yes. I forgot your lowly status.'

Eileen clucked her tongue as if to say 'so what'.

'Can I see him?'

'No. You must not meet him or contact him in any way. Certainly not until after your interview with Glasgow. Who knew that you were meeting him in London?'

'No one. I try to have a part of my life remain private.'

'Are you sure? Not, say, to a colleague...'

'No! I told you.'

'You are not to go to Dublin. When he contacts you, give an excuse of having to mark or prepare for your Glasgow interview. He will understand.'

'I understand. You told him about me?' Her mind was clear and thinking as normal.

'I can't tell you. It is an operational matter.'

'You are terrified of his reaction when he meets me. Knowing I betrayed him.'

Eileen was curt and dismissive. 'Don't give me that 'innocent little girl deceived' routine. You know the rules. You have betrayed plenty of your *comrades.*'

She stood up and took a step towards the bed.

'Only difference is that you didn't go to bed with them... or maybe you did. A shag for the cause.'

'Fucking, evil bitch!' A rare expletive.

'Yes.'

Eileen sat down again.

'I know what I am. What I do. But I don't try to cloak it with some false morality. To salve my conscience. Our job is to use people to... willingly mostly, unwillingly sometimes, even unwittingly. Even he knows the violence can't continue. He told you that in your own home. And that is what we are trying to do. My Service's job is to serve our country's interests. And despite the myopic attitude in our government and security agencies, it is in HMG's interests to end the violence. Even the sometimes blockheaded Arthur knows that.'

Immediately she regretted her disparaging of Godden.

' Thank you for trying to save...'

'Yes. Remember it was your people who caused this. Why didn't they stay in Scotland!'

'That's not fair. It's...'

Christine was not going to be allowed the time to defend her community.

'Is that why you were so keen to help the Catholics. Amends for the sins of your father.' She knew that she had gone too far. 'I'm sorry, Christine. I'm tired. I have... but that's not an excuse. It's not your fault. You are not responsible. We are just trying to resolve it... to end it.'

She paused feeling guilty.

'And you have played your part. We do appreciate your contribution especially considering the risks to your safety. Arthur has said that you should receive a decoration.' Again, she regretted saying it.

'That will be just fine. Ample amends.'

Eileen smiled at 'amends' being thrown back.

'I am sorry.' She was sincere.

'I just want my life back. To have a normal life. Not constantly looking over my shoulder. Wondering if the man approaching me has a gun and has been sent to kill me. I rarely see my father and mother. They have aged. I have aged. He, my father, told me once that he regretted making that telephone call. He thought that he was saving me, instead it brought Arthur and...'

She looked around the hotel room.

'... all this into my life. I want to be normal. To rediscover my love of literature.'

'It would be crass of me to say that I understand.'

Eileen did to a certain extent and empathised because she too wanted a normal life, being determined to resign. The letter was written.

'Your stint with us is at an end. And I can assure you that comes from the top. But, we don't think it's in your interest to be extracted immediately. Your former comrades might ask questions. It's for your safety.'

Christine knew that it was to protect their new source but she did not want any further arguments.

'If you get the job in Glasgow, then that provides the perfect cover for your move.'

Eileen decided not to inform her that some pressure was going to be applied to the university. The Service still retained some, though fading, influence in the older universities but it was better not to mention it to Christine who no doubt would not take the job in such circumstances. Pride.

'After a while he might be able to come over. You could go to concerts. I do know that there are concerts in Glasgow.'

'Do you.' Christine said in a mocking tone.

'Certainly. I did my degree there.'

She knew that she should not have told her but she would not tell her that they had been contemporaries, nor that she had spied on Christine. Passing her name to *the accountant* for his ledger.

'And of course, there's Edinburgh.'

'Of course. And it would be convenient for you... him coming over.' Thinking of her trips to London for debriefings.

'You might be able to look up Ian. Please, it was not intended as a malicious remark.'

Eileen looked at her watch.

'I need to go.' She stood up. 'Please follow the instructions. You can go out. We can arrange for you to visit your parents.' It was an impulsive offer to tempt her.

Christine did not respond immediately.

'Will you? That... I can tell them about Glasgow and South-ampton. I know that they will be pleased. Cheer them up. Yes. Thank you, Eileen.'

Eileen knew that she would have to clear it with Godden but was confident that he would not object. If he did, she would do it herself.

'Probably tomorrow. Please don't phone your parents.'

'No, I won't. It will be a pleasant surprise for them. God

knows that they have not had many over the last ten years.'

She wasn't sure if it had been ten years since the meeting with Godden in her bedroom.

'Good. I'll arrange a car and driver.'

There was no need to mention the shepherding vehicle: Christine would know.

'Will it be that nice soldier? My guardian angel.'

Eileen did not straightaway catch that she had said 'soldier'. Then she realised Braco must have told Christine and she would need to have a word with him.

'No. Sorry. He is not available.'

'Ok. Promise me one thing.'

Eileen's hand was on the door knob. Eileen half-turned.

'Yes.'

'Don't recruit him. In any way.' Both her eyes and voice were pleading, 'Please don't corrupt that boy.'

− 37 −

The vehicle would be waiting for him in the car-park. It was simply a case of going to look for the vehicle with the driver outside, waving to attract his attention. If it was two up, then one normally waited outside the terminal exit door.

He thought that she must be flying out when he saw Eileen Kanna, and thought that she had better hurry up and go through security if she wanted to catch the London flight on the aircraft that he had just come off. He would simply say hello. She spotted him just before he reached her. There were no pleasantries only, 'Let's go.'

She walked briskly and silently to the Volkswagen Passat. Once he was in the passenger seat with Eileen behind the wheel, she said, 'Your gun's in the glove compartment.'

She had left a weapon in an unattended vehicle, and normally he would have reminded her in a jocular manner that it was not a gun; but there was something in her demeanour that warned him off.

'Have you heard?'

He thought it might be to do with the choirmaster.

'No.'

'Christine has been shot.'

'Shot? Wounded?'

'No. She's dead.'

'When?'

'Today. It was on the main BBC news.'

'I haven't seen any news today.'

He thought the only reason it was an item on the news was because she was a university lecturer. People in GB did not hear most of what went on in the Province. The first shard of guilt was pricking him.

'I'll brief you once we are out of the car-park.'

The murder had happened at or just after lunch-time. The full details were not yet known. The RUC were still investigating. The lecturer was on her way to the university. So far there appeared to be no eye-witnesses. Bill, the caretaker, was the first to her. He was out for a walk and in another street, approaching the corner to turn into Christine's street. He heard two shots, a gap then another shot. He knew that it was a handgun. He thought immediately that it was Christine. He only knew her as a Sinn Féin activist. As he rounded the corner, he almost collided with two youths who were running away from the scene. They were shouting. He could not quite remember what they were saying. Clearly excited and agitated. He did not see a weapon.

Christine was lying two doors up from her house. Bill said he knelt to check her pulse and tried to administer first aid. She had been shot in the side of the head. He shouted at the elderly woman in an open doorway to telephone for an ambulance. He thought that Christine was trying to speak so he raised her to cradle her head. But she was gone: it was the last embers of life leaving her, not words. Then he realised that she had also been shot in the back. By this time there were others around; clearly students who were distressed. A lady came out of a house shouting that she was a doctor. And a RUC landrover was there almost from nowhere. The police took control and moved others back to allow the doctor to attend the casualty. Bill decided to drift away.

There had been no protection. The team could not spare anyone because they had to complete the route recces, and the Colville/Ormsby axis did not want to risk drawing any attention to Christine. Anyway, it was unlikely that a single operative could have saved her. There might have been more deaths. Neither had to say what the consequences would be of a lone, undercover soldier shooting gunmen who were likely to be loyalists, or being shot himself. There would be questions asked and even if the press could be contained, the IRA would be asking why the secret soldiers were following Christine. She was not important. The IRA were likely to decide not following but protecting her, which would result in one conclusion: that she was an informer and this almost certainly would eventually lead to the choirmaster.

Braco was going to be based in Lisburn for the rest of his tour. The *Mythical* team was being assumed into the Group but in reality being disbanded. Braco was being re-assigned as liaison to the Group to ensure the merger, take-over, ran smoothly. His accommodation had been arranged.

Despite knowing that it was unlikely that he could have prevented Christine's murder, he could not shed the pangs of guilt.

'If I had been there.'

'It wasn't your fault.'

'I know. But If I had been there. I might have been able to save her.'

He pre-empted Eileen from responding.

'And provide a cover-story. I have been seen around the university, in the library. It could have provided a cover story. Was shepherding someone else. Must have other assets in the university and around there. I was passing... on my way home when I intervened.'

He looked at Eileen. 'I know. It's happened. In the past.'

Braco had learned a very good lesson from an outstanding company commander: what is done is done. Cannot change the past but can be guided by it.

Eileen reflected that the soldier was thinking like her people, and remembered Christine's plea.

'You know Christine's last words to me were about you.'

Braco did not respond just looking straight ahead.

'I think she liked you.'

She would not tell him the context.

'Probably most females like you.'

She was glad that he did not respond thinking the comment was a little gushy. But she was pondering another of his comments. For future action.

38

'Oh. It's you.'

Braco had waited till Mayne's wife had left in the car with their child.

'Come in.'

'How long will your wife be away?'

'Hour or so. Gone shopping. Probably two or three because she is dropping in on her sister. The kids can play.' The suspicious tone kicked in 'Why?'

'Can we talk?'

They were in the same position in the living-room as on Braco's last, only, visit to Peter Mayne's home. The visitor refused any type of drink and Mayne decided not to have the planned whiskey on his wife leaving.

'You know about Christine Latham. Sorry. A stupid question.'

'Yes. It's my station. Know the guys who were first at the scene.'

'The police seemed to get there quickly.'

'Yes. Well, they were... hold on. Just stop fucking there. If you have been sent by er... Godden or whoever is your master now. Leave now.'

Mayne stood up.

'There was no collusion. Don't even think that. They're good lads. I know them.'

Mayne was looking down at him and Braco feared that he might actually try to throw him out.

'Sorry.'

'Just tell me what you have been sent to say. Then you can go.'

'That went well.' In an attempt to defuse the situation. 'May I start again. And we know there was no police collusion. Peter, will you just hear me out?'

Mayne sat down and said, 'I'm listening.'

'Christine Latham was one of us. I know that you won't repeat it.'

Mayne wagged his head several times looking to his right at the bay window.

'One is never surprised at who is who. The whole place is a web of lies and deceit.'

Braco ignored the home-spun philosophy.

'You knew her.'

Mayne turned back towards the soldier, a smile on his face. 'Oh they are letting you read the files. No longer sitting in a bush.'

He ignored the sarcasm.

'She told me.'

That brought a facial reaction from the policeman.

'She didn't know that I knew you. She was telling me about her university days in Glasgow. She spoke highly of you. She seemed to think that you were funny.'

Mayne stifled his retort instead saying, 'Very good.'

He laughed, as did Braco.

'And you want to know why I didn't tell you?'

'No.'

Mayne ignored the reply.

'Why should I? I didn't know of your interest in Christine – professional of course.' Another smile. 'I compartmentalise my life. That was in the past. Anyway it was a need to know and you didn't need to know.'

He did not speak for a short period reflecting on his time in university.

'Who else did she mention?'

'Oh. Another Irish girl. – You called her Belfast Bernie but she wasn't from Belfast.'

Mayne laughed.

'I knew. Of course I knew. I liked Bernie. If things had turned out differently... well that's in the past. Mention anyone else?'

'An Ian Barclay.'

'Ian. Yes. He was more intense than Christine. You know I recommended him – indirectly – to your bosses. Wonder what happened to him.'

Another interlude.

'I let Ian down. I betrayed him in a childish sort of way. I suppose I betrayed Christine when colleagues were slagging her off as 'a féinan slut, a traitor to the Queen and Protestantism'. I probably joined in when I had had a few of these.'

His hand went to the table in front of him.

'Oh. Forgot. Didn't get my drink. Sure you don't want one?'

'I'm sure. I need to go soon.'

'Okay. What do you want to know?'

'We know a few things about it. Can you tell me the stage of the police investigation?'

'Sure. But not to be repeated.' Both smiled.

He started with the police vehicle to dispel any idea of collusion. The vehicle had stopped, which they did from time to time, always in safe areas. Sometimes just to write up notes or in support of an operation or to foil an operation. Two of the policeman were outside the vehicle on guard. They heard the shots, though were not certain they were actually shots, so decided to investigate.

'That's what police officers do.' Said with a sardonic grin.

There were no eye-witnesses.

It *was* two young guys. Both on the fringes. They are known to the police but they don't mouth off. They keep a respectful distance from the police. Special Branch seemed to think that it was an opportunistic shooting. They were told to pick-up a weapon and take it somewhere.

Mayne paused to look at Braco before saying, 'Don't repeat this.'

Braco nodded.

'There was one witness to the actual shooting though it's being kept tight. Probably somebody looking out their window. Unless... it wasn't your guys? Looking after her?'

'I'm almost certain it wasn't.'

'That would create an almighty shit-storm if it came out the... or whoever lost a source.'

'Peter, it wasn't us. I know. I was looking after her till last week.' His eyes were down. 'I wasn't replaced for the few days I was on leave. I don't know why.'

'God! Sorry mate.'

Mayne could see the soldier felt guilty. He had known other soldiers and police who held themselves responsible for a death, for not preventing an attack; the 'if only' syndrome.

'I know we have to put it behind us. I'm sure that you have been told to forget it; what's done is done. Easy to say but difficult to do. Most people, even the police, think when the squaddies go back to England, they forget this godforsaken place. Some do, others don't. *They* are haunted by the "if only".'

The two boys had been walking past Christine's house just as she was leaving. The boys kept walking then stopped, looking back at the female who had left the house. The witness seemed to think they were discussing whether they knew her. The taller, dark haired one seemed to be in charge and kind of dragged the smaller, fair-haired one back towards Christine. The witness thought the taller one said something to Christine. The witness thought that he might have called her name. Christine Latham half-turned and the dark-haired boy fired two shots.

'One hit her in the left hand side of her face. The other missed. The taller one then almost forced the handgun into the other boy's hand and according to the witness, was pointing to the body on the ground telling him to fire which he did, hitting her in the back. The witness thinks they had a problem with the gun, a stoppage. Then they ran away. Shouting.'

'Do the police know who they are?'

'Yes. As I said they are known.'

'Are they going to arrest them?'

'You've been here long enough: knowing is easy, proving is difficult.'

'What about the witness?'

Mayne did not disclose that the witness was related to a policeman. 'Standing up in open court. It's a death sentence... especially as the victim was IRA.'

'Sinn Féin.'

'All the same to those boys. I doubt they have degrees, even an O-level between them on the fine distinction between the IRA and Sinn Féin. Anyway the only distinction is in the number of letters.'

'So nothing will happen to them?'

'No. I didn't say that. Once they are sure. They will pick them up for a three, more likely a seven day stay in Castlereagh. Remember Castlereagh is usually booked up weeks in advance. And there is nothing worse than them walking after three or seven days. It would boost their egos. And of course the UVF or whomever would want to know who told the police.'

Braco said, 'Surely, if they are young punks, they'll break.'

Mayne chortled.

'Often it's the weak who are the strongest. I was involved in a case when we arrested some loyalists. For serious offences. One was a young, small, weedy, pathetic being. This wee guy stuck it out while others, the so-called hard men, broke. It was reckoned the wee guy had been so abused throughout his life, that Castlereagh was a holiday-camp. You can never be certain who will talk.'

'So. It could be a while.'

'Yes.'

Braco was not quite ready to make the approach so asked, 'How come you know all this!'

Mayne laughed. 'I told you I have friends. And my family is a spy net-work. I could find out about you and your role.'

Mayne produced his wide, all-knowing grin, a sort of dare me.

'Bluffing bastard,' thought Braco but still a sliver of doubt. Even in the battalion Mayne seemed to know things beyond the reach of the ordinary squaddie. Also, they, SIS, had tried or did recruit him and thereafter, he thumbed his nose at them. It took a solid, inner core to do that.

'Peter, I would be grateful if you could keep me up to speed with the investigation... actually with the two's movements.'

' I can't do *that*.'

His face was grave projecting his policeman's authority.

'And I wouldn't do it for Ormsby, Godden and the...'

'It's not for them. They are not in the need to know category for this.'

'I need a drink. No. You are playing with fire. I should caution you... At least throw you out of my house.'

Mayne maintained his stern policeman's expression.

'Let it go. Why?'

'For Christine.'

You didn't know her. For a short time maybe.'

'She was a very brave... a courageous woman. I saw the effect, the tear in her face. I'm supposed to be a tough, special forces soldier. I couldn't have done what she did... and for so long.'

'How long? When you told me I thought... assumed that it was recently. When?'

'Almost ten years.'

He wasn't sure. Possibly Christine could not remember exactly.

'So what are you going to say when your colleagues say that féinan slut got what she deserved?'

Mayne was silent, ignoring the soldier, pondering. He was glad that he had not been drinking. The whiskey would have eliminated the caution, ignored his warrant card, to be replaced with bravado and misplaced loyalty.

'Who... er no. How many is in this need to know group?'

'Two.'

'One of your mates. Wracked by guilt also.' He held up his right hand. 'No. I don't want to know and you wouldn't tell me.'

Another interlude then a smile

'Not many to have in your gang of corner boys.'

'Sorry?'

'Remember Murray talking about the corner boys. The IRA, the Branch.'

'That's right. He was... is probably right.'

'Why not approach him? Think he has some form in this.'

'No outsiders.'

He had thought of Tamworth but quickly rejected him: he was too decent and honourable.

'For Christine. It's personal.' A slightly mocking tone.

Braco ignored the jibe.

'Here's a phone number.' Braco held out the small slip of paper which had been ripped out of his small, black note-book.

Mayne took it and held it up. 'You know this is evidence?'

Braco ignored the question.

'You can phone at any time. Ask for Ian. If I'm not there they will get me. You know not to ask any questions. Phone again in an hour. I am not going to be far away. Whoever answers won't ask any questions. Belfast accent preferred. It won't be recorded.'

'It *is* personal.'

Mayne thought the choice of 'Ian' was deliberate but thought best not to ask. He recalled Braco as a good soldier. Now, he had a controlled, authoritative hardness. It made him think of an outstanding major in the battalion. He had served in the SAS and projected the same image. It could be chilling at times.

'You know some of my colleagues might turn up at your door.'

Braco now standing, disregarded the inferred threat.

'It is your choice. If you do call, I promise that I will never enter your life again.'

He opened the door to the hall.

'It *is* personal. We need to defend *our* corner.'

39

He had been given a 15 minute slot to brief C before the latter departed for lunch with his counter-part at the Security Service, who was hosting the lunch in his office.

'Well. What happened in Dublin?' C asked Simon Ormsby.

'I am off to lunch with the Director-General. He prefers it to be a proper working lunch with an agenda. In his office. I know he hates my choice of restaurants. He is right: they are ghastly. But even we have to economise if we want our operations. Instead of Godden briefing Colville direct, he wants us to follow the proper chain of command – Service to Service. So be it. So. Did *Danube* want to retract? A quickie divorce? Is he still *Danube* or has he become... what are we calling him?'

'No, C. Still *Danube*. He has to produce. Earn his crust.'

'Or moniker.'

Ormsby smiled in appreciation of his superior's wit, which mostly he failed to find amusing. More resonant of the sixth form.

'I much preferred it when we gave them numbers. I am not equipped for the modern service. Time for Tunbridge Wells.'

Ormsby doubted if C had ever been there, but did not doubt C's determination to remain in post.

'*Danube* is even more committed. And I think Irwin is just

the right man for him. He is very impressive. I don't understand why Hong Kong wanted rid of him.

'He's a bloody fool. Too much sun and too many cocktail parties with the taipans and a myriad of chancers and conmen. But he does not know his sojourn will soon be at an end. He has produced heehaw. If it were not for our listening stations, we would know nothing about what's happening out there. He probably realised Irwin was producing, and that would never do. Upset the applecart. Or is it the rickshaw.'

Another smile from Ormsby.

'I was thinking that Godden might be a suitable replacement. He's an old China hand.'

'He wasn't actually in Hong Kong.'

'Same area. And he would not be seduced by the temptations of the orient.'

A pause while C removed the file on the centre of his desk and placed in a tray .

'Always think of Godden as a Calvinistic Scot. Dour and disapproving. He's not a Scot?'

'No, sir.'

'It was the Scots who were responsible for Hong Kong.'

'I know.'

'Responsible for most of the empire. Should have been called the Scottish Empire, not British. So our new man is happy and raring to go. Good. Godden can give Colville the details. And I shall tell that to the DG. You know he insists on us calling each other by our titles at the beginning and end of the meeting. A strange man. Just typical of a glorified policeman. You want us all under the same umbrella.'

'Well, C ...'

'Never do. You know my thoughts on that.'

'Yes, C.'

'Anything else?'

'Godden thought a decoration might be in order for *Mighty Midget*.'

'Simon. You know I hate these code-names. I think that you do it to drive me out. I know what you are all up to, my loyal assistants. Problem is that you are all too busy fighting with each other so that you are unable to organise a palace coup. What do you think of Godden's idea?'

'Well. Certainly deserved. But I have always thought that the value of a gong was the recognition and plaudits. A good table in a restaurant... of course not a ghastly one. Not much use if you are dead, and in her case not able to publicise it for another ten, twenty years. Her parents might appreciate it. But again they couldn't tell anyone that their daughter was actually on the side of the righteous. Would be quite frustrating for them.'

'Let me think about it. You know, Ormsby, despite your polished, urbane veneer, you are a cold-hearted bastard. And don't thank me.'

'Sir.'

'At least her death removes a risk to... I am not going to say it.'

'*Danube*. And he provides distance and insurance for Dublin.'

'Yes, indeed. The others don't know about Dublin?'

'We are not yet under the same umbrella.'

The Audi lingered three cars behind the blue Hillman Avenger, both vehicles stationary.

The single shot as instructed, to frighten the post office staff and ensure no one either inside or outside would follow them or attempt to impede their getaway.

The black haired robber who had fired the shot crumpled onto the pavement, killed by two shots to his chest. Braco, using the car roof for support, refocused his 9 mm automatic to his right, to the second robber.

The fair-haired, freckle faced 19 year old, his hand shaking, pointed his empty revolver in Braco's direction but he did not see the soldier; his eyes were fixed on the body of the boy who had been his best friend since they were five.

The second double tap sent the fair-haired boy back into the post office doorway, half-bent but still.

The police landrover blocked the path of the Hillman Avenger as it tried to pull out. The driver raised his arms, screaming from inside the vehicle, 'Don't shoot! Please don't…' Now sobbing.

The second police landrover drove past the post office to stop at the next junction.

A sergeant left the first landrover. A crowd was gathering and people were pointing at Braco, now wearing a baseball hat, his weapon reholstered and concealed, with his hands up, shouting, 'Army! Army!' whilst walking towards the RUC sergeant.

A near-by army patrol, having heard the shots, were running towards the second police landrover.

Braco showed his identity card to the police sergeant, explaining he was on a recce and had stopped to get cigarettes. He had not shouted a warning because the terrorist had already discharged his weapon. He knew that he would have to make a statement but it was SOP for them to get out of the area. He could be contacted via Lisburn. The sergeant understood, having dealt with undercover soldiers before. The police had been parked up just round the corner because they had been tipped off but had not been expecting firearms to be involved.

He opened the driver's door of the Audi before looking towards the police driver seated in the landrover, who was speaking into the radio handset. Their eyes met briefly. The deed was done: to avenge the murder of a valuable agent and to seek justice for a friend. This would be their last communion.

The Audi pulled out, the driver's eyes straight ahead. The police driver noticed the black haired woman leaving the newsagent's, her hands stuffed into the pockets of a parka type jacket, her head erect looking forward, taking no notice of the commotion on the street.

In his rear-view mirror, he saw the Audi had stopped four cars behind his vehicle and the front passenger door opened for the unconcerned lady.

The last time he had seen her was in a house near Waterloo Station.

This was a simple act of retribution. She had not sought authorisation. Her corner boys had prevailed on this occasion. He was surprised that he did not feel any guilt.

Oddly, he thought of it as a chivalrous act. The corner boys and chivalry were uncommon bedfellows.

Printed in Great Britain
by Amazon